"I'm sorry a

"I was rude," Dean sai tomorrow at 8:00 a.m. and we'll talk about the job."

"Sure. Thanks." Annabelle shifted and bit the inside of her cheek.

"You got family who could help you out?" he asked, wishing he hadn't. It wasn't a good idea to get too acquainted.

She chuckled wryly. "Nope. My mom died a few years ago and my daddy was a bit of a rambling man. I haven't seen him since I was about seven. I have a younger brother, but the less I see of him the better off my pocketbook is." She shrugged as if admitting that her family was less than desirable wasn't a big deal. "I learned to rely on myself a long time ago."

He believed her. Dressed in a denim skirt that was too short and a blouse that fit too tightly across her breasts, she looked like a white trash prom queen, but there was a sense of dignity clinging to her that dared anyone to pass judgment.

Closing his eyes briefly to block out the image of her as she stood before him, he bit out a terse "Don't be late" as his goodbye and walked—no, practically ran—from the restaurant.

Dear Reader,

I'm a sucker for a love story between two good people who really deserve a happy ending. Dean Halvorsen and Annabelle Nichols are two such people. Writing their story was incredibly easy. The scenes fell out of my head faster than my fingers could type, simply because these people were meant to be together. It was an exhilarating ride from the start and I feel lucky to have been invited to play.

As the oldest in my sibling group, I understood Dean's need to be the responsible one—the one with the broadest shoulders and the wisest counsel—but it was good to see how sometimes being stoic closes us off to bigger emotional experiences and payoffs. Annabelle was a joy to discover. Although feisty and her own woman, I loved that Annabelle was particularly vulnerable when it came to perceptions about herself. Those revealing moments are manna to a writer as a story unfolds and I had a few of those moments with their love story.

I hope you enjoy reading it as much as I did writing, and I hope that the town of Emmett's Mill has become your cozy retreat when the real world proves much too hectic. I know it has for me.

Hearing from readers is one of my greatest joys (aside from really good chocolate), so don't be shy. Feel free to drop me a line at my Web site—www.kimberlyvanmeter.com—or through snail mail, P.O. Box 2210, Oakdale, CA 95361.

Happy reading,

Kimberly Van Meter

AN IMPERFECT MATCH
Kimberly Van Meter

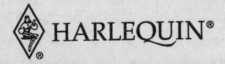

HARLEQUIN®

TORONTO • NEW YORK • LONDON
AMSTERDAM • PARIS • SYDNEY • HAMBURG
STOCKHOLM • ATHENS • TOKYO • MILAN • MADRID
PRAGUE • WARSAW • BUDAPEST • AUCKLAND

ISBN-13: 978-0-373-71513-8
ISBN-10: 0-373-71513-7

AN IMPERFECT MATCH

Copyright © 2008 by Kimberly Sheetz.

This is a work of fiction. Names, characters, places and incidents are either the product of the author's imagination or are used fictitiously, and any resemblance to actual persons, living or dead, business establishments, events or locales is entirely coincidental.

This edition published by arrangement with Harlequin Books S.A.

® and TM are trademarks of the publisher. Trademarks indicated with ® are registered in the United States Patent and Trademark Office, the Canadian Trade Marks Office and in other countries.

www.eHarlequin.com

Printed in U.S.A.

ABOUT THE AUTHOR

An avid reader since before she can remember, Kimberly Van Meter started her writing career at the age of sixteen when she finished her first novel, typing late nights and early mornings on her mother's old portable typewriter. Although that first novel was nothing short of literary mud, with each successive piece of work her writing improved to the point of reaching that coveted published status.

Kimberly, now a journalist, and her husband and three kids make their home in Oakdale. She enjoys writing, reading, photography and drinking hot chocolate by the windowsill when it rains.

Books by Kimberly Van Meter

HARLEQUIN SUPERROMANCE
1391—THE TRUTH ABOUT FAMILY
1433—FATHER MATERIAL*
1469—RETURN TO EMMETT'S MILL*
1485—A KISS TO REMEMBER*

*Emmett's Mill stories

Special thanks must go to RJ Murdoch
for taking time out of his tremendously
busy schedule to educate me on the big world of a
successful builder/contractor. Any deviations from
the way things are truly done are my own and no
reflection on what anyone has taken the time to
teach me. Thanks for all your help!

To Dawn Henley for being the best
"office roomie" a person could ask for
and helping me brainstorm when my own brain
went on hiatus.

To Marg Jackson for the laughter, friendship and
overall good company from day one.

To the Leadin' Ladies for their unwavering support
that never fails to humble me and buoy my spirits
in one fell swoop. You ladies are the best!

CHAPTER ONE

DEAN HALVORSEN'S day soured just about the same time his breakfast burrito heartburn kicked in, and he realized as he fished around in his pocket that he'd left his antacids at home.

"Eagle came in with a lower bid. You know how it goes. Times are tough. The bottom line is tight and we had to go with the lowest bidder. You understand, right?"

Dean bit back what he wanted to say and gave a short nod to Petey Simonsini. No, he didn't understand. What he did understand was that Eagle Construction had snaked another job out from under his company by somehow coming under the Halvorsen Construction bid. Which was damn near impossible since Dean had cut the bid to the bone in an attempt to get the job.

"Aaron beat us fair and square, I suppose," Dean said, though it made his teeth grind just to say it. Aaron Eagle never did things the right way. He cut corners, hired unlicensed subcontractors and bought shoddy materials to punch holes in the budget. No. Dean didn't figure Aaron had beat him square at all, but there was no sense in whining about it. Except, as he rubbed at the spot on his chest where the acid pooled, he knew his temper was about to get the best of him.

Damn him. The man was on a personal quest to put Halvorsen Construction out of business. This was the third bid they'd lost to Eagle in six months. It seemed every time Dean put in a bid, Aaron was right behind him, even on the out-of-town jobs. The man had an agenda and it was starting to piss Dean off. Pretty soon he was going to have to start bidding on state jobs and that idea didn't appeal at all—not because he hated the unions, which wasn't entirely true, but because of all the red tape that came with those jobs.

By the time he arrived at the office, his heartburn had reached four-alarm status. As he burst through the door, intent on one thing—to find his antacids— he pulled up short and choked on what he saw.

His younger brother Sammy looked up and grinned broadly, daring Dean to yell, and then introduced the woman sitting behind the desk.

Beth's desk.

"Dean, meet our new office manager, Annabelle Nichols."

She stood and extended her hand, but Dean wasn't in the mood to play nice anymore. Too bad for her. And he was going to have one less brother in about two minutes.

"I don't remember hiring an office manager,"

Dean said stonily, and she withdrew her hand with a nervous glance at Sammy.

"Aw, c'mon now. Don't be a jerk in front of Annabelle. There's plenty of time to show her just how difficult and surly you can be. Why start with the first day?"

Sammy—ever the comedian. But Dean wasn't laughing. Sammy had broached the subject of hiring someone new last week, and Dean thought he'd communicated quite clearly his thoughts on the subject. They didn't need anyone new.

As he eyed the woman in front of him, Dean realized he must not have been clear enough.

Ignoring Sammy, he said to her, "Ma'am, I'm afraid there's been a miscommunication between me and my idiot brother. We're not hiring right now. I'll pay you a full day's wage for your trouble."

"Excuse us, Annabelle. This will just take a minute." Sammy lost his good-time grin and strode to Dean. "I own a stake in this company, and I say we *do* need someone. Beth's been gone two years and the business is slowly falling to crap because you've refused to hire a full-time office manager. The temp agencies were fine for the short haul, but the constant flow of people that have come and gone through here is killing us. We're losing too many jobs because of stupid mistakes that wouldn't have been an issue if we'd had someone like Beth in the office."

"There's no one like Beth," Dean all but growled, appalled that Sammy would even suggest such a thing. He avoided looking in the woman's direction but he could smell something fruity in the air—melon, perhaps—probably coming from that long curly hair, he noted with a frown. It was making his nose itch. "Everything's fine. You're overreacting."

"Bullshit," Sammy said, his temper flaring. He gestured to the desk that was littered with Post-its, paperwork, bits and scraps of note pages and job sheets. "You couldn't find a brick on that desk much less anything important, like contracts and subcontractor bids!"

"All you need is a good file system," the woman interjected quickly, drawing Dean's attention away from the need to place his fist squarely into his brother's face. She swallowed and gestured, her hands moving like little birds as she gathered piles. "And I was just telling Sammy when you came in that I may have an idea that might work to organize your system."

"The system's fine the way it is," he answered, giving her a hard look, which she—surprisingly—returned.

"Not from what I can see," she said. "Your system is cataloged by job number, which makes it hard to find later for reference. If the files were alphabetical, it would be much more efficient and you wouldn't have a Post-it forest growing on your desk, the surface of which, I might add, has completely disappeared. It's no wonder you're losing jobs."

Dean sent a quick look to his brother. Sammy had told her about Gilly's? That was low. Embarrassment at that incident made his heartburn feel like a mild tickle.

"Yes, I told her about Gilly's," Sammy said without a hint of apology, his gaze clear but concerned. "Beth's gone. We all loved her but we can't let the family business go down the tubes because you don't want anyone else to sit at that desk."

Dean caught the quick widening of Annabelle's eyes and he felt terribly exposed. Beth used to keep the office running smoothly. They had been a team: a well-oiled machine that had helped take his father's company to another level of business. She was not only his wife, but his best friend and business partner.

No one could replace her. Especially not a woman barely out of her teens. Dean assessed Annabelle with a quick, dismissive sweep. She wasn't a day over twenty-five, he'd wager, though there was something about her—the way her dark eyes caught everything without missing a beat—that made her seem older.

"Sorry," he said to her, as he pulled his wallet from his back pocket. "I said we don't need anyone else." Throwing a wad of cash to the desk, he turned on his heel, saying over his shoulder to his brother, "She's gone by the time I get back."

ANNABELLE felt the slam of the office door reverberate, and she exhaled heavily, pursing her lips against the awkward moment sitting between her and Sammy.

Sammy was married to Annabelle's best friend, Dana, but Annabelle didn't know him or his family very well, having only just moved to Emmett's Mill. Obviously, he'd offered her the job without consulting his brother.

And now she was in a strange town without a job. If that wasn't a continuation of the stream of bad luck she'd been cursed with, she didn't know what else was.

"Let me talk to him," Sammy said, his mouth grim. "He'll come around."

"It's fine. Don't push it. He seems pretty set in his mind. Besides, I've never been the type to stay when I'm wanted to go. Thanks for trying, though. I appreciate it."

Sammy shook his head resolutely. "No. I'll talk to my dad. He'll get him to see reason."

Annabelle shuddered at the thought of Sammy doing such a thing on her account. "God no. I don't even know your brother, but I wouldn't much like it if someone tattled on me like that. I'll be fine. There's gotta be something else available. Restaurants are always hiring, right?"

Sammy grimaced. "Maybe. But Emmett's Mill is a tourist town. It practically shuts down in the winter. Hell, I'm sorry, Annabelle. Dana and I pretty much talked you into moving here on the promise that you'd have a job. I never figured on Dean being such an ass about the whole thing. I mean, I knew he'd be resistant but not this bad...."

She patted Sammy on the shoulder and scooped up the cash on the desk. "My rent's paid for the month. I'll find something else. Besides, I like it here. It's a perfect town for a fresh start."

Sammy smiled but there was worry in his expression. Pocketing the cash, she grinned without showing a hint of the true panic starting to blossom, and did what she could to allay his concern. Dana had married a good man. It wasn't his fault things hadn't worked out as they'd hoped.

If anyone was well acquainted with disappointment, it was Annabelle. But she never dwelled on the past. And as she closed the office door to Halvorsen Construction she considered the unfortunate incident with Dean Halvorsen well on its way to history.

She paused briefly at her car. For some reason, she'd thought this was going to be the place where she could put down roots. Talk about being way off.

Family, roots, stability. She snorted. An illusion. All of it. God, when was she ever going to learn?

CHAPTER TWO

DEAN HEARD her voice before he saw her. Returning to his double cheeseburger, he tried to ignore the flash of guilt but it had already ruined his lunch.

Annabelle was talking earnestly to Steve Gerke, the manager of The Grill, and by the look on Steve's face, whatever they were talking about didn't bode well for her. Dean pushed his plate away, ready to leave. He signaled for the waitress, but she motioned that she'd be a few minutes. *Great.* Annabelle drew his gaze despite his resolve to pretend he didn't see her trying to find a job.

"I learn fast," he heard her say. Her voice was husky yet melodic. A strange contradiction he hadn't noticed the other day. His ears pricked again. "Anything? Dishwasher, maybe? How about line cook? I can make a mean plate of hash browns."

"I'm sorry, Ms...."

"Nichols. Annabelle Nichols."

"Ms. Nichols. We've already hired all the staff we need at the moment. Good luck with your search. Leave your number with Maria up front and I'll let you know if anything changes."

Tough break. He tried not to see the sharp disappointment on her face but she kept forcing his attention toward her. She looked like one of those fine-boned porcelain dolls that cost so much you shouldn't touch them. He shook off the thought and motioned again to the waitress, ready to get back to the office, when Aaron walked in. *Ah hell.*

Dean must've racked up a serious deficit in a past life for all the karmic crap he'd been served lately.

He stiffened, determined to ignore the man, but Aaron had a knack for pissing people off—a talent Dean was sure he perfected in the privacy of his own home—and right now, Aaron was doing a bang-up job of rubbing Dean the wrong way.

Aaron's expression lit with a dark zeal when he saw Dean, and it was all Dean could do to remember his manners and not deck the guy right then and there. There was no love lost between them, and both men knew why.

Dean wasn't the smooth talker in the family. That was his younger brother Sammy's forte. And he left him to it for good reason. He'd never excelled at smiling and playing nice when he wanted to do the exact opposite. This was something Aaron knew and exploited whenever possible.

"Great job landing that new plaza contract, though I don't know how you managed to talk old man Tucker into selling that slice of land. I've been trying for years and the old sucker wouldn't budge. Mind sharing any tips?" Aaron asked with feigned casual interest.

"You seem to be doing fine on your own," Dean said tightly, his gaze returning to the woman giving Steve one last chance to decide that he couldn't live without her on the payroll. He had to give her points for tenacity. She didn't give up easily. "You don't need any help from me," he added, signaling an end—at least on his part—to the conversation.

Aaron tracked Dean's stare and noticed Annabelle, appreciation for her lush curves and ample breasts evident in his lingering look. "Who's that?"

"Dunno." That was mildly correct. Dean didn't actually know her. Didn't want to know her. Aaron continued to stare and Dean's patience slipped. "A little young for you, don't you think?"

"Not a crime to look." Aaron smiled. "I'd say a body like that was made to draw attention. Maybe someone ought to welcome her to the community. Seeing as you're heading out, I'll take care of it." He clapped Dean on the shoulder, which was at best annoying and made Dean want to growl at the liberty, and then headed in the young woman's direction.

Good sense told him to leave. But watching Aaron sidle up to Annabelle made his blood boil. Dean looked away, ready to leave, but there was no way he could walk out the door with Aaron sizing her up. Biting off a silent string of curses, Dean followed Aaron, intending to warn the woman off whatever Aaron planned to offer, and, if it worked, he'd enjoy ruining Aaron's day as a bonus.

Aaron's smile faltered briefly when he realized

Dean was standing beside him, but he didn't veer off course.

"What seems to be the problem, Steve?" Aaron asked the manager with a wide smile but his attention never left Annabelle. "You giving this beautiful woman trouble?"

To her credit, she didn't seem impressed with Aaron's chivalrous act and actually inched away to provide a wider buffer between them as she answered for Steve. "No problem. Just looking for a job. Thanks though."

"And I told her there aren't any openings right now," Steve said, shooting Annabelle a regretful look. "But, like I said, leave your name and number with Maria and we'll keep you in mind."

Steve left and Annabelle's expression showed her disappointment, which Aaron was quick to capitalize on.

"I'll bet I could find some work for you. What's your name, sweetheart?" Aaron asked. "Are you new in town?"

"Annabelle Nichols," she answered, glancing at Dean for a brief second. Her soft brown eyes seared into his with a force that threatened to knock him back, but she didn't acknowledge him otherwise. She had freckles, he noted with surprise. Faint dots of color sprinkled the bridge of her nose in a way that could only be described as terminally cute, but her long red hair fell in loose, inviting waves—

He jerked imperceptibly at the direction of his

thoughts, deciding he was no better than Aaron, thinking things he shouldn't about someone who was young enough to be…well, a sister.

At forty-one, he didn't need to be lusting after a woman in her early twenties. That sort of thing begged for trouble, and trouble he didn't need.

"Where you from?" Aaron asked, looking the part of a politely interested passerby, but Dean didn't buy it. The man had no shame. "Can't be from around here. I'd remember someone like you," he said with a boyish smile, and Dean's desire to punch him intensified.

But, seeing as he couldn't deck the man in a restaurant, Dean skewered Aaron with a short look and asked, "How're Gina and the new baby?"

Aaron's gaze narrowed at being caught in his game and a dull stain colored his cheeks. "Doing fine. Thanks for asking," he answered with a tight smile but didn't take the opportunity to bow out with his tail between his legs. Instead, he recovered with a grin. "So, what can you do, sweetheart? I might have an opening."

"She already has a job," Dean blurted, ignoring Aaron's irritated stare and Annabelle's startled one. He was damn sure not going to let Aaron try to worm his way into Annabelle's pants under the guise of doing something nice. Yet even as his mouth moved he wondered what the hell he was doing. He'd made himself abundantly clear to Annabelle yesterday, yet here he was looking like an indecisive ass with a bad temper today. To hell with it. That was all before

Aaron stuck his nose into it. He eyed her intently. "Don't you?"

"I…uh…yeah. I guess so," she answered. Though clearly confused, she was willing to play along.

Aaron shot Dean an accusatory look. "You said you didn't know her. Now she works for you?"

"I just met her yesterday. I forgot Sammy hired her." Again, mostly true. *So piss off, you philandering prick.* Dean looked at Annabelle. "If we're not paying you enough I'll see what we can do. No sense in you working two jobs if you don't have to."

"Thanks," she said, watching him curiously. "So, I'll see you tomorrow morning?"

"Yeah."

Aaron's smile returned, not quite ready to call it quits. Adjusting quickly, he changed tactics. "Trust me, darlin', you don't want to work for this grouch. He's no fun. Come with me and I'll show you how working for Eagle Construction is better. Besides, from what I've been hearing, Halvorsen Construction has had a run of bad luck. No such problems with Eagle. You'd never have to worry about your check clearing."

Dean caught Annabelle's look of alarm and it took everything in him not to clench his fists. Instead, he smiled thinly and said, "Well, it's true we've lost a few bids to an unscrupulous contractor, but at least with Halvorsen Construction you don't have to worry about the boss trying to look down your shirt or up your skirt."

Annabelle moved away from Aaron with a small

smile and her next comment made Dean's respect level go up a notch. "Thanks, but I'm not looking for a good time. I'm just looking for something to pay the bills."

"Fair enough," Aaron said, tipping his baseball cap to her and spearing Dean with a black look. "Maybe I'll see you around." To Dean he said, "You ought to come by and see how Gilly's turned out. We managed to pick up the contract when the original contractor crapped out. See you around, Dean."

Dean didn't bother with a rebuttal. There was no sense in playing Aaron's game. Dean liked to think he was better than that, that his parents had raised him to be a better person, but the urge was strong to do something he'd regret later.

"I take it you're not buddies."

"No. Can't stand the man."

"Listen, I'd love to hear that story sometime, but right now I just hope you were serious about the job, because if not I need to track down that Steve guy again and try harder to convince him that he needs me here at the restaurant. I'm not quitting this day until I go home with a job."

It wasn't his style to butt his nose into other people's business, but the thought of Annabelle even considering working for Eagle Construction was worse than disobeying his own tenet to keep to his own affairs. Not that she was really in any danger— the woman was no pretty bimbo. Sharp intelligence flared behind her eyes and the longer he stared, the harder it was to tear himself away. That in itself should've been a big enough warning to back off, but his pride warred with his guilt until he raised his hands in surrender. He'd used her to win a small battle with Aaron; the least he could do was give her a job until she could find something else.

"I'm sorry about yesterday," he said gruffly. "Sammy should've warned me. I reacted badly. Be at the office tomorrow at 8:00 a.m. and we'll talk about your duties."

"Sure. Thanks." She shifted and bit the inside of her cheek absently, the action reminding him that she was truly much younger than him. "I'll keep an eye out for something else though."

"You got family who could help you out?" he asked, wishing he hadn't. It wasn't a good idea to get too acquainted.

She chuckled wryly. "Nope. My mom died a few years ago and my daddy was a bit of a rambling man. I haven't seen him since I was about seven. I have a younger brother, but the less I see of him the better off my pocketbook is." She shrugged as if admitting that her family was less than desirable wasn't a big deal. "I learned to rely on myself a long time ago."

He believed her. Dressed in a denim skirt that was too short and a blouse that fit too tightly across her breasts, she looked like a white-trash prom queen looking for a date but there was a sense of dignity clinging to her that dared anyone to pass judgment.

Closing his eyes briefly to block out the image of

her as she stood before him, he bit out a terse, "Don't be late," as his goodbye and walked—no, practically ran—from the restaurant.

CHAPTER THREE

DEAN GLANCED at the dusty wall clock and noted the time. Five past eight. She was officially late on her first day of work. That didn't bode well for her future with Halvorsen Construction. He sighed. So much for helping a person out. He grabbed the plans for the building site he was scheduled to survey today and had only just rolled them out the length of his conference table when the front door flew open. Annabelle came through carrying more things than she had hands.

Then he noticed the small bundle in her right arm was wearing tiny shoes and his mouth dropped open.

"I'm so sorry," she started, setting down a stuffed diaper bag and a long rectangle of a contraption that Dean had a sinking feeling was a playpen. "Dana was supposed to watch Honey, but she was called out on the ambulance and I didn't have time to find another babysitter. But I swear she'll be no trouble at all. I brought toys and snacks and her favorite blanket and…and…please don't fire me. I really need this job."

"Honey?" Dean stared at the little girl who was staring at him with the biggest blue eyes he'd ever seen. "Did you say her name was Honey?"

"That's right," she answered, smiling without a hint of bashfulness. "From the moment I first laid eyes on her I thought she was the sweetest thing I'd ever seen and immediately knew Honey was the right choice. Honey Faith Nichols. She's my girl."

"How old is she?" he asked.

"Sixteen months. Her birthday is in February. She's an Aquarius. I'm a Cancer. Do you know what your sign is?"

"Uh, no. I don't believe in that stuff."

"Oh, I do. I think it gives a lot of insight to your personality. When's your birthday? I know a bit about astrology. I could find out—"

"No, that's okay. So, Honey… Aren't you worried about what other kids might say about a name like that?"

She frowned. "No. Should I be?"

"Well, I don't know, it's just a little odd."

At that she chuckled. "It's only odd to those who like everything to fit in preordained little spaces. I want to encourage Honey to do whatever inspires her. I don't want anyone ever to tell her that she can't or shouldn't do something simply because she might not fit a stereotype."

He didn't know what to say. Annabelle didn't seem to notice. She smiled as she looked at her daughter. Love was evident in her expression and voice as she said, "Besides, it's who she's meant to be. Can you imagine her as a Christie or a Sarah?"

No. Actually, he couldn't. Naming a kid something like Honey was a little too hippy-dippy for his sensibilities, but the longer he stared at the child he realized the name fitted her well. The kid was downright cherubic. He couldn't remember if all kids that age were that cute or just this one. He glanced at the clock and his odd musing fled.

"Uh, well, as long as she stays in that playpen," he said, not quite sure of what else to do. "This place isn't baby-proof and it's not safe. I'm not even sure if we're insured for this sort of thing. God, I'm betting we're not. Just keep her contained, will you?"

"Absolutely," she agreed, bobbing her head. "You won't even notice she's here. I promise. She's the best baby. Thank you."

Dean eyed the baby and all the gear that came with her and was thrown off-kilter. His son, Brandon, was seventeen and self-sufficient. Dean hardly remembered what it was like to have a baby around. And that's just the way he wanted to keep it, he almost growled.

Grabbing his coat, he was stalking out, ready to get to the job site and back to something he understood and felt comfortable with, when he realized he hadn't told Annabelle her duties. Stopping at the door, he gestured toward the mess, saying, "Don't touch anything. I have a system and I don't want anyone messing with it."

She gave his cluttered desk a dubious look but nodded to indicate she wouldn't touch it. "So, what should I do?" she asked.

"You can make coffee, answer phones, take messages, scrub the bathroom, general office stuff."

"I don't consider scrubbing the bathroom general office stuff," she retorted, frowning. "I could file things for you. Type up whatever you need. I'm pretty handy with the computer, too. What computer programs are you running?"

"Uh." He glanced down at his watch and swore. "I don't know. Sammy does all that stuff. You'll have to ask him. Don't file anything. Like I said, you'll mess up my system. Just…just…I don't know, stay out of things. I'll be back in a while. I'm late!"

Dean got to the job site and although part of his brain was on work and he managed a coherent conversation with the foreman, another part of his brain was stuck on the woman sitting in his office with a toddler.

She should've mentioned she had a kid.

Why?

Because…well, there was no defensible answer because it was none of his business. Still, it became his business when that kid ended up in his office.

This wasn't something that could become a habit. He hadn't wanted to hire her in the first place and now he had a woman with daycare issues.

He glanced skyward at the clouds rolling in for an end-of-season storm and knew it would be raining before he returned to the office. It wouldn't be a cold rain, but rather a mild soak promising some muggy humidity afterward.

Sammy drove up, raucous music blaring from his truck loud enough to split an eardrum, and Dean was ready to take out his frustration on his youngest brother.

"What's up, big brother?" Sammy asked with typical good humor. Sammy had been born with an innate ability to find the lighter side in every situation. "I hear you hired Dana's friend? Good. Sounds like a win-win situation on both sides."

News traveled fast. Especially between women. "You know she has a kid?"

"Yeah? So? You like kids. You got one of your own, remember?"

Dean glowered. "I didn't expect her to show up for her first day of work with a baby on her hip. That's not professional by my standards."

"You need to loosen up. You're wound so tight if you were a clock you'd bust a spring. Listen, Dana told me a little about her story and she deserves a break."

"What do you mean?"

Sammy shrugged. "For being only twenty-six, she's had a hard life."

"How so?"

"Why don't you ask her?"

Dean backed off. "I don't want to get involved."

"Too late. She's your employee now. I'd say you're involved…at least a little." At Dean's sour look, Sammy chuckled. "So she's packing a kid around. Big deal. What counts is she's a good person looking for a fresh start, right?"

"Yeah, I guess so," Dean said, softening just a little. He admired people willing to work hard and earn what they wanted in life, but he also knew that sometimes luck played a part. By the sounds of it, she hadn't had much in that department. "All right. She can stay—for a while. We'll see how good an office manager she turns out to be. No promises, got it?"

"No problem. I've done my part by talking her up. The rest is on her. Dana understands that. I think," he added with a slight frown.

Dean eyed Sammy speculatively. "Everything okay? With you and Dana?"

"Yeah, sure," Sammy said, waving away Dean's concern but then added, "You know, this marriage stuff isn't as easy as you and Beth made it look. I guess I figured as long as you loved someone all the other stuff would fall into line. Besides, the other stuff is petty, right?"

"Sometimes it is and sometimes it isn't. What's going on with you two?"

Sammy shrugged. "Sometimes I don't get Dana. I ask her 'what's wrong?' and she says 'nothing,' but then glares at me for the rest of the day as if I haven't asked. She's got me so turned upside-down I don't know which end is up anymore."

"You love her, right?"

"More than I thought possible. It's kinda scary, actually. I never thought I'd feel this way about anyone."

Dean remembered those early days when he and Beth were two dumb kids playing house rather than two adults trying to foster a good marriage. "Then stick with it. It gets better with time. You get to know each other and then you fall into a rhythm. There were times when Beth and I could almost finish each other's sentences we were so in tune with each other," he said. "And then there were other times when it seemed we were talking different languages. It's a dance, brother. When you have a good partner sometimes you lead, other times you follow, but it's always a beautiful song."

A moment of silence passed between the brothers as a wave of loss rippled between them. Inhaling slowly, Sammy clapped Dean on the shoulder. "Beth was one of a kind. No doubt about it."

"That she was," Dean agreed, his throat closing. He looked at Sammy. "Hey, enough of this serious stuff. We're sitting here sniffling like two old ladies when we've got work to do."

"Ever the hard-ass." Sammy smiled. After a short pause, he sobered, saying, "Thanks for giving Annabelle a chance. She needs it. And I think she'll be good for the office."

Dean nodded grudgingly, not quite sure where he sat on that score. He hoped it went smoothly. He'd never been one to fire someone, which was why he preferred to work with family. He knew they wouldn't let him down. All three Halvorsen men were dependable, even Sammy, despite his wild streak. In fact, he was really missing his brother Josh, but he couldn't fault the man for wanting to spend time with his new wife, Tasha. He sighed, his thoughts returning to his new office manager, hoping he wouldn't regret his decision.

Time would tell.

ANNABELLE sat behind the incredibly messy desk and wondered what she was supposed to do if she couldn't actually do anything. Honey was playing quietly in her playpen, content for the moment with the plethora of toys and books Annabelle had brought, so Annabelle took the opportunity to walk around the small office space.

It was nothing fancy and it was plainly evident men were the primary occupants. The bathroom was, for lack of a better word, gross. The seat on the toilet was up and if she hadn't noticed before trying to use it she'd have been swimming in the toilet bowl.

She was returning to the desk when the front door opened and a tall, good-looking teen walked in, then did a double take.

"Who are you?" he asked without preamble, a scowl deepening on his face. "Where's my dad?"

Annabelle jumped from the chair and extended a hand toward the boy, but he chose to ignore the gesture and ask again, "Who are you and why are you sitting in my mom's chair?"

"Oh, uh, I didn't realize someone… Uh, well, Mr. Halvorsen didn't actually specify where I should sit,

I just assumed I should sit here. My name's Annabelle Nichols. It's my first day. And you are?"

"Brandon Halvorsen. My dad owns this place," he answered, plainly still ticked but doing his teenage best to keep it under control. Too bad for her he wasn't doing a great job. She felt like a first-rate interloper. "When's he coming back?" he demanded, and she managed a shrug.

"He didn't say." Great. The kid hated her for some reason. For the sake of keeping her job, she tried making amends for whatever he thought she'd done. "I'm sorry I caught you off guard. Your dad offered me the job yesterday and it's my first day." She hesitated. "I'm sorry about your mom," she offered—Dana had told her Dean's wife had died in a car accident—but the boy was plainly not in the mood to receive condolences.

He grunted. "Yeah, well, that's life, right?"

"Sometimes. My mom died a few years ago. I know what it feels like to lose someone special. If you ever need someone to talk to…I can relate."

He looked at her as if she was crazy, and she wished she could rescind the offer. This kid was determined to be pissed at her no matter what she said. Fine. She wasn't one to push against a brick wall. She sighed. "Well, nice to meet you. I'd better get back to work. Do you want to leave a message for your dad that you came by?"

"Don't bother. I'll call his cell," the boy said and abruptly left, slamming the door behind him.

She glared at the door and wondered if taking this job was more trouble than it was worth. Surely, there had to be something else in this town that she could do. Obviously, Dean had forgotten to mention a few key points about this job. Such as a bad-tempered teenager who didn't approve of anyone taking over where his mom left off. She glanced around the office, noting the disarray, and wondered how long the office had been running without a rudder. She knew how lost she'd felt when her mom died. She couldn't imagine losing a spouse and a business partner at once.

She turned to Honey, who was watching with an owl-like stare that was her signature. Annabelle often wondered if her daughter was an old soul. Sometimes, it seemed the girl knew more than she should at such a tender age. Her mouth twitched with a confused smile as she asked, "What are we going to do, kiddo? Stick it out with these people or just call it a day?"

Honey blinked and then returned to her toys, seemingly content with what she had been doing.

"All right," Annabelle said, pursing her lips slightly as she decided to stick it out and see where things went. "We stay. But don't get too comfortable. I have a feeling this just isn't the place for us."

CHAPTER FOUR

"IT'S JUST temporary," Dean said to Brandon's sullen, accusatory glare from across the dinner table. "Your uncle Sammy seems to think we need a little help around the office. And Annabelle is a friend of Dana's so it seemed like a good deal for both of us."

"We don't need anyone messing around with the office," Brandon said. "She'll screw up Mom's system. Besides, what happened to the temp service you were using?"

"The temps weren't working out as we'd hoped. There was too much turnover. Besides, there wasn't one I felt was a good enough fit. As much as I hate to admit it, we're in bad shape. And we can't afford to lose any more business. But don't worry, she's not going to change anything. And, if things don't work out, we don't have an obligation to keep her. I made that clear."

Dean pushed away from his plate, his appetite disappearing at the direction of the conversation. He drew a deep breath. "Like I said, it's temporary and there's nothing wrong with helping a person who's down on their luck. Your mom would've wanted us to lend a hand. You know she would."

Brandon softened imperceptibly at the mention of Beth, but Dean could still see the storm raging behind his son's eyes. "I don't want her there," he said. "It feels wrong seeing her sit in Mom's chair. Doing Mom's job. It's just not right."

"You didn't have a problem with the temps."

"She's different. The temps were usually old ladies looking for a supplement to their retirement. This woman is no old lady."

Dean leveled his gaze at Brandon and hoped his son never found cause to doubt his word as he said, "No one is going to replace your mother. Ever. She's always here in our hearts and no one can ever take that away. But, as much as I've tried to ignore it, the office is falling apart. We lost two bids last week to Eagle Construction, and as far as I can tell Aaron's hot on the trail of any unsecured contract. We can't keep taking hits like this for much longer if we want to stay in business."

A long pause sat between them until Brandon relented with a slow nod of his head. His boy was headstrong but not stupid. "So, you're saying she's only staying until we get things organized, right?" Brandon asked.

"Well, that's the plan," Dean answered with complete conviction, but Brandon still seemed troubled. "What?" he asked, wanting to do whatever he could to allay his son's fears.

Brandon shifted in his chair, plainly uncomfortable with whatever else was rattling around his head. "She's pretty," he finally blurted, but the way he said it didn't make that sound like a good thing and Dean knew what his son was afraid of.

"She's attractive," Dean acknowledged, shutting out the image of Annabelle as she'd been dressed the other day. All legs and breasts. "But I'm not looking, if you know what I mean."

Brandon sighed with obvious relief and he grinned for the first time since the evening began. "Thanks, Dad. I needed to hear that. I got a little freaked out when I saw her. A lot of guys would think she's hot or something, but I should've known you're too old for her anyway."

Dean forced a chuckle, trying not to let his son's innocent statement sting. Hadn't he told himself the very same thing? "Glad we got that out of the way," he said a bit wryly, signaling the end of the conversation.

Brandon smiled. "Me, too. I guess she can stay until you can find something else for her. You're right. Mom would've wanted us to help if we could. She was always looking out for everyone but herself."

Dean nodded and swallowed the sudden lump in his throat that never failed to choke him when he thought of Beth. God, he missed her. It didn't seem fair that she'd been taken from them so young, but since it never brought her back, he'd long ago stopped railing against the injustice of God's plan.

Some things just weren't fair and that was that.

His thoughts wandered to Annabelle and what little he knew of her. Sammy had implied that life hadn't been particularly fair to her, either, but she didn't seem the type to cry about it. He had to admit he admired that in a person. Anyone could sit and bawl. It took guts and a strong character to pull themselves up and move when all they wanted to do was quit.

Where was Honey's father? Was he in the picture at all? Sighing, he realized it wasn't his place to wonder such things. No good was going to come from him poking his nose into Annabelle's business, especially after promising his son that she wouldn't be around long.

ANNABELLE ARRIVED on time the following morning, earning a curt nod of approval from Dean as she entered the office. He also didn't hide his relief that Honey was not with her. She withheld a sigh for his obvious dislike of her baby and tried not to take it personally. It was his loss. Honey was an amazing kid.

Dean gestured toward a ridiculously small desk and she looked at him quizzically. "That's where I'm supposed to sit? Which sixth-grade classroom is missing a desk?"

"I know it's on the small side, but I wanted you to have a space to work from while we get things figured out. It's all I could find on such short notice."

"What's wrong with that desk?" she pointed at the large and still cluttered desk he was behind.

"It's not a good idea."

"Why not?"

"Because it's not."

She inhaled a short yet frustrated breath. "Listen, this is a little crazy. You can't possibly expect me to sit at that baby desk when there's a perfectly good, adult-size desk right here."

"My wife used to sit there," he said bluntly.

She tried to tread carefully, but his odd territorial stance on the furniture was wearing on her patience. If she'd had anything else to go to, she'd ditch this job in a second. But she didn't and therefore was stuck with the need to make a go of it. With as much delicacy as her annoyance would allow, she said, "I'm sorry for your loss. Dana told me your wife died. But I can't really do the job you've hired me to do without a proper place to sit. I promise I won't change anything. I won't move pictures around or kill her plants—although, you seem to be doing a pretty good job of that yourself—and I'll even do my damnedest to learn your kooky system, but you have to loosen up, too."

He stared and she held her breath, knowing the next words out of his stern mouth were going to be something along the lines of *Don't let the door hit your ass on the way out,* and resigned herself to another serious job hunt.

But he didn't.

"You've got a point," he slowly agreed, though it looked like the admission was painful. "All right, I'll haul that kiddie desk out of here."

"Thank you," she said, thinking privately it seemed an odd thing to be grateful for, but she accepted the victory just the same. "Now, show me how to run this office."

An hour later, Annabelle had a headache.

"But why don't you just file the jobs alphabetically?" she asked, not quite understanding the inefficient way they were doing things. "This number system is bound to screw things up. No wonder you're losing stuff. Look here, this job and this job—" she gestured to two different slips of paper "—have the same number but they're different contracts. If you used an alphabetical system by company or client name you'd have less slipping through the cracks."

"Beth devised this number system and it worked before so it'll work again. Now, instead of fighting me on it, just listen and learn."

Annabelle bristled. It wasn't in her nature to allow someone to talk to her as though she was an idiot. And it didn't matter that Dean was the kind of man who could make her look twice on a crowded street— he was seriously pissing her off with his dogged refusal to see what was plain in front of his face.

"I'm sure this system worked peachy for the woman who conjured it out of her head but for us mere mortals, it's a bit confusing. Even you can't seem to figure it out."

Dean's face flushed a dull red and she knew she'd crossed the line. Damn it all to hell. But even as Annabelle prepared for the roar of indignation she was sure was heading her way, he seemed to choke down whatever had been dancing on his tongue and uttered a grunt of some sort that may have been an agreement.

But he didn't look happy about it. "Well, she made it look easy. And all the files are numbered in this way. To start over would take an inordinate amount of time that I don't have."

At this Annabelle brightened. Finally something she could work with. "No problem. That's what I'm here for. I'll get this system turned around so that anyone coming in after me could easily figure it out, and you can concentrate on getting the jobs."

He shifted uneasily, but there was a glimmer of interest in his brown eyes that Annabelle had to admit made her insides flip-flop oddly. "You think you could do that?"

She smiled. "Of course. I wouldn't have made the offer if I couldn't deliver. I've worked in an office before and I have an eye for efficiency. I guess you could call it my gift."

He grunted, but she couldn't tell if it was a noise that qualified as approval or disapproval and so she said, "You know, if we're going to work together we need a better communication style."

He blinked. "What do you mean?"

"I mean the grunting has to stop. I know guys have their own language, but for the purposes of ensuring that I don't misunderstand you, let's try for a mutually agreed-upon language. Like English."

Dean scowled, but Annabelle wasn't deterred or intimidated. She'd been around men more coarse and meaner than Dean Halvorsen could ever manage to be, and she wasn't going to back down. Besides, her mom had always said, men needed to be reminded every now and again of the rules, otherwise they ran amuck. Much like dogs.

Although, now that she thought about it, her mom might not have been the best for advice about men— she never seemed to be able to hold on to one or find one worth keeping.

She sighed privately, pushing that particular thought as far away as she could manage, and returned her attention to Dean.

"So, what's it going to be?"

He sighed with annoyance but answered quite clearly, "Fine. Can we get back to work?"

"Absolutely." She graced him with a wide smile that wasn't the least bit coy or suggestive but suddenly he seemed caught, and when he tore his gaze away from hers, she wondered whether she was imagining things or Dean might actually find her attractive.

Did she want that? Good God, no. But…a lonely voice protested softly, Dean was one of the good guys. She could feel it in her bones. Her intuition was usually spot-on—having had to dodge creeps and toads on a regular basis growing up—but she'd let her guard down and Thad had somehow gotten past her defenses. She thought of Honey and she couldn't regret her choice in that regard, but she'd be a liar if she didn't say that she wished she'd found a decent man to father her child.

But messing around with the boss was a giant no-no.

"I see you found a babysitter."

Dean's voice broke into her thoughts, a welcome distraction. She nodded. "Dana is watching her for me on the days that she isn't working."

"You and Dana grew up together, right?"

"Yeah," she answered, moving away from Dean and grabbing a handful of files. She wasn't in the mood to share her dismal upbringing. Besides, he probably already knew all the highlights. No sense in sharing the lowlights as well. "Well, I'd better get started redoing this system or else it'll take all day."

DEAN MOVED to one side of the office and tried to ignore the way Annabelle's skirt swished around her legs as she went about her business, filing and lightly humming as she went. There was something earthy and comforting about her confidence, in spite of her wardrobe choices. It wasn't her skirt that was the problem, he thought, averting his eyes, searching for anything that might be more appropriate than what kept drawing his gaze.

Autumn was in the air but it was still warm enough to cause beads of sweat to coat his brow if he stood in the direct sunlight, which was probably why she had chosen the strappy number clinging to her breasts like a second skin, molding to the firm, plump flesh as if it were painted on, but it was damn distracting and not exactly professional, he groused. Jamming his baseball cap on his head—intent on getting out of there to meet a client at the job site—it took a moment for him to realize that his groin was reacting in a most inappropriate manner, reminding him painfully that he was a man with needs he'd been ignoring for far too long. He'd been sure after Beth's death that that part of him was pretty much down for the count, too. Apparently, that was not the case.

Shame at his bodily reaction caused him to inhale sharply, and guilt for thinking of another woman in a sexual manner made him feel that he was no better than Aaron Eagle.

Echoes of Brandon's concerns floated into his panicked brain and he spun on his heel toward the door, only to slam his shin into the leg of a chair.

She turned at the sound to ask, "You okay?" Her eyebrows arched in concern, causing the tiniest wrinkles to mar her otherwise perfect face.

"Fine," he answered, biting back the swear words he wanted to yell because his shin was throbbing in time with the blood rushing to his cheeks…and other places. He managed to say, "I'll be back later," and then slammed out the door.

ANNABELLE STARED after Dean as he walked—no, limped—stiffly from the office, and she shook her head. Men. Would she ever understand them?

Probably not. Annabelle shrugged her shoulders, and said, "I don't think that man likes me." Then she turned to the file cabinet and focused on finishing her filing.

CHAPTER FIVE

ANNABELLE didn't mean it to, but a wistful sigh escaped her as she caught a private moment between Dana and Sammy in their kitchen.

Sammy, his eyes shining with love and desire, feasted on Dana as if she was a rack of lamb and he was a starving man.

Thad had never looked at her like that. Not truly.

Sure, she'd seen lust in men's eyes, but it had never gone further than that, and young as Annabelle was, she'd always known the difference. She'd had no use for men with mouths full of pretty words aimed at only one thing.

But even as she was slightly envious of the fairy-tale romance Dana seemed to be enjoying, she couldn't really remain that way. Dana deserved a good man. She'd had a rough childhood, too. That's probably what bonded the two of them so tightly. She'd do anything for Dana, and vice versa.

She forced a smile and cleared her throat as she lifted their dirty plates. "Sorry. I didn't mean to interrupt. Just trying to help out."

Sammy grinned and pinched Dana's behind as she tried to move past him. She jumped a little and her cheeks colored, but there was a high flush to her features that made her simply glow. Annabelle's eyes threatened to water. "You guys have to stop that. I think I'm still hormonal," she teased, allowing Dana to take the plates from her hand. "Isn't there some medical text that says a woman's hormones can go haywire as far as a year and a half after the birth of a baby?"

Sammy eyed Dana as if he were mentally undressing her and said, "Dunno. But we'll let you know once I manage to get this girl to squeeze a few out."

"Samuel!" Dana exclaimed, whirling long enough to snap him with a dish towel. "Get out of here before you scare my best friend away and she never comes back for dinner."

"Whatever you say," he said, as he sauntered out of the kitchen and went straight for Honey's makeshift high chair, pulling her out to gobble her little tummy with loud smacking noises. Honey's delighted giggles faded as the two disappeared to make mischief in the living room.

Dana's gaze softened and Annabelle felt her nose stuff up from the tears that weren't far behind. Damn, where'd all the waterworks come from? She rubbed at her eyes. It hurt knowing Dana wanted a baby so badly yet hadn't conceived. "Soon," Annabelle promised, meeting Dana's stare with absolute conviction. "Just give it time."

"I know," Dana said. "It's just hard. I see you with

Honey and she's such a wonderful baby and you're a great mom.... I want that, too."

"And you will. I'm sure that Halvorsen sperm is pretty industrious. Just give it a little more time. You've only been married six months. I mean, you guys should be spending more time getting busy than worrying if you're ovulating. Takes all the fun out of it, I hear."

Not that Annabelle would know about anything like that. She'd gotten pregnant distressingly easily.

"You got that right," Dana agreed. Eyes clearing, she linked her arm through Annabelle's and led her away from the dishes that needed washing and the remains of dinner that still needed to be put away, ignoring Annabelle's protests to the contrary, saying, "Tell me about working with Dean. I'm dying to know how you two are getting along."

"I'd rather wash the dishes," Annabelle said under her breath. At Dana's troubled look, Annabelle brightened with a customary grin. "Just kidding. He's...well, gruff and can't seem to stand the sight of me, but at least he changed his mind about giving me a job. That's all that counts in my book."

"So practical." Dana sighed, then gave her a subtle look that bordered on sly if Annabelle was to wager a guess and Annabelle stared her down.

"Don't even go there," Annabelle warned, knowing that look well enough to fear it. "I mean it, Dana. Do not try and play matchmaker."

"What?"

"Drop the innocent act, Collins. I know you too well."

Dana's nose wrinkled at the use of her maiden name but she didn't deny that something had been percolating in her brain. Yet she couldn't help but add in a rush, "He's single, very available, not to mention good-looking. Doesn't get better than a Halvorsen. They're good, honest—"

"Not interested," Annabelle stated firmly, interrupting Dana's Halvorsen PR spiel. "He's my boss. In other words—"

"Off-limits," Dana finished for her. "I know."

"I knew you'd understand. I just can't go there. I'm over my quota for stupid moves and I'm not about to start adding the mistakes of my mother to my own."

"You're not your mother," Dana said. "You know I loved her even more than mine but she was terrible when it came to guys. It's a wonder there weren't more like Buddy in and out of her life."

And, by proxy, mine. Annabelle shuddered at the thought of her mother's last boyfriend.

Evil, drunken bastard. That about summed it up. *Trailer trash,* Annabelle added, unable to help herself even in the privacy of her own head.

"He's still in prison, right?" Dana peered at Annabelle anxiously and Annabelle gave a short affirmative jerk of her head.

"Yeah, but he's up for parole in a year," Annabelle answered, adding with as much humor as she could muster in light of the subject matter, "I'm hoping he'll meet the business end of a pointy object before that happens. Prison, I hear, can be a dangerous place."

"Are you worried he'll come after you?"

Annabelle scoffed, but her insides quivered. "Of course not. He'd be the biggest idiot on the planet even to come near me. I wouldn't hesitate to shoot him."

"You don't own a gun."

Annabelle sent Dana a short look. "I'd buy one."

Dana chuckled. "I bet you would."

Shaking off the memory with visible effort, Annabelle returned the conversation to Dana and Sammy and their plans to remodel the little house they'd bought.

As Annabelle knew she would, Dana quickly warmed to the subject and soon her own troubles were forgotten as she simply enjoyed the company of her good friend and the quiet satisfaction that she'd secured a job without having to resort to cocktail waitressing, as she'd feared.

And she pushed all thoughts of Buddy King far from her mind.

THE NEXT DAY Dean got to the office early in hopes of being gone by the time Annabelle arrived, but, as often happened, the minute he stepped into the small building, he got distracted and wasn't able to get out before she arrived.

He grimaced as the door swung wide and Annabelle, carrying Honey, walked inside loaded down with various baby items. The look on her face was vaguely apologetic, but there was a hint of defiance as well.

"Let me guess. Dana was called into work unexpectedly," Dean said as he removed what he'd learned earlier was the playpen apparatus from her shoulder. She smiled briefly in thanks and he tried not to enjoy the feelings it sparked. "Do you need some help finding a babysitter?" he asked.

"I don't feel comfortable letting just anyone watch my baby," she said and he jerked against the subtle rebuke. "She's no trouble. Besides, Dana is coming at lunch to pick her up for me."

Dean thought of Beth and how protective she'd been of Brandon. In fact, he remembered Beth setting up a playpen for Brandon in nearly the same spot Annabelle was setting up a space for Honey. He sighed, realizing his argument was petty and if Beth were here, she'd agree that Honey, as young as she was, needed to be with her mother.

"She can stay," Dean said. "But since I'm guessing this could become a habit, I might as well childproof the office."

"You don't need to do that," she protested softly, distress in her expression. "I don't want to inconvenience anyone."

"Don't be ridiculous. It's not safe. You don't want to keep her in that pen all day, do you?"

"No, I suppose not." Her face broke out in a surprised yet gentle smile. "Thank you."

"Don't mention it." He resisted her attempt to take

the playpen from him and made quick work of setting it up for her. Seemed these kinds of things hadn't changed all that much since Brandon was a baby. "Beth was the same way. Never felt comfortable leaving Brandon with anyone."

She gave him a smile, uncertainty hovering at its edges, and placed her daughter inside the playpen. "So, you have just the one son?"

Dean nodded. "One seemed like enough. Beth had troubles. We didn't want to risk it."

"What kind of troubles?"

Dean shifted, hating the memory of those long-ago scary days when he worried that he might have to choose between his wife and his unborn child. "Ah, a bad case of placenta previa. Brandon was sitting right over Beth's…" His cheeks colored a little. "Um, cervix. It never got better like in some cases and we didn't know it because back then they didn't do scans routinely like doctors do now. They both almost died during the birth."

"That's awful. I can understand your reluctance to try again."

"Yeah." He almost said that Beth had been willing, but he figured he'd shared enough on that score. He gestured to Honey. "The dad in the picture?" he asked bluntly, needing to know for some reason.

Annabelle met his gaze and answered without flinching. "No. Being a daddy didn't appeal to Thad beyond the novelty. It's just me and my girl. And we like it that way."

The way her chin tilted up, as if daring him to say something, made him want to smile, but he controlled the impulse. The woman had pride. He understood that. "So, he's not bound to show up in Emmett's Mill wanting to play house again, right?"

She shook her head. "No. Thad was relieved when I told him we were leaving."

If Annabelle felt a flicker of sadness at her failed relationship, she hid it well. Dean wondered what kind of partner she'd been. He sensed she'd put everything she had into it, giving up only when she felt the relationship was a lost cause. She was a trouper, he could feel it.

But there was more to Annabelle Nichols than just her steel backbone and it was that other aspect of her that bothered Dean the most.

Without conscious effort, she exuded a sultry sensuality that echoed in her husky voice, making him shudder in a most uncomfortable manner. Everything about her was lush—from her sweet-smelling hair to the firm, wish-you-could-touch-them breasts barely contained by her too-tight tops.

Today she wore a sundress, faded by many washings, but still pretty. Honey wore a newer outfit in a matching sunny yellow with a floppy hat that she was now examining with quiet diligence, and Dean realized that Annabelle probably spent most of her money on her daughter, leaving little for herself.

"It's none of my business, but I'm curious just the same," Annabelle broke into his thoughts, peering at him with complete candor as she organized paper-work. "What's the deal between you and that other construction guy I met in the restaurant?"

SHE TOLD herself she was making conversation but she really wanted to know why Dean's eyes had glit-tered with anger despite his obvious effort at control. He'd nearly vibrated with violent energy he'd not acted on. Since she was new in town, she didn't know people's histories and felt at a distinct disadvantage.

Dean didn't seem compelled to answer at first, but, after a pregnant pause, he shrugged. "I don't care for his business practices or the way he conducts his personal life."

Annabelle nodded and resumed her task, but she kept a watch on Dean through lowered lashes. He was a big man, with broad shoulders—not surpris-ing for someone who'd been raised in the construc-tion business—fit and lean, hard with muscle.

One would never guess he spent most of his time on administrative tasks. Dana hadn't lied the other night. Dean Halvorsen wasn't hard on the eyes. Thick brown hair threaded with silver and in need of a quick snip framed a handsome face that didn't smile nearly enough and showcased a stubborn jaw that Annabelle had learned spent too much time clench-ing when he was trying to hold back something he shouldn't say or do.

Annabelle's gaze strayed to the framed photo of Beth on the desk and she swallowed instinctively as a strange lump bobbed in her throat. Beth Halvorsen had been pretty but not classically beautiful. Her blond hair hung to her shoulders and lines framed her blue eyes from a lifetime of laughter, with smaller ones around the firm mouth tipped in a smile at whoever was taking the picture. From the confident, slightly conspiratorial expression on her face, Dean had probably taken the photo. The light shining from Beth's eyes spoke of countless private conversations whispered in hushed tones meant only for a lover to hear.

Unable to look any longer, Annabelle glanced away. She knew from Dana that a car accident had claimed Beth too young and the entire Halvorsen family felt her loss. She considered briefly her own family and how when her mother had died, no one but she and Dana had gone to the funeral. No one had mourned the loss of Sadie Nichols. No one had even noticed. It had made Annabelle stiffen in fear that that would be her fate as well. Alone, used up, forgotten and thrown away.

"You okay?" Dean asked, drawing her attention from the paperwork in her hand that she had actually ceased to see. She shook her head and refocused on her job with a mumbled affirmative but Dean persisted. "You look a little pale. Do you need something? Coffee? Water? A soda?"

She risked a brief smile at his concern, but her heart ached for something she'd never known and probably never would. She knew deep down that Beth Halvorsen had experienced a true and abiding love, and it seemed downright shameful that Annabelle could even for a split second yearn for something similar with the woman's husband.

Disgrace flooded her cheeks, and she waved away Dean's offer on the pretense of needing to use the restroom. With a quick glance at Honey, who was playing quietly in her pen, Annabelle closed the door behind her and leaned against it. Drawing deep breaths, she willed away the despicable show of tears that crowded her sinuses, reminding her that she was a mess on the inside no matter how hard she tried to prove otherwise. She vowed she wouldn't dare leave this dirty, disgusting bathroom until she could emerge the happy, secure and strong person she desperately wanted to be.

A self-deprecating smile tinged with hysterical panic twisted her lips as she realized she could be in here awhile.

CHAPTER SIX

DEAN TRIED not to notice how Annabelle had practically run from the room to disappear into the bathroom, but it was pretty hard. His eyes seemed to find her no matter where she went and no matter how hard he tried to ignore her.

Tried to ignore was about the right choice of words, too. Removing her from his mind was the only thing that kept him focused. But of course the more you try to avoid something, the more your mind makes you ultrasensitive to it. All this failed avoidance strategy was giving him a headache.

Honey made a distressed sound and he turned to regard her with apprehension. "Yeah?" he asked, as if she could answer him.

She toddled to her feet and pressed her little body against the side of the playpen, raising her chubby arms. She wanted him to pick her up. Dean glanced at the closed door and willed Annabelle to return, but she didn't, and he wondered if everything was all right.

Honey's big blue eyes widened and she shook her

hands at him with an expression that couldn't get any clearer.

"Your mama should be out in just a minute," he said and tried focusing on the paperwork in his hand, but when he glanced back at the kid he could've sworn he saw her lip tremble in disappointment. His heart did a little uncharacteristic stutter.

"I get it, you're tired of being in that pen. I don't blame you. Brandon never did like these things, either," he said, reaching down to pick her up. He expected the baby to stiffen in alarm since he was a stranger, but she snuggled up to him, quite content in the crook of his arm. "Haven't you ever heard of stranger-danger?" he asked with a chuckle as Honey cooed up at him and offered a grin full of tiny white teeth. "Yeah, you're pretty cute and you know it."

He didn't remember babies smelling this good, he noted in surprise. Maybe it was true that boys and girls were made of different stuff because he remembered Brandon smelling...less sweet.

He bent down and sniffed at Honey's crown, and his suspicion was confirmed. This baby smelled like powder, sunshine and rain on a summer day all wrapped up in one. "No wonder women go nuts over babies," he murmured, taking Honey with him to the file cabinet where he'd left off.

There was something nice about holding Honey. She watched as he searched through the cabinet with his one free hand and seemed content just to hang out while he did whatever he needed to do.

He shifted her to the other side and fell into a rhythm, a part of him starting to worry about Annabelle and the other wishing he and Beth had been able to have more kids, when the main door opened and Brandon walked in.

"What are you doing?" Brandon asked, gesturing to Honey. "Why are you holding her kid?"

Her—as in Annabelle. Dean shifted Honey again and she offered a sweet smile to Brandon, which his son ignored. "Annabelle is in the restroom. There's no reason for you to be rude to Honey."

"Honey? What a stupid name. Is your new office manager a hippie or something? Is this kid her love child?"

Dean stiffened at the ugliness in Brandon's tone, and he pinned him with a short look that communicated how much he appreciated his attitude. "You were born in the wrong era even to know what a love child is. She's a cute kid. Once you get to know her, the name actually fits. What are you doing out of school?" he asked, redirecting the conversation.

"It's a pro day. I told you that yesterday," Brandon answered, his scowl still firmly on his face. "I guess you had other things on your mind."

"You got something you need to say?" Dean asked, getting straight to the point of Brandon's attitude. "Because your mom and I didn't raise you to be so ugly to an innocent child."

Instantly chastised, Brandon made a visible effort

to shake off whatever feelings were rioting in his brain, and Dean let up.

"I need a couple of bucks," Brandon said, still eyeing Honey with faint distrust. "Me and Jessie want to go down to Merced and catch a movie. I'm short a few until payday. Can you front me?"

Dean nodded and grabbed his wallet from his back pocket. Tossing it to Brandon, Dean instructed him to pull out two twenties. "Home before ten, right?"

"Yeah."

Brandon was doing a better job of hiding his feelings but Dean knew his son well. "Brandon, I'm not adopting her. Relax."

Brandon swallowed but nodded. "Sorry, Dad. It just freaked me out for a minute. You're right. She is kinda cute. For a baby."

Dean smiled, his chest loosening from the pent-up tension between them. "Hey, why don't you and Jessie sign up for D-Day? You know your nana could use a couple of young hands to help out."

"Sure, Dad. I'll see what Jessie says and I'll get back to you."

Brandon left, and Dean turned to see Annabelle standing by the bathroom door, watching with a slightly frozen expression on her face.

"She was fussing," he said by way of explanation but he moved to return Honey to the pen, feeling distinctly as if he'd trespassed. "I waited for you to come out, but she seemed pretty upset...."

"That's fine. Thank you." Annabelle flashed a bright

smile and settled behind the desk, once again the model of efficiency, yet Dean sensed something was off-kilter. "Don't forget you have a subcontractor meeting at 3:00 p.m.," she said, adeptly avoiding meeting his gaze. She double-checked the calendar. "Dayton Plumbing. They're going to meet you at the job site."

"I haven't forgotten. What's wrong? Are you sick?"

Beth had always accused him of being Neander-thalishly blunt when it came to some things, and he could almost hear his wife's annoyed sigh as the words tripped out of his mouth.

Annabelle pinned him with a short look. "I'm fine. Please stop asking. I don't like to be badgered, especially when there's nothing wrong." She added stiffly, "Thanks for your concern."

Case closed. Dean shrugged. Plainly, there was something bothering her, but out of the two of them she was being the smart one by not inviting him into her business. He knew when to stop pushing his nose where it didn't belong.

"Good. I'm heading out after my meeting with Dayton. I probably won't return to the office. I'll come in tomorrow before you get here to baby-proof everything."

She offered him another smile by way of gratitude and he accepted it at face value.

Women were too complex for the likes of him. Beth hadn't been high-maintenance and he'd loved that about her. For a fleeting moment he wondered what kind of woman Annabelle was. There was an air of mystery about her, so different from Beth, who'd been completely down-to-earth and practically an open book. An odd tickle at the base of his spine warned him away from delving too deep into Annabelle's secrets. Something told him he might not like what he found.

THAT NIGHT Annabelle sat staring into the darkness of her rundown duplex and sipped a glass of wine. It wasn't like her to be so maudlin, allowing her thoughts to wander into dangerous territory, but seeing Dean holding Honey as if it were the most natural thing in the world had made her sad in a way that was too close to self-pity for Annabelle's comfort.

Dean was not hers. Nor would he ever be. Annabelle would no sooner wish for the moon to fall into her hands than wonder what could be between them.

That had been Sadie's problem. She was always looking for love in the wrong places. Her mother's romance track record—God love her—was as clichéd as a country song.

Fatigue pulled at her body and Annabelle couldn't keep her thoughts straight. She'd lied to Dana, but only because she didn't want her to worry. Buddy King was up for parole much sooner than a year. It had been just another reason to leave Hinkley behind. She doubted he'd try and track her down. Annabelle didn't suppose he enjoyed prison so much he'd want to return to it.

The night air had the scent of rain, though Annabelle hadn't heard that a storm was coming. Emmett's Mill was so different from the dustbowl nothingness of Hinkley. Sadie Nichols would've called it God's Country, a scenic place with wondrously wild smells, its Sierra Nevada greenery broken only by the vibrant fall colors of changing leaves on the trees and spots of dry earth as it hungered for moisture.

It was a place anyone would love to call home. She glanced at her half-empty glass and wondered if such a place existed for her. As a child she'd prayed for a fresh start for her and her mom but it had never come. Now Annabelle had found that perfect place, but she still felt like an outsider looking in—a beggar child pressed against the windowpanes of a cozy house belonging to someone else.

She drained her glass and reached for the bottle sitting on the scarred coffee table, but, as her fingers curled around the neck, she decided against a refill. One glass was enough.

A twig snapped outside and Annabelle jumped as she peered nervously into the dark. The sound of a tomcat yowling echoed in the night. Heartbeat thundering in her ears, she forced a light laugh at herself for acting like the heroine in a scary movie. There were no boogeymen in Emmett's Mill.

Not even ones named Buddy.

WHATEVER had been bothering Annabelle the day before was gone today and Dean was thankful. She wore another sundress, only this one she wore with a light cardigan that covered her most bountiful assets and Dean told himself that was a blessing. Except, when she smiled she brought the sunshine with her and he momentarily forgot what he'd been saying or doing. Flustered, he returned to his calendar, ready to hit the job site. He noted Annabelle glancing in puzzled amazement at the various baby-proofing items throughout the office: latches on drawers, doorknob protectors, plastic covers for electrical outlets, a gate blocking off the bathroom. Granted, he might've overdone it.

"You really didn't need to go that far," Annabelle said, although her eyes were shining. "Clients are going to think you run a daycare on the side."

He chuckled. "I just don't want Honey stuck in that pen all the time. Babies need to stretch their legs, too."

Annabelle nodded, appreciation evident in the way her mouth played with a subtle smile. "I'm sure she'll love it."

For a split second a violent hunger to taste those full lips ripped through him and stole the air from his chest. He cleared his throat with difficulty on the pretense of having something caught, and made a concentrated effort to get the hell out of there before he did something stupid—like give in to his baser needs—but he was met at the door by his mother.

"Dean, sweetheart, just the person I wanted to see," Mary exclaimed, moving around him with the ease of a woman who knew what she was doing. She approached Annabelle with a warm smile. "You must be Annabelle. Sammy and Dana have told me very good things about you."

Annabelle looked clearly nervous and Dean could understand why. Mary Halvorsen was a woman to be reckoned with. After raising three boisterous sons, each of whom had grown to over six feet tall, she didn't scare easily or get sidetracked from her purpose. And right now, she had her sights set on Annabelle for some reason.

"Mom, don't be wrangling Annabelle into one of your committees. I doubt she wants to spend her time in a quilting circle with a bunch of old biddies."

"Watch your tongue, Dean Emmett Halvorsen," Mary said in a dulcet tone threaded with steel. "Besides, I didn't come to invite Annabelle to the Quilters Brigade, unless, that is, you would like to join...." Mary pinned Annabelle with an expectant stare until Annabelle shook her head. "Right. I didn't think so. Although it's a stereotype that only old women quilt. Dean knows this. He used to quilt himself."

Dean bit back a groan, unable to believe his own mother had outed him like that. His cheeks flooded with warmth. "Not to rush you, Mom, but what did you come by for?"

"Well, I came by to see if Annabelle would like to volunteer on D-Day. We still need volunteers and I haven't heard from Brandon and his girl, Jessie. We need some young, strong backs to carry supplies and run refreshments to the crews."

Bewildered, Annabelle asked, "D-Day? As in the battle of Normandy?"

Mary chuckled, her stout body jiggling with mirth. "Goodness no, child, but kudos to you for knowing your history. No, D-Day in Emmett's Mill is Restoration Day. We're restoring the mill next month."

Annabelle stared blankly. "What mill? And why do you call it D-Day? Shouldn't it be R-Day or something like that?"

Mary gave Dean a look that said he was falling down on the job if Annabelle didn't even know about the town's namesake and why they were restoring it. "My dear, Emmett's Mill was named after our very own Waldon Emmett. The Halvorsen family is directly descended from the original Emmetts who settled here, which is why Dean's father and I chose Emmett as Dean's middle name. As for why we call it D-Day, the committee wanted something grand to commemorate this auspicious day in our local history, and since Waldon Emmett was of French descent, well, we thought calling it D-Day would give it a sense of importance."

"I see." Annabelle looked a little lost and Dean didn't blame her. The committee's logic was tenuous at best. "Well, it certainly does sound grand," she agreed, looking to Dean as if for a sign that she hadn't somehow offended his mother. It was endearing but unnecessary. Mary Halvorsen had skin thicker than a rhino.

"Mom, don't bore Annabelle with our family history," Dean said, smothering a chuckle. "Not everyone is fascinated with other people's history. It's like watching home movies of total strangers. Those kinds of things are barely tolerable for the people who are in them."

"Oh hush. No one asked you," Mary retorted, eyes dancing as she returned to Annabelle. "Am I boring you, dear?"

"No, I think it's fascinating. Please do continue." Annabelle reached down to pick up Honey, who had begun to fuss a little. "I think it's great that you know so much about your family and that your history isn't something you'd rather hide."

Mary turned a triumphant smile Dean's way before continuing. "Thank you. So, as I was saying, Waldon Emmett built the flour mill in 1832 and made his fortune selling freshly milled flour to the neighboring cities, except by the time he died his son, Waldon, Jr., wasn't much of a miller and quickly drove the business into the ground. Wallie, as he was called, spent most of the family's fortune on a host of get-rich schemes that inevitably failed. All that remains is the mill. It was finally donated to the historical society and we've formed the nonprofit organization heading the Emmett's Mill Restoration project."

"Aren't you sorry you asked?" Dean asked Annabelle wryly, but she looked taken in by the story. "Are you a history buff?" he asked.

"Not particularly, but I enjoy hearing about local history. It must feel wonderful to have such deep roots here in Emmett's Mill," she murmured.

His mother jumped in, loving her captive audience. "You should come to dinner tonight—"

"Mom," Dean interjected, alarmed at where the conversation was headed. Mary blinked at him in annoyance for interrupting her, but he wasn't about to let his mom drag Annabelle to a family dinner. A Halvorsen dinner wasn't for the faint of heart. It was loud, chaotic and usually there were at least three conversations happening at once. He couldn't see Annabelle feeling comfortable at all. Not to mention he was having enough trouble dealing with his inappropriate mental wanderings, he didn't need to complicate matters. "Leave Annabelle with a flyer. I have to get going."

"So go." Mary dismissed him, alighting on Honey without missing a beat. "Who is this angel?"

Annabelle smiled with genuine joy. "This is my daughter, Honey. She's sixteen months old."

Mary sighed with longing. "A granddaughter. That's what I'm missing. I adore my grandsons but I've never had anyone to pamper. I'm holding out hope that one of my sons will deliver. Your mom must be thrilled to have a granddaughter."

Annabelle shot Dean a quick look, which he wasn't sure was one of distress or one of annoyance for his mother's questions but she answered just the same. "My mother died before Honey was born."

Mary's expression lost some of its happiness. "Oh dear. That settles it. You have to come to Sunday dinner this weekend. I won't take no for an answer."

She turned to Dean with instructions. "You'll bring her? I don't want her driving that road at night with a baby. You know how those twists and turns can be tricky for people not used to them."

She pulled a flyer from her purse and placed it in front of Annabelle with a warm smile. "I have to go. Here's the information about the project. Please give it some thought. It's a wonderful way to get to know your new community and it's a worthwhile project."

And then she was gone.

Dean expelled a heavy breath and suddenly felt the all-over body fatigue that always happened when he got caught in the maelstrom that was his mother.

He turned to Annabelle, hands spread in apology. "She's pretty passionate about some things," he said by way of explanation, but he realized Annabelle hadn't minded.

"You're so lucky," she said with a catch to her voice. "Tell your mom I'd be honored to be a part of the restoration project, but I'll have to pass on dinner. I don't think it's a good idea to cross the lines," she said, shocking him with her refusal. He'd thought he might have to somehow dissuade her, but she'd beat him to it.

He couldn't agree more. So why did he feel so disappointed?

"Are you sure?" he heard himself blurt. "There's plenty of food. My mom cooks enough to feed a platoon. It's a miracle none of us grew up to be fat. It's probably a good thing we all work in jobs that are fairly physical, otherwise all that good eating might've gone straight to our waistlines."

"I didn't think guys cared about stuff like that," she teased lightly.

"Are you kidding? We care. We just hide it better. No guy likes to see his gut hanging over his belt. And that's the truth even if we don't want to admit it."

"Really? Well, from where I'm standing, you don't have anything to worry about."

The innocent comment made his mouth dry up. Had she been checking him out? Noticing him in the same ways that he couldn't help but notice her? He started to stammer a response with all the eloquence of a prepubescent boy but Annabelle unwittingly saved him from himself when she sighed wistfully.

"I really like your mom and I'm betting dinner would be great, but it's just not a good idea, you know?"

He did. Thank God, one of them was thinking clearly. "Don't worry, I'll let my mom down easily."

"Thanks."

"No problem."

No problem—except for the part where he wanted her to come to dinner. Wanted to ignore that blinking caution light in his brain. And wanted to get to know Annabelle in a way that was more than professional.

Dean wanted everything he'd told his son he absolutely didn't want from Annabelle.

And that didn't feel so good.

CHAPTER SEVEN

"WHERE'S your friend?" Mary Halvorsen asked as Dean stepped into the dining room for Sunday dinner. Her disappointed tone spoke volumes. "I set an extra place setting."

"She's not my friend, Mom. She's my office manager. *An employee.* You don't invite George or Paulo over for Sunday dinner. I don't see why you felt the need to invite Annabelle."

"George and Paulo have their own families to go home to," Mary answered with a slight clip, making him feel like a kid again. How did mothers manage to hold on to that tone even after their kids were grown? "It's obvious that young woman needs a family. She's alone and needs someone to take her under their wing. Besides, she's a friend of Dana's so she's practically family anyway."

Dana smiled at Mary. "That's so sweet but I know Annabelle and she'd never cross the line between employee and employer. It's something she's a bit of a stickler for."

"Oh? How come?" Mary asked, intrigued by

this bit of information. Truth be told, Dean was curious, too.

Dana must've realized she'd divulged too much for she looked to Sammy for help.

"Anyone hear from Josh and Tasha?" Sammy asked, giving Dana a subtle wink.

A shrewd light entered Mary's eyes but she allowed the subject change, answering with good cheer. "I did this morning. They're still in Punta Gorda but they'll be leaving soon."

"Why can't they go to a normal place for a vacation?" Dean grumbled, mostly because Josh was his best welder. "What's wrong with Hawaii? Or Oregon? South America is nothing but a jungle."

"You know why. Tasha loves Punta Gorda and this was the first time she's been able to get back since the wedding. She may have quit the Peace Corps to marry Josh and raise a family here but I think a part of her heart is still with those jungle people."

Dana giggled at Mary's use of *jungle people* but Dean was surly and didn't find the humor in anything. He gestured to Sammy. "You get that cement guy to come down on his price?"

Brian, the Halvorsen patriarch, came in from his study and after clapping each of his sons on the shoulder, took his place at the head of the table. "Who are you using for cement?" he asked, his ears perking at the construction business talk, but Mary put her foot down.

"No shop talk at the table. You know that. Where's

Brandon? I expected to see him tonight. With Christopher gone to visit his mother for a few weeks I feel deserted by my only grandsons."

Dean smiled. "Brandon is having dinner over at Jessie's house tonight. He told me to tell you he promises not to enjoy anyone else's mashed potatoes as much as yours."

"Smart boy," Mary said with no small amount of pride. "I like that Jessie. She's a sweet girl, though watch that those hormones don't go and get him into trouble."

"Brandon's a good kid. He won't do anything stupid," Dean said, though a frisson of alarm followed. Maybe he needed to have a talk with Brandon, make sure that they were using protection if they were sexually active. Ugh. The thought made him feel old. For some reason he'd always assumed Beth would be the one to tackle that conversation. She'd been good at handling the things that made Dean squirm.

Dinner conversation flowed around him and he participated with one-word answers, wishing he'd called off dinner with his parents. He wasn't good company tonight. And it came down to one simple reason. He'd wanted Annabelle there. And that made him angry with himself.

The woman became more beautiful the more time he spent with her, which should've been impossible as she was already prettier than anyone had a right to be. Moments went by when he lost track of his thoughts simply because he'd caught a whiff of her skin or hair and an irrational desire to bury his nose in it always followed. He wondered how she got her skin to sparkle as if it had been dusted with sunshine, or how her brown eyes could appear softer than warm chocolate. Worse, he wanted to know what memory left that haunted look behind when it visited.

Heaving a private sigh, he returned to his mostly untouched plate and swore at his dilemma.

He had no business being attracted to Annabelle. The reasons were many and varied but the biggest reason had to do with his heart. When Beth had died, his heart died with her.

Annabelle deserved more than he could offer.

ANNABELLE, with Honey at her hip, walked into the small deli, and quickly found Dana in the back already sipping an iced tea.

"Starting without me?" Annabelle joked as she settled Honey into a baby chair.

"Sorry. I was parched." Dana assessed Annabelle openly. "You look good. I see working with Dean agrees with you."

"Having a steady paycheck agrees with me," Annabelle corrected her but smiled, knowing Dana was just giving her a hard time. "So, I've joined the D-Day committee. Tell me, have I made a huge mistake or what?"

"Depends. I think it's a good way to connect with the community. The whole town seems to be involved, but on the other hand, do you want to be *that* involved? I mean, no offense, AnnaB, but you've never been what anyone would call a joiner."

"I've never been somewhere I felt welcome to join," Annabelle answered. "It's not like Hinkley was a wealth of open arms. When was the last time anyone cared what happened to the people living on Bleeter Street?"

"Ain't that the truth," Dana muttered. "God, I hate that place."

"Yeah, me, too." Annabelle's thoughts went immediately to the single-wide mobile home of her childhood that smelled perpetually of stale beer and musty carpet no matter how many times she'd tried sweeping it out. Dana's mobile had been two trailers down. Sometimes Annabelle could hear the muffled shouts that came from Dana's family as they brawled within the claustrophobic space. The next day, Dana had often had bruises.

Dana broke the silence first, saying, "Well, good for you for joining. So, what has Mary put you in charge of?"

"Refreshments." Annabelle shifted in her chair with a frown. "But I'm not quite sure what that entails. I was going to ask but the meeting got a little chaotic and I forgot. Those quilters are a wild bunch."

"You'll be in charge of bringing drinks to the construction crew. Lemonade, water, stuff like that. But don't worry, you'll have a bunch of kid volunteers at your disposal. It's going to be like an old-fashioned barn-raising, except we're not raising a barn, we're relocating a mill."

"I still can't believe they're going to do that," Annabelle said. "Makes me nervous just thinking about it."

"I wouldn't worry. A company from out of town is going to do the actual moving and then once the mill is on the museum property, that's when everyone else will get involved."

"It's hard to believe so many people care," Annabelle said.

The two women caught each other's stare. Dana reached over and grasped Annabelle's free hand. "No place is perfect but Emmett's Mill comes close. This is a town where people care about their neighbors. If I hadn't seen it myself I wouldn't have believed it. This town takes care of their own pretty well. It feels good."

Annabelle was wary of anything that sounded too good to be true even if she wanted to believe. She tried pulling away but Dana wouldn't let her.

"You're so used to being on the defensive that you don't know how to feel when no one is trying to attack you. I know. I felt the same way until I met Sammy. He showed me that not everyone has an agenda."

Annabelle forced a laugh and pressed a kiss to Honey's head as she gestured for Dana to stop. "I surrender. This talk is too serious for lunch. C'mon, I don't want to spend my lunch hour arguing the merits of Emmett's Mill. I agree with you, it's a great town, otherwise I wouldn't have moved here. Although," she said, pausing with pursed lips, "I think I got a prank call last night."

"What do you mean? Did they say anything?"

"No. But I could hear them breathing. It was probably just some kids playing a joke but it was a little creepy. I was weirded out for a while afterward but now that I think about it, it's probably nothing."

"Maybe you should tell Dean."

Annabelle rolled her eyes. "And why should I do that?"

"Because maybe he could look into it for you."

"Dana, I don't need a man to chase away bad-mannered teenagers. That's all it was. I almost didn't mention it."

Dana looked worried. "Well, I'm glad you did. If it happens again, please tell me you'll let Dean know. I don't like it."

"Fine," Annabelle grudgingly agreed, though only for Dana's benefit. A prank call was nothing to get worked up over. She felt silly for even mentioning it. And the fact that Dana wanted Dean to be her champion was transparent.

All this baby business had given Dana a one-track mind, it seemed. Annabelle would have to be an idiot not to see where this was going. She didn't need Dana's help in the matchmaking department. Annabelle could screw up her own love life, thank you very much. And as much as she ached to be a part of a wonderful family like the Halvorsens, it wasn't right to try to insert herself into a picture where she didn't belong.

Besides, it didn't take a rocket scientist to figure out that Dean was still nursing a broken heart. Annabelle wasn't about to sign up to be Dean's rebound woman. God, the thought gave her chills. Rebound women always got the shaft in the love department because people who never should've been together in the first place inevitably realize this fact and that's when everything falls apart. In that situation, someone ends up the loser. And that wasn't going to be Annabelle.

"In case I haven't told you, I'm so glad you moved here."

Annabelle looked up at the catch in her friend's voice. Dana blinked back tears but the sincerity in her eyes nearly bowled Annabelle over. They were each other's closest family and didn't need blood to bind them. Despite how she might mature and change, a part of Annabelle always felt like the kid living in the trailer park with next to nothing to call her own. Dana understood this because she struggled with it, too. "You don't have to tell me. I already know. And I'm glad, too. But I don't want you to be disappointed if my happy ending isn't the same as yours. I don't want you to worry about me, either. I'm a survivor and I'll always land on my feet. With or without a man to help me."

HE'D TRIED to be understanding, but each time Brandon saw Annabelle sitting at his mom's old desk he saw red. She was trespassing. And her kid was a nuisance, too. Brandon's dad had baby-proofed the entire office until it took a degree in engineering just to open a drawer. Brandon wanted things to go back to the way they were before *she* got there.

"Hi, Brandon," Annabelle said with a smile as if she wasn't aware that he could barely tolerate her. That baby actually smiled at him, too. Like they were working together to mock him with their nice routine. Annabelle looked around him to gesture toward Jessie. "This your girlfriend?"

He gritted his teeth, hating even to answer, but his dad kept getting after him for being rude so he jerked his head in the affirmative, but turned his attention to his dad. "Me and the guys are heading over to Buckley's for a few hours. That okay with you? I'll be home by curfew."

Dean paused to regard his son but then returned to his paperwork. "As long as your homework is done and you're home by ten o'clock. What did Coach say about your shoulder?"

Brandon rotated the muscle and shrugged. "It's nothing. Just a strain. The PT guy said there's nothing ripped or torn. Everything should be fine for the game tomorrow."

"That's good but I don't want you playing if you're hurt," his dad warned him. "One game isn't going to kill you."

"Dad, I'm not stupid. Don't worry about it. Everything is fine." He looked to Jessie, who had been quietly chatting with Annabelle, and gestured that it was time to leave. "See you later. Thanks, Dad," he added over his shoulder as he left, Jessie right behind him. Once they were out of earshot, he nearly snarled at Jessie, who blinked in surprise at his tone. "Don't get chummy with her. She's not sticking around," he said. "She's just a charity case that my dad's taken on because he felt bad."

"That's a crappy thing to say," Jessie said, frowning. "What's gotten into you?"

He drew a deep breath and apologized for snapping, but inside he felt no different. The sooner Annabelle Nichols was out of their lives, the less chance Brandon had of getting a stepmom. The thought made him queasy.

The only thing that kept him from totally freaking out was that his dad had promised him there was nothing going on between him and Annabelle. If only she wasn't so pretty…and nice.

CHAPTER EIGHT

ANNABELLE had just snapped Honey into her car seat and slipped the key into the ignition when her old Ford Escort made a horrible racket that ended in a guttural wheeze.

"No, you will not do this to me," Annabelle muttered, trying to turn the ignition again despite the ominous clicking it was making. "You were just given a clean bill of health last week after the oil change. There's no reason for you to be acting like this," she said, talking to the car as if it were a recalcitrant child rather than a machine that had just expired. She clenched her teeth and leaned into the steering wheel. "I do not accept this. You *will* turn over and we *will* drive home!"

Dean appeared beside her window with a puzzled expression. "Everything okay?"

"Yep. Just great," she lied with a bright smile. "Just having a difference of opinion with my vehicle."

"Come again?"

She shook her head and waved him on. "No worries. I'll get this figured out. Go on home."

But just as she feared, Dean wasn't about to leave her without knowing she had reliable transportation, and, while that chivalrous routine was endearing, she really didn't want him to feel obligated to stay. She glanced at her watch. Dana was working tonight. It was a five-mile walk from the office to her craptastic duplex and it was already getting dark. She considered her meager checking account balance and immediately discarded the thought of calling a tow truck.

"Annabelle, pop your hood."

"No, it's okay, really," Annabelle called out, but Dean refused to budge and gestured impatiently. "Well, uh, okay. But I'm sure it's nothing."

The latch snapped and Dean propped the hood. Needing to feel useful, she grabbed the flashlight from her glove compartment and climbed out of the car to stand beside Dean as he inspected the engine. She peered into the coiled machinery and wondered if he knew what the heck he was doing. Thad hadn't been much of a mechanic but he had always liked to pretend he was.

"Fan's not broken and your battery cables are fine. But we'll have it towed to Mountain Motors and see what Jonas can make of it." He carefully closed the hood. "I'll take you home. Go ahead and grab your stuff and I'll get Honey."

She wanted to decline politely, but that would really be stupid. There was no way she was going to walk five miles with a toddler who was a half hour away from becoming really cranky, not to mention,

Annabelle wouldn't be able to see two feet in front of her once she headed out of town. She might end up in a ditch or something. "Thanks," Annabelle said, though it came out not at all grateful sounding. He didn't call her on it and she was at least glad for that.

Honey gurgled with pleasure as Dean strapped her into the back of his king-cab monster diesel truck and then Annabelle hopped in, trying not to notice how comfortable his ride was in comparison to her own. Of course it was comfortable. It was practically brand-new, while hers was…not.

There was nothing wrong with her little Escort. It was her first car and she'd bought it with her own money. It probably just needed a tune-up. Everything would look better in the morning. The thought was very Scarlett O'Hara–esque of her, but sometimes that Southern belle had had the right of things.

"Where do you live?" Dean asked, pulling out of the driveway and onto the highway.

"Uh, just on the outskirts of town, in those duplexes off Morning Glory Road."

He appeared troubled but didn't comment. The first time she'd seen the duplex she'd nearly cried. But she'd lived in worse and with a little elbow grease, she'd rationalized that it could be very cozy.

As they pulled up to the duplex, Annabelle grimaced. Well, it was safe to say the duplex—despite her efforts—had never quite reached her aspirations.

She opened the passenger door and dropped to the ground from the dizzying height of the truck, then

went to her front door to unlock it while Dean unbuck-
led Honey from her car seat. She accepted Honey
from his arms while he unlatched the car seat from the
truck. She tried taking the car seat, too, but he wouldn't
let her and simply followed her into the house.

She tried not to cringe when she caught him
openly assessing her unit with a critical eye.

"Who's your landlord?" he asked, his hands going
to his hips as he stared at a crack in the ceiling. "Is
this structurally sound?"

She laughed nervously, but she'd wondered that
herself. "It's fine. You're paranoid. Thanks for the lift.
I'm sure Dana can take us tomorrow."

"No need. I'll come get you. I have to come by this
way anyway."

"No, you don't. You're being ridiculous. I don't need
you to be my taxi. Dana can get us or maybe Sammy."

There was a loud bang and Annabelle jumped. Ordinarily, she wouldn't have reacted like that, but having
Dean in her space put her on edge. She felt him judging
her and her humble home. This place was a palace
compared to where she'd grown up. If he thought so
poorly of her duplex what would he think of her background if he knew? She tried not to let it bother her,
for who really cared what others thought? But knowing that Dean might harbor the slightest amount of pity
toward her was enough to make her defensive.

"What was that?" he growled, moving past her to
peer out the small kitchen window. "Are your neighbors rowdy? Have they given you any trouble?"

Annabelle sighed. It was sweet, really, that he was worried. But her neighbors were nothing compared to the riff-raff she was used to putting up with. Hell, she could handle those yahoos next door with her eyes closed. "Dean, everything's fine. Thank you. I appreciate your concern but it's unnecessary."

He paused and for a wild moment Annabelle wondered if he was going to grab Honey and her, toss them both back into the truck and burn rubber out of there. No doubt that's what he wanted to do. Dana had all but said the same thing when she'd first seen the place, but Annabelle was determined to make things better on her own.

He must've read that in her eyes for he backed down—grudgingly. With one caveat. "I'm picking you up. Be ready at 8:00 a.m."

And then he closed the door behind him with instructions to use the dead bolt when he was gone.

She slid the dead bolt into place and shut the thin drapes across the kitchen window to create some semblance of privacy before making Honey and herself a quick bite to eat.

After a shower, she put Honey to bed, double-checking the window latches before she turned off the light, and then she took a seat by the window to stare into the night.

The duplex was squalid—not even three passes with a rented steam cleaner could get the carpets completely clean—but the view was beautiful. From the ridge above Emmett's Mill, the lights of downtown twinkled like stars and the moon illuminated the dark sky with a soft glow.

A sigh escaped her as her thoughts returned to Dean. He wasn't a man of many words, but that was okay. Sammy seemed to do most of the talking for everyone. But Annabelle appreciated a man who spent less time talking and more time working. Her mom had been a sucker for sweet talkers. Poor Mom. Always looking for a knight in shining armor to rescue her from the way her life had turned out.

Stop it. Shaking off her melancholy, Annabelle reached for her mail and started to sift through it. She was still receiving the previous tenant's mail but the landlord hadn't much cared. They had left in the middle of the night, skipping out on the last month's rent. So Annabelle had had to pay two months in advance. Tossing the misdirected mail in a growing pile to return to the post office, she got to the last envelope in her small stack and slid it open, barely registering the label from the district attorney's office in Hinkley.

Unfolding the letter, she scanned the contents and her heart began to thunder uncomfortably in her chest as three simple words scared the living hell out of her.

Out on parole.

The phone rang, jangling her nerves. She rose on unsteady feet to answer it.

"Hello?"

Nothing. But Annabelle could hear someone breathing. Damn kids. She gripped the phone tighter and said, "This is juvenile. Do your parents know—"

"Bitch!" And then the line went dead.

Annabelle drew back in startled silence. Swallowing, she glanced out the front window before hanging up the receiver. Kids, she thought shakily. With a mean streak.

Suppressing a shiver, she double-checked the flimsy lock on the front door but still felt exposed. Forcing a short laugh, she told herself she was overreacting, but her gaze strayed to the letter on the coffee table and her heart beat painfully against everything she was trying to convince herself of.

A prank call. No big deal. She could handle it.

DEAN ARRIVED at Annabelle's place a little early, but he hadn't slept well the night before and found himself up earlier than usual. Downing a quick cup of coffee and burning his taste buds in the process, he made the short drive to Annabelle's and then wondered if he should wait outside or knock on the door.

After a minute of arguing with himself on the merits of waiting or knocking, in the end, he went to the front door and tapped on it hesitantly.

A few moments later, Annabelle peered around the door frame clutching a towel, and he cursed his impatience. He should've waited in the truck.

"Are you early?" Annabelle asked, biting her lip. "Or am I late?"

"I'm sorry, Annabelle. I'm early. I'll just wait in the truck until you're ready." He turned to leave, positive he felt the tips of his ears reddening when she called after him.

"It's okay. I was running a bit behind anyway. I overslept. Why don't you come in and keep an eye on Honey for me while I take a quick shower? It'll be much faster if I don't have to take her with me. She likes to play with the shampoo when I'm not looking."

"Uh…okay," he said, though his Adam's apple bobbed uncomfortably in his throat as he dutifully tried to avoid the imagery jumping to his overactive imagination. Annabelle with her lush curves and creamy skin—naked. The blood rushed from his ears to his groin and he almost did an about-face. But then he saw Annabelle grab Honey from her crib as the toddler rubbed at her eyes, smiling sleepily when she spotted him, and his heart warmed in a pleasant way. The kid was too darn cute. A person would have to be made of stone not to like Honey Nichols.

"Look who's here," Annabelle said, pressing a kiss to Honey's wild hair. "Mama's going to take a quick shower. Can you sit with Dean for a minute? I won't be long. I promise."

Honey didn't even hesitate but went straight into Dean's arms. Annabelle's expression faltered, surprise at Honey's reaction evident in her eyes. She met Dean's gaze with a puzzled smile. "She must really like you. I've never seen her so open with anyone. Not even her da—" Annabelle stopped, plainly disturbed by how much information she was sharing. "I'll just be a minute."

"Take your time," Dean said, holding Honey against his chest and walking the perimeter of the small duplex as Annabelle disappeared. The bathroom door closed and Dean busied himself with studying her unit.

Despite Annabelle's attempts at livening up the place with a few pictures here and there and a vibrant handmade afghan draped across the top of the faded sofa, the duplex maintained a stale atmosphere that spoke of the countless inhabitants before her who hadn't cared as much as she did for their living conditions. Apparently, upkeep wasn't the landlord's top priority. Peering out the window, he realized it didn't have a screen. Drawing away, his mouth formed a tight line as his blood pressure rose. Window screens were required in residential rentals. He wondered who owned the property and how hard it might be to find out. His cell phone was in his hand before he realized what he was doing. Seconds before he got more involved than he wanted to be, he came to his senses and snapped the phone shut. He glanced at Honey with a light smile. "Let's get your seat in the truck, kiddo. We can wait for your mom there."

It was only a few minutes later that Annabelle appeared at the front door, locking it before making her way to the truck gingerly on spindly heels, wearing another of her short skirts that showed off a lean pair of smooth pale legs. Dean groaned and looked away. He didn't know how he was supposed to keep his mind in neutral when she kept shoving it into overdrive. She had to know that she was driving him crazy with those flashes of cleavage peeking out from behind that flimsy V-necked blouse and those impossibly short skirts that rode up her legs.

Dean swallowed with difficulty but managed to keep his attention on the road with ruthless determination.

"You need screens on those windows," he said, startling her with his gruff tone. "It's dangerous with a baby in the house."

"I know. That's why I keep the windows closed on that side."

"That's no solution. Who's your landlord?"

Annabelle sighed. "I don't know. I go through a property management company, Grafton Realty. Besides, I've called the manager and he told me that the owner isn't interested in replacing the screens because the tenants keep ripping them out. He said if I want screens I have to buy them."

Dean balked. "That's bullshit."

She shrugged as if she was used to this sort of thing. "It's not that big a deal. We just work around it."

"Honey could fall. This isn't something that can be ignored, Annabelle." He earned a sharp look, but he didn't care. He already hated the idea of Honey and Annabelle living in that place because of the neighbors on the other side. They looked a little rough.

"It's not your concern. Thank you, anyway," Annabelle replied curtly, sending him the clear message that she didn't like to be treated like a pet project.

"Besides, with the weather turning soon, I won't have much need for open windows anyway."

"There are liability issues," he argued. "It's not as simple as you just choosing not to open your windows. And then there's also the issue of the landlord refusing to provide the basics of his responsibilities to his tenant. My dad used to own plenty of rental properties. Trust me, I know all the work that goes into owning them. When I was growing up, my brothers and I spent many of our weekends helping Dad do repairs. Your landlord is a bad one," he finished.

"Be that as it may, I don't need you poking your nose into my business. Bad landlords have a tendency to kick out their troublemaker tenants, if you catch my drift."

"That would be a blessing," Dean muttered.

"Not for Honey and me. In case you haven't noticed, there's a shortage of rentals in Emmett's Mill. We were lucky to find this place."

Dean opened his mouth, ready to argue some more just for the sake of keeping his mind occupied, but she had a valid point. He thought of his expansive home and the two spare bedrooms gathering dust, but before he could continue in that direction, he shook himself loose of that particular brand of crazy. Annabelle and Honey could not move in with him and Brandon. For one, Brandon would declare a mutiny and two, it was just plain stupid.

Focus on what you can fix, Dean told himself. Like window screens and broken cars.

Yeah, Halvorsen…stick to those.

CHAPTER NINE

"SUGAR?" Annabelle exclaimed, staring in dismay at Jonas, the head mechanic at Mountain Motors as he wiped the grease and motor oil from his fingers. "How does sugar get into the gas tank? Is that something that happens naturally?" she asked, knowing she was teetering on the edge of desperate with her questioning. Deep down she knew the answer but she was praying she was wrong.

She wasn't.

"Uh, no." Jonas shook the dirty mop he called a head of hair regretfully. "Someone put it there. Screwed up your fuel intake valve, too. Possibly even your fuel pump."

Annabelle groaned but didn't have time to cry. Her lunch was only an hour and she had to get back to the office. "Let's get down to brass tacks. Two questions. What's this going to cost me and how long will it take to fix it?"

Jonas sucked his front teeth as he mentally counted the beans in his head and answered, "About $800, give or take a few."

"A few what?"

"Hunnerd."

It might as well be a million. She didn't have it. "Right." She drew a deep breath, her brain whirring fast. If it weren't for bad luck she wouldn't have any. "I don't have that kind of cash right now," she said, going straight to the point. "But, uh, we could work out a deal, like trade for something?"

Jonas's eyes widened and he shook his head in alarm. "You're pretty and all but I'm a married man. I don't reckon my wife would take too kindly to any sort of *arrangement*, Miss Annabelle. I'm sorry."

Annabelle's cheeks burned as she grasped what Jonas thought she was offering. "God, no, Jonas. I didn't mean *that*. I just meant if you had some office work you needed some help with, computer work, or, hell, I don't know, maybe someone to clean up a bit, then I could help out in that way in exchange for the repair."

Jonas relaxed but he shook his head again. "Sorry, no computer. We do everything by hand, and, well, we already have a cleaning lady who comes once a month to scrub the toilets and such. We aren't that picky and she does a good enough job. I'm right sorry, Miss Annabelle." He paused, then added with a grin that showed off the gap in his front teeth, "I won't charge you for the diagnostic or the tow. It's on the house. I'll even take it back to your place for you. I heard you don't live too far out of town."

She swallowed around the lump in her throat

even as she fought to keep her voice strong and bright. "Don't be silly. You performed a service. You should be paid for it. You're not running a charity, Jonas. It's a business. How much do I owe you?"

Jonas sighed heavily as if he hated to tell her. "Seventy-five."

She winced privately but grabbed her checkbook. "Check okay?"

"Of course. I know you're good for it. Dean Halvorsen wouldn't have hired you if he didn't think you were good folk." She smiled tightly and handed him the check. He gave it a cursory glance before saying, "Listen, when you get the money, you bring the car back and I'll give you the newcomer ten percent discount off the total repair. It's the least I can do."

"Thank you, Jonas. Just leave the keys in the car when you drop it off."

"Sure thing, Miss Annabelle. Take care."

DEAN WAS packing up the last of his work tools when Sammy walked over to him, his expression puzzled. "You know anything about what went wrong with Annabelle's car?"

Dean shook his head. "No. Why?"

"Dana just told me that Annabelle said someone put sugar in her gas tank."

Dean stopped to stare at his brother. "Sugar?"

"Yeah. That's pretty deliberate. Who'd want to do that?"

"I don't know." But he agreed with Sammy. Whoever did it meant to do something mean.

"Dana already took Annabelle and Honey home for the night so you don't need to take them," Sammy said, his expression still worried. "I gotta tell you, brother. This bothers me."

"Me, too," Dean admitted, glancing at Sammy. "You said something about Annabelle and Dana coming from troubled backgrounds. Anything I should know about?" Sammy's silence was telling. Dean sighed. "Sammy, if she's in some kind of trouble…"

"You gotta ask her, man. Dana swore me to secrecy and it's nothing that's Annabelle's fault, but she should be the one to tell people if she wants them to know. Understand?"

"Yeah. I do."

Sammy nodded, his relief evident. But as Dean went to climb into his truck, Sammy stopped him, his grave expression distinctly at odds with his usual jocular attitude. "No matter what, she's a good person. Loyal to a fault I'd say. In some ways, she's a lot like Beth."

At the mention of his dead wife's name, Dean tried not to stiffen. He knew Sammy was just trying to draw a parallel, but Dean was like a wounded bear inside when it came to the memory of his wife. Sometimes he couldn't help but lash out at the people trying to reach out to him. "They're nothing alike," he said, pushing away the ache he felt inside. "And never will be."

KNEES TUCKED into her chest, Annabelle willed the panic away. Someone had deliberately sabotaged her car. No one knew her here, which led her to surmise that someone from Hinkley had done this. And there was only one person she could imagine who hated her so much that they'd do such a thing.

Buddy. Her gaze strayed to the slip of paper lying on her coffee table. He was out on parole after serving eight years of his sixteen-year sentence. The prison system's reward for good behavior.

And if it had been Buddy, this little stunt was simply a calling card. An ominous reminder that they had a score to settle, and he was ready to collect.

Shivering, she drew her knees tighter and squeezed her eyes shut to block out the fear that when she least expected it, his face would pop into view. Snarling, or worse, grinning with his jackal smile as he stalked her with revenge in his heart.

A knock at the front door nearly sent her hurtling to the floor in one startled movement as her heartbeat thundered in her ears. It was too late for visitors and it wasn't like her neighbors were the sort to borrow a cube of butter. Her eyes watered and she wiped at them angrily. *Get hold of yourself!* It was highly unlikely Buddy was on the other side of that door, she told herself as she walked on wobbly legs to answer. "Who is it?" she asked, her voice still a bit high-pitched to sound normal.

"Dean."

Relief was instant, but it served to make her knees even less stable. "What are you doing here so late?" she asked, opening the door and letting him in.

"We need to talk."

"About what?" Annabelle asked, sincerely puzzled. "Is this about the new phone directory? I know I didn't ask but your Rolodex is outdated. It's a pain to go through and try to update those little cards when everything today is done digitally. The computer program I downloaded can be hot synced with your PDA—"

"I'm not talking about the damn phone directory. I want to know who would want to hurt you and Honey."

She swallowed, stunned at his blunt question and how easily he managed to zero in on her biggest fear. Her eyes widened and she shook her head. "I don't know," she lied. The less Dean knew about her childhood in Hinkley, the better off he'd be. It was her burden to bear. No one else's.

Crossing into the living room, she curled into a ball on the sofa. "It was probably some dumb kid playing a prank," she said, trying to throw him off the true reason for her fear. "I admit, it's a pretty nasty prank." And an expensive one, she almost added, but didn't want him to offer to pay for it because she could almost sense that's where he was going. "And here I thought small towns were full of nothing but nice people. Hmm, guess not."

Dean exhaled, regarding her with that steady gaze, seeming to pierce right through her flimsy excuse until she fought the urge to squirm. "Are you in trouble?" he asked quietly.

She laughed, but the sound was ragged even to her own ears. "No more than anyone else who just found out someone had tried to mix baking ingredients in her gas tank. This is more of a nuisance than anything else. It really puts a cramp in my travel plans." She tried joking but, damn the man, he wasn't laughing. Suddenly tired of her own game, Annabelle dropped the act. "Dean…I don't know who might've done this. All I know is I'm without a vehicle in a town without public transit. That's what I'm focusing on right now. Okay?"

"I'll help you."

"I don't want your help."

"Why not?"

She sighed, wishing for a millisecond that her principles weren't so ironclad, that she could just allow herself to sink into his strong arms, even for a moment, to let someone else shoulder the weight crushing her. But it was a foolish wish because Annabelle could never do that. She'd never allow herself to depend on someone else so completely. "Because I'm not the kind of woman who looks for someone to save her. I will save myself. I've been doing it for years and I've had plenty of practice."

"I have a car you can borrow while yours is in the shop," Dean said as if she hadn't just spoken. "It's in good shape and you need a reliable car."

"What did I just say? Stop trying to save me! I

can't borrow one of your vehicles. What would people think?"

He looked at her incredulously. "Who cares?"

"I do."

"Has it ever occurred to you that you worry about all the wrong things?"

She drew back. "Excuse me?"

"If you're so worried about what people think why do you dress like you do?"

"I beg your pardon?" She could feel her cheeks pinking as a wave of mortification rolled over her. Suddenly, she was back in high school and the popular girls were criticizing her wardrobe. It was stupid to draw the parallel—she was not in high school any longer—but the feeling his statement evoked was pretty much the same. "Who are you to criticize my clothes?"

"Your boss," he answered bluntly and she could only stare. Her momentary silence prompted him to continue though Annabelle was quite certain she didn't want to hear any more of what Dean Halvorsen had to say.

"If you don't want men to stare at your breasts don't put them on a platter. If you don't want people to think that you're less than who you are, don't give them an opportunity. You come to work decked out in hooker heels and tight tanks that leave nothing to the imagination and then act all indignant when men like Aaron Eagle come sniffing around."

"I never encouraged that man's attention. If you

recall I was quite clear on how I stood in regards to his advances." Stung, she blinked back angry tears. "And, excuse me, but I didn't realize my wardrobe was so offensive. I thought I was dressed nicely," she added, the starch in her tone disintegrating with a watery hiccup that made her cheeks burn that much more hotly for the pitiful sound. Grinding the moisture from her eyes, she pulled the afghan her mother had knitted from the top of the sofa and tucked it around herself as if the soft yarn could protect her from further insult, hoping the gesture was enough to communicate that he was no longer welcome.

But he didn't leave. Damn the man. She sent a nasty look his way. "Anything else you have a problem with? My hair perhaps? Or my eyes? Maybe those aren't to your liking, either." Too bad. There was nothing she could do about those. Not that she could change her wardrobe, either. It wasn't as if she had room in her budget for new clothes.

A long enough moment passed between them that Annabelle started to feel the silence as if it were a living, breathing thing and she wasn't happy with its presence. She risked another glance his way, this time not as angry but still hurt, and she caught the open chagrin in his expression. She softened, knowing without having to hear the words that he felt bad, but she wasn't ready to make the first move. Luckily, she didn't have to.

Dean drew a deep breath. "You were dressed

nicely. I'm sorry. I shouldn't have said it like that. Hell, I suck when it comes to saying things the right way."

"You got that right," Annabelle agreed softly, not quite ready to let him off the hook. She eyed him curiously. "So, what did you mean? Do you really hate the way I dress?"

"That answer is complicated."

"Try simplifying."

"It's like this…" He drifted toward her, but she remained rooted where she stood. Soon, she was staring into a pair of eyes that were far too extraordinary to be called brown as they flared with brilliant flecks of hazel. She forgot herself and why she needed to keep her distance as he spoke again. "Annabelle, you have to know that you're a beautiful woman with a stunning figure, but that's just what's on the surface and I know that's probably all a lot of people see. I strive to keep things professional between us, but some days when you're dressed like that…hell, woman, I'm just a man and all I can think of is you and it kills me. I shouldn't be thinking of you in that way. I'm your boss."

His eyes had the look of a man tortured by his admission, ashamed even by his perceived weakness, and Annabelle had a startling revelation. He was fighting as hard as she was to keep the lines drawn, but there seemed a current flowing between them that kept pulling them near to one another.

Annabelle was falling even though she was standing still, which was patently ridiculous. She realized with a breathy start that her gaze feasted on the promise of his lips, aching to know what it felt like to have them pressed against her own. Valid points. He made valid points, a voice in her head reminded her even as her feet seemed to move in the same direction, pulled on an invisible current toward one inevitable course.

"I like my clothes," she said in a soft voice, looking up into Dean's gorgeous eyes and wondering how she had never noticed their unusual color before this moment. "And I'm not going to change."

"Yes, you will," he murmured with a low growl that excited her in a way that defied explanation. His arms closed around her in a perfect fit, their bodies molding against one another until Annabelle struggled to remember why this was a bad idea. This was safety, a different voice whispered. This was home. No, this was a man who was off-limits and dangerous.

But it was too late. She was a goner. Probably hadn't even had a chance from the moment he came toward her. Her fate had been sealed. But as far as fates go, she thought weakly, as his lips touched hers in a firm exploration that sparked little tingles up and down her body, this isn't half-bad.

Shoot, if she was going to send her life to hell in a handbag, having Dean ride shotgun wasn't a terrible idea.

What did she have to lose?

CHAPTER TEN

DEAN WAS a bundle of nerves. He wasn't accustomed to acting like an idiot. Usually, he was the responsible one. The one who shouldered the family load without complaint.

And yet, here he was, itching from nervous apprehension over one stupid move.

What the hell was he thinking? That was an easy one to answer. He hadn't been thinking. He didn't know what came over him. It was as if he were under a spell or something. Yeah. That was it. A spell of stupidity. A wave of disgust rolled over him and he wondered if this was what happened to middle-aged men when they hit a midlife crisis. First comes the motorcycle, then the younger woman. Except, he'd skipped the wheels and gone straight to the hot babe.

Scrubbing his hands down his face, he tried focusing on the day ahead. Dana was bringing Annabelle and for that he was grateful. He needed a little time to get hold of himself. He'd spun away from Annabelle the moment his brain reengaged with a resounding *What the hell are you doing?* and after stammering some kind of lame excuse he'd practically run out of the house.

Judging by the stunned expression on her face, he doubted that was the reaction she'd expected. It probably made her feel like dirt, but he couldn't help it. His feet had gone on autopilot and his body had had no choice but to follow. He'd screwed up. Dropped the ball. And now he had the aftermath to deal with, which would be awkward as hell as soon as she got here.

His heart pounded as the sound of Dana's car in the driveway told him Annabelle had arrived. Under normal circumstances, he would've gone out to help with Honey, but he wanted to postpone this face-to-face as long as possible. *Coward.* He forced his attention to the bid sheet and not to the sound of footsteps coming toward the building.

But as the moment he'd been dreading arrived, Annabelle shocked the hell out of him when she did the exact opposite of what he expected.

She smiled as if nothing had happened.

"Good morning," she said, placing Honey's diaper bag in the corner and Honey on the floor while she constructed the playpen. "Don't forget you have that lunch meeting with that new concrete guy over at The Grill and Brandon is going to be late tonight. He's going over to Jessie's after school."

Startled by the ease with which she pretended nothing had happened between them, Dean could only stare for a moment until Honey climbed into his lap and his arms went around the toddler as she grabbed at the items scattered across his desk. So, was this how they should address the issue? Pretend?

It should've been the answer to his dilemma. Obviously, they were on the same page. Neither thought what they did was appropriate, and it was better just to let it go. So, why did he suddenly want to talk about it?

It didn't feel right to act as though nothing had changed. Or maybe it hadn't for her, which left him feeling like the complete sap for letting it affect him in such a visceral manner.

Jerking his gaze away from Annabelle, his mouth softened as he looked at Honey. She smelled of baby shampoo and powder. Her silky blond curls hung in lazy ringlets against rosebud cheeks and he was reminded of something far more pressing than his momentary lapse in judgment.

"You should file a police report," he said to Annabelle as she finished with the playpen. She straightened and offered a brittle smile but little else, which told him that despite her seemingly sunny disposition, she was rattled as well. "I don't feel comfortable knowing someone deliberately sabotaged your car."

Annabelle laughed and brushed past him accidentally, sending his whole body on alert, as she traveled to the file cabinet. "You worry too much. I told you it was probably just a prank. I'm not going to bother the authorities over something like this. Besides, it's not your problem, okay?"

Polite but firm, the message was loud and clear. Back off.

Honey voiced her opinion with a string of nonsensical babble and he renewed his efforts. "What if it hadn't been sugar in your tank but your brake line cut, or your tires? What if you were driving down the road with Honey and you careened down a cliff? There're bigger things at stake here, don't you think?" Annabelle blanched and Dean knew he'd made his point. "What's it going to hurt to talk with a deputy? Besides, you might need a police report for your insurance company to cover the damages."

"Insurance covers stuff like this?"

"Some. Depends on your policy. Did you get full coverage or just liability?"

"Full."

"Well, then, I'd say it's probably covered under comprehensive. I'd bet you have a $500 deductible, though."

She chewed her lip. "Well, that's a little better than the $800 Jonas quoted me," she said, thinking out loud. "All right. I'll make a report but not because I'm worried or anything. Just for the insurance. No one is out to get me or Honey," she assured him, but the subtle quiver told him differently. Since she'd agreed to make the report, he decided to stop pressing the issue. The end result was to his liking so he figured he'd let the rest go. For now.

"Good." He checked his watch. Time to go. He had appointments one on top of another and he was glad. Annabelle might be able to pretend that they hadn't locked lips, but he was having a hard time doing the same. Now that he'd tasted those plump, pouting lips, it was all he could do not to lean in for another. She smelled like a sexy fruit salad—if there was such a thing—and it was hard to ignore the sensory overload.

He stood and gently handed Honey over to Annabelle, swallowing the impulse to babble all sorts of ridiculous stuff about last night, and headed for the door.

Her voice—oddly forlorn and at odds with the strong woman he knew her as—stopped him.

"I know you didn't mean to kiss me."

He wished that were true.

"It was probably just one of those spur-of-the-moment, high-emotion kind of things. I know it didn't mean anything."

A part of him desperately wished he'd felt nothing but uncomplicated desire as their lips touched. It would simplify the situation by half. But he knew the truth. He'd never been the kind of man who could be intimate without involving his heart. Sex for the sake of physical release never felt right.

Closing his eyes for a split second, he opened them as he turned to face her. She stood, cradling Honey on her hip, backlit by the sun coming in from the far window, and his throat closed at the sheer beauty of the picture she made. He couldn't lie. "Kissing you was my choice." *And given half a chance I'd do it again.*

ANNABELLE stared, not quite sure she'd heard that right. But the tight set of Dean's jaw and the piercing look in his brown eyes told her differently.

"So why do you look as if you just admitted to something awful?" she asked, putting Honey into her playpen for the time being.

"It *is* awful," he said simply, his gaze tracking her movements, sliding over her like a caress. "It's inappropriate given our working relationship, but it wasn't an accident. There's no sense in lying. I wanted to kiss you."

Heat curled deep in her belly and pooled in her pelvis but she managed to nod. She'd wanted to kiss him, too. But where did that leave them? The question must've flashed in her eyes.

"We go back to the way things were. It shouldn't be that hard. We hardly know each other, right?"

"Right."

"So, we just tuck this incident away in our private thoughts and leave it there. We both know it can't go any further and there's no sense in chasing after something that's doomed to fail."

Very sensible. But her chest felt leaden. Had she hoped for more? Flustered by her own reaction, she offered a breezy smile that she certainly didn't feel, and nodded. "Absolutely, that's the best idea. I'm completely on board with that. Much less complicated. Good thinking."

He eyed her with suspicion and she wondered if

she was smiling too brightly to be taken at face value. What did it matter what he thought? They'd agreed to a course of action and it seemed the most logical given their circumstances, so whatever else she was feeling—disappointment, chagrin, frustration—would just have to dissipate on its own.

"Glad we agree," he said slowly, though he didn't make a move to leave as she'd expected. In fact, the air between them felt heavy with unfinished business and Annabelle knew what was missing.

"Just one question," she started, her heart rate kicking a tango in her chest as she closed the short distance. He regarded her with wary interest, his whole body tense. She swallowed, wondering what the hell had gotten into her.

"Yeah?"

The tight scratch of his voice rubbed against her raw nerves and sent heat curling through her body.

"What if I didn't want to pretend that nothing happened? What if…I wanted to try it again?"

Dean's eyes darkened, and she could tell he fought a war against himself. She sensed the battle between propriety and desire, and the fact that he struggled made her want him all the more. It was insane and went against every principle that she stood for. Don't lust after your boss. The rule was very simple. Sticking to it was not so easy.

"Annabelle…"

"I know." She lifted on her tiptoes and did the

very thing she knew she should never do. But as her lips touched his, she wondered if being good was overrated.

CHAPTER ELEVEN

"ANNABELLE? Did you hear me, dear?"

Annabelle started, embarrassed to have been caught daydreaming during a committee meeting by none other than Dean's mother, Mary. She adjusted Honey on her lap in an attempt to look as though the baby had needed her attention. Shameful to use her own daughter that way, she thought ruefully and pressed a quick kiss on Honey's head.

"I'm sorry. I didn't catch that," she admitted, feeling her cheeks heat. She couldn't very well tell Dean's mother that the reason she wasn't paying attention was because she was replaying that day's activities in her head. Repeatedly. Well, mostly only a few select moments. But they were really good moments.

"Would you like us to bring the lemonade canisters to Dean's office or to your house?"

"The office would be fine," she murmured.

"They're heavy once you fill them," Mary said, then looked to Dean. "You can help her, right, son?"

Dean caught Annabelle's gaze and she felt the power of his stare all the way down to her toes.

Before she knew it, a smile was curving her lips and all but announcing to the room that something was going on between them.

"No need," Annabelle said quickly, dropping the smile in favor of something more businesslike. "I'm sure I can manage on my own. I'm stronger than I look."

A wave of light laughter filled the room but all Annabelle could see was Dean as he told his mother that he'd help in any way the committee might need him.

He was an incredible kisser. Sweet, yet firm; gentle yet demanding. He'd possessed her mouth with nothing less than mastery and Annabelle had had to fight to keep her expression carefully schooled lest it drift into something akin to blissfully dreamy.

"You look like you have something juicy to share," Dana whispered out of the corner of her mouth. "Tell now? Or later?"

"What are you talking about?" Annabelle said, trying to bluff, but Dana wasn't buying. She tried harder to throw her best friend off the scent. "I'm just happy to be involved. Feels good, you know?"

Dana nodded but a shrewd light shone from her eyes. "Mmm-hmm" was all she said, but Annabelle breathed a secret sigh of relief that Dana didn't seem inclined to press just yet. The operative word being *yet*. That was okay. By the time Dana got around to squeezing something out of Annabelle, whatever was going on between her and Dean would likely be over. Annabelle wasn't a fool. Well, at the moment she was certainly acting like one, mooning over her boss, but in the long run, she knew where things really stood. This was a fling. Plain and simple. Ordinarily, Annabelle wasn't one to play that game, but there was something about Dean that robbed her of the ability to think straight. Especially when he hit her with those smoldering glances that all but screamed he was thinking of one thing.

And that should piss her off. She hated being objectified. But coming from Dean it didn't feel like something cheap and tawdry, though a part of her was petrified that it was exactly that, but she was too googly-eyed to notice it for what it truly was. *Ugh.* She rubbed her temple as her own dizzying logic sent a stabbing pain straight to her brain.

Somehow the meeting ended and she managed to make all the appropriate head bobs and agreements though she couldn't for the life of her recall what had been the topic of discussion. Something about refreshments? Cucumber sandwiches? Who eats those? Sounded dreadful. Hope she'd heard that wrong.

They filed out of the community hall, which was really a glorified barn that had been retrofitted for the town's purpose of a meeting center, and Annabelle said her goodbyes to everyone, hoisting Honey higher on her hip as she awaited Dean. She hated being dependent on him, but they'd arrived together, and he had the car seat in the truck. It didn't seem right to arrive and leave together. She didn't want people to talk.

"Maybe Dana could give us a ride home," Annabelle suggested, hating the nervous quality of her voice. When he looked at her oddly, she explained with a fair amount of awkwardness. "Well, you know, I don't want you to think that I expect you to drive us around all the time. Dana and Sammy would surely take us home if I asked. And, I don't want people to think…" She blushed. "You know. In the absence of facts, people make up stories."

Instead of answering, Dean gently took Honey from her arms and said, "Are you hungry, monkey? I am. Let's get something to eat. All that talk of cucumber and aram sandwiches has made me hungry for some real food." He turned to Annabelle with a twitching grin. "You coming? Or would you rather stand out here in the dark discussing the merits of the Emmett's Mill gossip grapevine? Which, I might add, started talking the moment Sammy hired you. Since there's nothing we can do about it, let's eat."

Smart. And utterly frustrating because he was right.

"I'm uncomfortable with everyone knowing my business," she said quietly when she caught up to him. "I'd rather whatever is happening between us—if anything—is kept between you and me. People might not look at me very kindly if they thought I was trying to move in on Emmett's Mill's favorite widower."

"No one would think that."

"Yes, they would. I know how people think about strangers in small towns. Guilty until proven innocent and I don't want anyone to judge me or Honey."

He shot her a quick look that was incredibly protective and warmed her heart in a silly way. "No one is going to say a word about either of you. I wouldn't allow it."

Dean buckled Honey into her seat and Annabelle climbed into the truck, struck by how comfortable this moment was. They felt like a family. Shaking off that ridiculous—and dangerous—thought, she strapped on her seat belt and exhaled a short breath. "Well, thanks, but you can just take us home. I'll just throw in a pot pie for me and Honey to share."

"How about you let me take you and Honey to dinner?"

Annabelle balked. "Out? In public? That's just begging for tongues to wag at my expense. No thanks. Are you ready to answer questions about…*this?*" Not that she knew what *this* was herself.

His mouth compressed into a tight line and she had her answer, though it poked her in a vulnerable spot. She straightened. "See? Home is best."

"Right." He sighed and put the truck in gear.

DEAN COULD smell whatever fragrance Annabelle always wore, whether it was simply her shampoo or perfume, and it made him want to bury his nose in the waves that fell down her back in an inviting tumble. He'd gone and screwed things up royally, but he couldn't say he regretted it. No, he could admit it hadn't been smart, but he couldn't say he wouldn't want to do it again if given the chance. Annabelle was under his skin in the worst way and he hungered to know more.

But she was right. He wasn't ready to answer questions. Not even his own.

Honey was already asleep by the time they reached Annabelle's house. Frowning because Honey hadn't eaten before she conked out, he wondered if they should wake her. He followed Annabelle inside, casting a wary eye around at the premises, then went straight to Honey's crib to put her down.

"Shouldn't she eat first?" he asked softly, moving aside so Annabelle could put the baby into her pajamas. He watched as she maneuvered Honey deftly into a sleeper without waking her. Beth had been able to do that, too. He'd always managed to wake Brandon every time he tried to do the same. He smiled. Must be a woman thing. Annabelle gestured for them to leave the room.

"I fed her before the meeting because I knew it might get late," she answered with a smile that was far too fleeting for his liking.

"Something's bothering you."

She avoided his stare and moved past him into the kitchen. "I'm just a little hungry. Do you want something? I have some pot pies that are pretty good for microwave food."

He shook his head, catching her hand and gently pulling her to him. He ought to leave. Stop complicating an already messed-up situation, but he wasn't going to. The breath hitched in her chest and the subtle movement created a cascading response in his body. He swallowed, feeling as if he was standing at the deep end of the pool and he'd suddenly forgotten how to swim. "I can't think straight when you're around," he said softly, dipping to inhale the sweet skin at her neck. "Why is that?"

She shivered and angled her head, glancing at him through thick lashes. "I don't know but it seems to be contagious," she said, her voice husky and warm.

He chuckled, loving the fact that even though they were both practically burning up, she still managed to hold on to her sharp wit. He could barely handle a coherent sentence at this point.

"We should stop."

He heard the regret in her voice. "You're right," he said, swallowing around the feel of his heartbeat banging in his throat. God, he felt like a damn kid again. "One kiss and we'll call it a night," he suggested and she nodded eagerly.

"One kiss. One kiss isn't going to hurt anything."

"One kiss…"

But Dean should've known that one kiss would never be enough. It didn't sate his appetite the way it should have; it increased it tenfold.

Slanting his mouth over hers as his arms wrapped around her body, he drew her flush against him until the ripe fullness of her breasts pressed against his chest, igniting the skin.

Her tongue slid along his, playing and teasing as much as tasting and devouring, and he spiraled in a heady dance of desire that made his eyes cross. She sucked his bottom lip between pearly white teeth, hinting at the way she liked to play, and the blood flow immediately stopped elsewhere in his body to reroute south. Feeling himself straining against the unforgiving fabric of his jeans, he grabbed her behind and hoisted her into his arms, loathe to break contact even as he took them out of the room and straight to her bedroom. Of all the crazy things he'd ever done in his life, this ranked in the top three, but he'd lost any chance of listening to reason. He wanted—no, needed her—the way a man on the edge had to have someone to talk him down before he jumped.

They fell to the small bed, sending pillows bouncing to the floor and he climbed her body until he was back at her mouth. Her lips, swollen and red from his attention, were sexy as hell, beckoning as she twisted and gasped in his hold to better feel him against her. The spaghetti straps on her sunshine-yellow top were little match for him as he easily divested her of the flimsy fabric, tossing it over her head to join the discarded pillows. A peach lacy bra with scalloped edges flirted with her creamy skin and he groaned at the beauty of the sight before him. Damn near perfection. Cupping both breasts, reveling in their full weight, he gently squeezed and nearly lost it when she arched and moaned, gripping his shoulders and digging her nails in with a breathy demand for more.

"Annabelle, you're amazing," he murmured, running the tip of his tongue along the shallow valley of her breasts, while he sent one hand sliding down her belly to the tops of her Capri pants. Her legs scissored languorously and she sighed with pleasure as he made short work of the buttons so he could work his fingers beneath the matching peach froth caressing her hips and hiding from view what he ached to see. He worked the pants down slowly, and she helped him by kicking them free until they fell to the floor. Gazing down at her body, her skin heated and flushed, he drank in the sight. As the moment cooled between them, Dean watched as uncertainty clouded her gaze. She tried shifting, but Dean held her still, going down to lightly kiss the faint spidery lines marking her belly, where Honey had grown safe and healthy in her womb. She trembled as his lips grazed the soft skin. "You have nothing to be ashamed of," he said, meaning every word. She was stunning and deserved no less than to believe it in her heart. "You're perfect."

She closed her eyes, but not before he caught the shine that betrayed her tender feelings. "Dean…"

Returning to her mouth, he gently explored her lips, needing to banish whatever had made her question, until she became pliant and yielding at his touch. Taking a brief moment to pull a condom from his wallet, he spent the next hour showing Annabelle in the most reverent way possible how much he enjoyed making love to a woman.

And judging by the scratches she left on his back, she appreciated his efforts.

CHAPTER TWELVE

BRANDON HEARD his father's truck pull into the driveway and he didn't need to see the time on his digital clock to know it was late.

His stomach churned as angry tears stung his eyes. His dad never went out late without telling him where he was going to be. He was a stickler for those kinds of things. So that led Brandon to believe that his dad hadn't wanted him to know where he was. And there was only one place Brandon wanted his dad to steer clear of.

The woman had finally wormed her way into his dad's pants. Brandon had known it would only be a matter of time. He wasn't stupid. His dad was probably lonely and Annabelle was hot. Half his friends were already panting after her, gazing in her direction as if she were a Greek goddess or some such shit, making up excuses to go with him when he had to go to the office. But Brandon saw through her game. She needed a man to take care of her. She already had a kid with some other loser, and now she was eyeing his dad like the top prize at a carnival booth.

It wasn't fair. Wasn't it enough that they'd lost Mom? She'd been the love of Dad's life—he was sure of it. He couldn't understand why Dad was forgetting that fact. Annabelle didn't hold a candle to Mom, he thought. Mom had been the kind of woman people could trust, the one everyone turned to when they needed help. A PTA mom, a woman who brought brownies for his class to share on his birthday. Annabelle was the kind of woman who was more likely to seduce the teacher than volunteer for lunch duty.

Jessie's voice broke into his angry thoughts as the echo of their earlier conversation came to mind.

"What's gotten into you?" she'd asked, irritation warring with concern in her hazel eyes. "You're going all mental over your dad's new office manager. I think she's nice."

"That's because you can't see her for what she truly is," he'd retorted in annoyance.

"Which is?" She crossed her arms and glared.

"A gold digger."

Jessie snorted and scoffed at the idea and his ears burned, but he didn't back down. "Oh, c'mon. You don't seriously think that, do you?"

He answered with a testy stare.

She shook her head. "You're way off base. Maybe you need to stop freaking out about stupid things and deal with your issues. You're creeping me out with all the ugly crap you've been saying about Annabelle."

"Can't help what's true."

She pinned him with a short look. "Yeah? Well, if you keep it up, you'll be spouting off to someone else because I don't want to hear it anymore."

And then she'd left. Brandon didn't blame her for leaving the way she did. He didn't much like himself the way he was feeling but he couldn't stop. It was as if Annabelle had burrowed under his skin like a parasite and was eating away at his ability to be a nice person. A flash of shame followed at the knowledge that his mom would have been very disappointed with him.

He countered by saying that if his mom knew how this woman had designs on his dad she'd want Brandon to protect the family however possible.

Which is exactly what he planned to do.

ANNABELLE couldn't seem to catch her breath. She suspected it had something to do with the fact that each time Dean came into the building her heart rate tripled and the urge to lick him like a giant piece of man-candy nearly overwhelmed her.

He glanced her way and her mouth curved.

This could be a problem. She allowed her smile to fade and busied herself with work. A fling was transient, fleeting and brief. Annabelle tried to focus but Dean was in her peripheral vision and her attention wandered.

When he looked up from his PDA, their gazes locked. A slow grin spread across his lips and she knew their thoughts mirrored each other's. She dropped her stare first. They couldn't keep doing this all day. For one thing, they wouldn't get any work done and for another, it was incredibly suspect. People were bound to notice.

"Have dinner with me tonight."

She started at his sudden proposition. "No."

"Why not?"

"You know why. We already covered that."

"At my house."

"Your house?"

He chuckled as if he'd surprised himself with the suggestion but immediately warmed to it. "Yeah. Let me cook you and Honey dinner. Brandon is staying at a friend's tonight and it'd be nice."

Tempting. Wildly tempting. Which is why she must decline but she wavered. "What's on the menu?"

"I can only do one thing well."

She blushed as her imagination provided a range of possibilities. Clearing her throat, she said, "Which is?"

"Barbecue."

"Barbecue? Chicken? Fish? Steak?"

"Anything that tastes good charbroiled," he answered. "Interested?"

Lord help me, yes. "Mildly."

Dean pocketed his PDA and grabbed his keys. "See you at five. Bring your appetite," he added with a wink.

Her breath hitched in her chest as she stared after him, trying not to gawk so hard that his jeans caught fire.

A woman could get used to a man like that. It was a full moment before her good sense returned and a regretful sigh followed. It seemed she had inherited her mother's deplorable compass when it came to steering clear of trouble after all. Only she hadn't gravitated toward a loser—quite the opposite. But it spelled trouble for Annabelle just the same.

So, what are you going to do about it? She worried her bottom lip and glanced toward Honey, who was playing with a set of toy keys Dean had picked up for her at the hardware store.

End it?

Yeah, how about trying that with a little conviction next time.

By THE TIME Dean returned to the office he was humming. He entered the building with a smile and went straight to Honey, picking up the toddler as if it were perfectly natural to do so at the end of a long day, and fought the urge to kiss Annabelle. Instead, he grabbed Honey's diaper bag and gestured for the door. "Shall we?"

"Are you sure this is a good idea?" she asked, hesitating as she followed. "I mean, this is going a bit fast. I don't want you to think that I expect anything from you just because..."

He glanced back at her, drank in the sight of her standing there backlit by the sun, her hair a fiery halo around her head, and his heart stuttered a beat. He transferred Honey to his other side and pulled Annabelle to him. She gasped, making an adorably feminine sound, and looked up at him with wide brown eyes. He lowered his head to hers and took her mouth firmly, leaving no doubt as to how he felt about her statement. "You worry too much," he said against her mouth. "It's just dinner, right?"

"One dinner, one kiss…I think we know how these things end up," she said wryly, though the corners of her mouth turned up playfully. She pushed away from him. "Fine. Dinner it is, but don't get used to this. I'm not your girlfriend."

"What are you then?"

Her mouth quirked as if she didn't quite know what to call herself and in the absence of knowing, simply shouldered the diaper bag and moved past Dean with a mumble under her breath that sounded a lot like, "office manager with benefits," and he felt laughter rumble in his chest. He liked her—more than he should—and he knew the consequences would likely make his heartburn feel like a mild flicker.

ANNABELLE, wineglass in hand, studied the pictures on the wall while Dean made all sorts of racket in the kitchen that didn't sound promising.

"You sure you know what you're doing in there?" she asked, pausing to glance at a photo of Brandon as a little boy. Judging by the missing tooth, he was probably around seven. Cute. Although, that wasn't surprising. Despite his crappy attitude toward her, he was a good-looking kid. He favored Beth, it seemed, with his facial features, but he'd got Dean's wide shoulders. Honey giggled as Dean's cat wound his way around her small body, twitching his ringed tail next to her face until she sneezed.

"Bless you, Honey-pie," she murmured, then sighed. Honey looked like Thad, down to her blue eyes and flaxen hair, but somehow a feminine version of Thad had turned out quite lovely. She walked to Honey and picked her up. "Let's see what culinary treat Dean is subjecting us to. Let's hope it's edible."

Annabelle needn't have worried, she realized, for, as she rounded the corner to the dining room, Dean had laid a cozy setting for three, though he had wisely left the candles that graced the oak table unlit. A steaming pot of green beans and another of garlic mashed potatoes sat beside a plate of roasted boneless chicken and Annabelle's mouth watered. "I'd say you can barbecue for me anytime," she said, taking a seat with Honey, wondering if she'd ever smelled anything so good. "If I ate like this every night I'd be fatter than a deer tick," she admitted with a rueful smile.

"I'm not one to complain about a little meat on a woman's bones," Dean said with a grin that made her feel naked. "Women are supposed to be soft and full of curves. You're just about perfect in that area," he added, and she blushed.

Dean disappeared, saying he'd be right back. Annabelle was grateful for the short reprieve so that she could get her head back on straight. How was a woman supposed to stay focused when the guy said things designed to make her melt? Dean returned with a beautiful wooden high chair and she lost whatever resistance she was trying to wage against falling for him.

"This was Brandon's." He plucked Honey from her lap before Annabelle could offer a weak protest, and slipped her into the old chair as easily as if he were accustomed to doing so every night. "Still works. Beth's father made this chair for Brandon before he was born. It's an heirloom we figured we could give to Brandon when he had kids but it's just gathering dust for now."

"Are you sure Brandon won't mind?"

"Well, until I give it to him for his family, technically, it's mine. I'd say he has no say in the matter," he said firmly, signifying an end to that particular conversation, but Annabelle was a little uncomfortable. She had enough issues with the teenager; she didn't need to compound them.

"Dean…"

"Annabelle," he said softly, stopping her from continuing. "Let's just enjoy dinner."

She nodded. He was right. Brandon wasn't here tonight, and it wasn't likely she'd make a habit of coming over for meals, so she'd just enjoy dinner, as Dean said. She smiled. "Pass the potatoes, please. Honey likes the kind that come out of a box, but I think she'll love these."

"Potatoes should never come out of a box," Dean said. "My mom would die before she put something out of a box on her table."

"Well, not everyone was raised with the Bradys," Annabelle said, placing a dollop of potatoes on her own plate. "My mom did the best that she could with what she had. And sometimes all we had came from a box."

"I'm sorry," Dean said. "I didn't mean to be offensive."

She shrugged. "No harm, no foul. But not everyone grew up like you did."

"Tell me about what it was like to grow up in your home," he said, and she immediately regretted her candid comments.

She waved away his request. "It's nothing worth talking about." True to a point. Her childhood was something right out of a Lifetime TV movie of the week. But who wanted to share that? Certainly not her. "Why do you ask?"

"Just curious, I guess. Can't help but wonder by your comment how different our lives were. When we first met, you mentioned that your dad left when you were seven. Did your mom remarry?"

Her throat tightened and her smile felt strained. "Ah, no. She didn't remarry." The succession of loser boyfriends had been worse than one deadbeat dad in Annabelle's opinion.

"So it was just you and your mom? You said you have a brother...."

"Robbie. Well, I heard he prefers to be called Rob now but it's hard for me to see him as anything other than my little brother...especially when he's asking me for money."

"What does he do for a living?"

"Nothing that I can tell. He stays with friends. I guess he's more like our dad in that he's a bit of a wanderer, too. He never really stays in one place long. I didn't even know where to find him to let him know our mom had died, so he missed the funeral."

"He'll come to regret that as he gets older."

"Yeah, well, by the time Robbie starts to realize stuff like that, I'm sure our mom's funeral will be just one of many regrets for him. Robbie hasn't made very good choices, unfortunately."

"How old is he?"

"Just turned twenty. He's still a kid. All he cares about is where to find the next good time. Honestly, I'm amazed he isn't in prison yet."

"Is that where your dad is?" Dean ventured carefully and Annabelle surprised him with a laugh.

"I have no idea where my dad is. He could be dead for all I know. And I don't really care. He abandoned us and didn't look backward once. He broke my mom's heart and I don't think she ever really recovered, you know?" He nodded and she continued with a short sigh. "There's nothing glamorous about being a single mom and sometimes it's harder than you thought it was going to be. A person bringing in a paycheck can make another person more tolerant of his…shortcomings."

"I take it your mom let a few bad apples into the house in order to make the bills."

Annabelle considered how to answer. She'd already shared too much. "One or two."

"Did any of them hurt you?"

She placed her fork down with an accidental clatter that made her stomach muscles clench. With forced gaiety, she said, "Dean, this is starting to feel more like the Inquisition than a pleasant dinner. How about lightening up with the third degree, okay?"

He leaned back in his chair, his expression thoughtful. "I'm sorry. When you grow up in a small town you tend to know a lot about the people around you simply because of circumstance. I just want to know more about you. I apologize for making you uncomfortable."

"It's fine. I understand. I'm just not the kind of girl who's into sharing all that much. The past is the past and it wasn't that great so I prefer to leave it there."

"So, if I can't ask about your childhood, what topics are fair game?"

"Well, that would depend…. What else do you want to know?"

"How'd you meet Honey's father?"

She winced privately, but figured this was safe enough territory. "He was the busboy at the restaurant I worked at," she answered, hating how clichéd that sounded. "My mom had just died and Thad was a shoulder to cry on. He was nice and I was vulnerable. I know…classic. But, I didn't expect to get pregnant, and when I did, I panicked at the thought of being a single mom. I'd avoided that situation for so long, I was mortified how easily I'd slipped."

"Is Nichols your married name?"

"No. We didn't actually get married. We were going to but I kept dragging my feet. I think subconsciously I must've known that it wasn't going to work out. And now I'm so glad we didn't tie the knot. If we were married still, Thad would no doubt want alimony."

"It's hard for me to understand how a father could walk away from his child. Brandon is the best thing ever to happen to Beth and me. He was a blessing from the moment he came into our lives."

Annabelle smiled at Honey, feeling much the same. "Yeah, I know. But Thad's just not that way and really, I'm glad. Makes things simpler on my end."

"Did you love him?"

"Why do you ask?"

He shrugged. "It just seems you aren't all that broke up about ditching the father of your baby. Makes me wonder if you ever loved him."

"Maybe I just deal with things differently than you."

"Is that an answer?"

"As much a one as you're going to get on the subject. I told you the past is the past. I prefer not to dwell."

"Fair enough. It's none of my business."

She smiled. "You're right. It's not."

"Since I'm already setting a precedent for asking questions that aren't any of my business, how about one more?"

He smiled in spite of his brashness and Annabelle replied with a low chuckle. "You can ask but there's no guarantee I'll answer. Go for it."

"All right. How'd you lose your mom?"

Annabelle's spirit dimmed as she remained quiet, always surprised by how that question still hurt. Sadie Nichols hadn't been the best provider, but she'd been full of heart and Annabelle had always felt loved by her mom. She just wished her mom had had a bit more sense when it came to men.

"I sense the odds of your answering slowly dwindling. Hard question?"

"Uh, sort of. Losing my mom was difficult."

"I can only imagine. Were you close?"

"Yeah," she answered softly, remembering how she, Robbie and her mom used to curl up on the sofa together before the accident and watch old movies. "When she died…I was really lost for a while."

"My mom is the glue that holds our family together. Without her, we would've been a bunch of unruly boys without enough sense between the three of us to fill a cereal bowl. Moms just have that special something. I'm sorry you lost yours so young."

"I have some good memories." Annabelle smiled. "Once my mom took us to Knott's Berry Farm with the money she got from her tax return. Some people might say she should've spent the money on things like bills and new clothes for us, but that weekend was the brightest spot in our childhood, and I'm not sorry we went without new jeans and shirts that year."

Silence followed and Annabelle realized she hadn't really answered Dean's question.

It would be easy to just say her mom had died from pneumonia complications due to her paralysis, but to do so would open her up to explaining how her mom had landed in that wheelchair and Annabelle didn't want to sully the evening with Buddy King's name.

It was bad enough he was in her memory.

Annabelle forced another smile. "Our food is getting cold. Let's eat, and while we're at it, let's change the subject."

CHAPTER THIRTEEN

"ALL RIGHT…although, I have to be honest, I'm not very good at small talk," Dean said, aware that Annabelle was intensely uncomfortable with topics that veered too close to personal, particularly about her childhood.

"Have you heard from your ex at all?" he asked, needing to know a little more about the man who was stupid enough to leave Annabelle and Honey. "Does he send you any money or anything?"

"I don't want anything from Thad. It's easier this way."

"He should at least be sending child support."

"Thad doesn't really have much of a work ethic. He barely makes enough to support himself much less a child. He agreed not to follow us as long as I don't pester him for support."

"What a loser," Dean muttered.

"New subject," Annabelle declared, simultaneously wiping a glob of potato from Honey's chin. "Tell me about Beth."

"What do you want to know?" he answered,

careful to keep his face neutral even when a spasm of grief followed her request. Talking about Beth only made her absence that much more real. Sometimes he liked to pretend she was going to walk through the front door, as if her accident had been some kind of bad dream. He cleared his throat and waited.

"What was she like?"

The exact opposite of you. Whereas Annabelle attracted attention without trying, Beth hadn't been the type of person who'd stop men in their tracks. Not that Beth hadn't been attractive, because she was, but hers had been a soft, wholesome, girl-next-door kind of pretty. Dean bit down on his tongue before his bumbling thoughts slipped out. Annabelle was likely to take a statement like that out of context. "She was a good mother, an excellent wife and my best friend." The tight feeling in his throat made that last part difficult to get out. He shifted in his chair. "A good woman."

"How'd you meet?" He sent her a short look and she merely laughed. "Turnabout is fair play. I answered your questions, now you can answer mine."

"I wouldn't say you answered all of them," he grumbled, and she shrugged as if that were a minor detail. "We met in our first year in college. She was an English major and I needed tutoring in that department. I plucked her name from an announcement board because she was the cheapest and I was short on cash. Ended up being the investment of my life."

"Did you pass your class?"

His cheeks colored a little. "No, but that wasn't Beth's fault. I was too distracted by her to notice what she was trying to teach me. I took the class over and got a different tutor—one I wasn't the least bit attracted to—and then got the balls to ask Beth out."

"That's a sweet story. So, you married a smarty, huh?"

"Yeah, I guess I did."

They laughed together and it felt good. The conversation flowed easily between them as long as they steered clear of the too-personal stuff, and before long it was time to clean up the leftovers.

Annabelle changed Honey into her pajamas and stuffed her toys into the diaper bag so they could get ready to leave. "It's getting close to Honey's bedtime. We should go," she said, and he agreed, though the greedy part of him wanted her to stay a bit longer. Honey's pink little mouth opened in a wide yawn that nearly toppled her over and he immediately shelved that part of him. Tucking Honey over his shoulder, he grabbed the diaper bag as well.

"Let's get this girl to bed, then."

A soft smile graced Annabelle's lips, and he was struck by how beautiful she was, even though she was as different from Beth as night was from day. Was he making a mistake in giving in to his feelings? He shrugged off the discomfort that the answer might've caused if he were in the mind to listen. He didn't want to think about the future. He just wanted to think about today. And possibly tomorrow as long as Annabelle was in it.

Guilt for abandoning a promise to Brandon made his heart drag in his chest. He'd never lied to his son before, and he didn't like the feeling it caused. But he wasn't ready to admit to Brandon or anyone else that he was starting to fall for Annabelle.

He'd just have to deal with it in his own way. In the meantime, he'd have to make sure they were discreet, which, by the sound of it, Annabelle was in favor of as well.

So, why did it make what he was fighting inside feel cheap and dirty?

A WEEK LATER, Annabelle was sitting with her fellow committee members chatting about the upcoming D-Day when Brandon and his girlfriend entered the community building. While he gave his grandmother a quick peck on the cheek, the look Annabelle received in return for her warm smile was nothing short of dismissive.

Jessie seemed embarrassed by Brandon's open snub but could only send an apologetic look Annabelle's way. Annabelle sighed and returned to her notes, determined to ignore Brandon's bad behavior, if only for Dean's sake.

Dana leaned over and whispered, "Why is Dean's son giving you the stink-eye? You run over his dog or something?"

Annabelle forced a smile. "Who can explain teenage angst? My guess is that he's afraid I'm trying to replace his mother."

"Any reason he'd think that?"

Annabelle refused to jump at the bait and answered with a shrug. "I sit at his mother's old desk. The kid seems to be terribly territorial. He'll get over it as soon as he realizes I'm not interested in taking Beth's place." *As if I could.* She wasn't blind or stupid. Dean might have enjoyed her body but he hadn't offered his heart. She ducked her head to avoid Dana's gaze, not quite ready to talk about what she'd done. A part of her burned with shame for caving so easily on her convictions. Was she any better than her mother in the decision-making department when it came to men? Already she'd say she was 0 for 2. And those weren't good odds.

"So, where is Dean tonight?" Dana asked, scooting over to chat more easily.

"He had a late meeting. He said he'd have Mary catch him up on anything he missed."

"Well, having your mom as the committee chair does help in that department. How did I get stuck on first-aid patrol while you got refreshments?"

"You're the paramedic. My only discernible skill rests with passing out lemonade. Be thankful you have a real skill to draw from," Annabelle answered dryly.

"Oh, quit the pity party. You have skills. I remember in high school you were so crafty. You always managed to make the most beautiful art projects without even trying. Didn't you win the local art council–sponsored contest for that pottery you did?"

Annabelle actually blushed that Dana would remember such a small detail. Honey tugged at her ear and Annabelle frowned as she answered, "It was just a small contest. Nothing big. I probably went up against three senior citizens. Not much of a competition, really."

"Oh, c'mon, don't be so modest. It was beautiful. What did you end up doing with it?" Dana followed Annabelle's gaze to rest on Honey as she toddled after an older boy with an interesting toy. "Honey seems a little under the weather. Is she okay?"

"I think so. Probably just the sniffles, and to answer your question I gave the bowl to my mom for her birthday." Annabelle smiled, the memory warming her until she remembered what fate the small ceramic bowl ultimately met. "It got broken and thrown away. I'd forgotten about it."

Not exactly true but she worked hard to forget anything associated with Buddy. He'd thrown it to the ground one night when he was fighting with Sadie. The blue bowl had shattered in spite of Sadie's pleas. The fact that her mother had begged and received nothing for the price of her dignity only made the memory worse.

"You should take up pottery again," Dana said, unaware that tears had begun to sting Annabelle's eyes. "I don't care what you say, you were good. Some people are just born with talent that others aren't. I think people would buy your work. I bet you could find a used pottery wheel on eBay.... AnnaB? What's wrong?"

Annabelle brushed at her eyes. "Nothing. I'm—"

"Lying," Dana interjected firmly. She turned to Mary. "Could you keep an eye on Honey for a minute? Annabelle and I are going to make a run to the car."

And with that Dana pulled Annabelle from her chair and out into the cool night air.

"Okay, you have a finite amount of time to spill your guts, and I'm not leaving until you tell me what the hell is wrong."

Annabelle should've known better than to try and bluff Dana. They had insights into each other's minds that few others could understand because of the bond they shared.

"I'm not sure Emmett's Mill was the fresh start I was hoping for."

"What are you talking about? You love it here."

Annabelle heaved a sigh, losing control and hating it. Her voice wobbled as she said, "I screwed up. I did the one thing I swore I would never do and now I don't know how to feel about myself because I'm all twisted up inside and if I'd never moved here I wouldn't be faced with this situation."

"Which situation is that?" Dana's concern seemed to grow as she pressed for an answer. "You're starting to scare me. Did you rob a bank or something?"

"I slept with Dean," Annabelle exclaimed, covering her face with her hands as if that alone could hide the way she felt inside. Dana gently pulled Annabelle's hands away and Annabelle continued in anguish. "And worse, I don't regret it. I mean, I do regret it because it was wrong but a part of me fell in love. And that's ridiculous! And surely a path straight to misery. Not to mention clichéd as hell. I mean, the office manager and the hunky contractor. Please. I couldn't even be original in my screw-up. Is this what my mom felt when she met Buddy? A part of me used to be so angry with her for falling in love with that man and now I feel like I can't help myself with Dean. I'm a hypocrite."

"First of all, calm down. Second, you are not comparing Dean Halvorsen to Buddy *effing* King. They're not even apples and oranges…they're more like apples and…*roadkill*." Dana acknowledged Annabelle's look of disgust but didn't back down. "True, Buddy was your mom's boss at first, but he was nothing if not a sleaze bucket who specifically targeted your mom for his own reasons and I will not allow you to compare the two. I'm sorry if I'm being harsh but I just won't."

"People will talk and say bad things about me like they did my mom. I heard the things they used to say about her around the plant and I refuse to let that kind of ugliness touch Honey. It's not her fault."

"No one is going to say shit about you or Honey. Neither Sammy nor Dean would let them. And if that didn't work, I'm not averse to putting in my two cents to whoever is stupid enough to open their mouth in front of me."

Annabelle's tears returned but for a different reason. Dana was a better friend than she deserved to have, and she reacted by simply wrapping the woman in a tight hug. "Thank you, Dana."

Dana's voice was muffled against Annabelle's shoulder but there was a wealth of emotion inside. "Don't mention it. You can always count on me to keep your head on straight because I know you'd do the same for me."

"You wouldn't even have to ask."

"I know."

They pulled apart and each wiped at their eyes. Finally, Annabelle looked at Dana and said speculatively, "So, pottery, huh? You think I have talent?"

"You know I would never lie to you. If you sucked I'd tell you that, too."

Annabelle laughed. "Yes, you would. I seem to remember you telling me in no uncertain terms that I couldn't carry a tune in a bucket."

"Dogs in three different counties are thanking me for that candid assessment."

Annabelle linked her arm in Dana's and they walked back inside. "What would I do without you?"

"Shrivel up and die. But don't worry, I'll never make you find out. You're stuck with me, girlfriend. Now, more about you and Dean…"

CHAPTER FOURTEEN

"ANNABELLE, don't be stubborn. Let me pay for the repair and you can pay me back. You need your car," Dean said, becoming increasingly annoyed at Annabelle's pointed refusal to accept either of his offers.

"I'm not going to let you pay for my car," Annabelle said, returning to the paperwork that she'd put into a neat pile before her. "End of discussion."

"Then at least let me lend you my spare car."

"That was Beth's car, wasn't it?"

"Yes." He drew a deep breath. "She was driving a rental car when the accident happened. I told her it was better to put the miles on someone else's car instead of our own. At the time I thought it was a great idea. Anyway…it's just sitting there in the driveway now, not doing anyone any good."

Annabelle slid her gaze away from him. "I'm not driving Beth's car. How do you think Brandon is going to feel if he sees me driving around town in his mom's car? The kid already hates me. Why make it worse?"

"He doesn't hate you," Dean countered, worried

that his son could be capable of despising someone so deeply with so little provocation. "He doesn't even know you."

"And something tells me he isn't interested in getting to know me, either."

"Give him some time."

Annabelle waved him away. "Don't worry about it. I'm not losing sleep about it, but you shouldn't kid yourself. Brandon certainly does hate me."

Dean ground his teeth against the urge to continue defending his son but he knew better than to waste time on a futile effort. Annabelle's mind was made up and frankly, Dean wasn't sure that she was wrong.

And that bothered him.

"If you're tired of shuttling us around I can get Dana to help out," she said and he reacted sharply.

"Did I say that?"

She glared. "Don't snap at me."

"Sorry. I don't understand what the big deal is…. It's just a car. You need transportation and I have extra wheels. It's a no-brainer in my book."

Annabelle quieted for a moment and he thought for a split second she was going to give him the silent treatment for snapping at her. He wouldn't blame her. This situation with Brandon had him on edge. Finally she spoke.

"You could never understand what it's like to be beholden to someone else for basic needs and, there-fore, to you, a car is just a car. But to someone who grew up with practically nothing and watched as her mother let one man after another into our home just because they could help put food on the table, the loan of a car from a man I've *slept with* is not simply a car. It's a statement that I'm no better than a whore and I refuse to let anyone make me feel like that."

He drew back stunned, his mouth opening but no words falling out. He didn't know what to say. She took his silence as something else and walked from the room with a terse declaration that she needed air and some privacy, leaving Dean to stare after her.

THE MIDNIGHT HOUR had come and gone but Annabelle was still awake. Flopping onto her stomach, she punched her flat pillow in the hopes of fluffing it into some semblance of comfort, but, even as her head sank into the pillowcase, it was nearly as comfortable as trying to catch some shut-eye on a tortilla.

If only she could blame her insomnia solely on the wretched state of her bedding.

Dean was the cause of her restlessness, and the realization that she was falling for the man in a ridiculously short amount of time. If colleges gave out degrees for plain, short-sighted stupidity, she'd surely have graduated at the top of the class.

Flipping again, sprawling across the bed, she tried not to recall how Dean had felt pressed against her, molding to her every curve as he'd memorized the hills and valleys of her body like a man determined to know every inch. Thoughtful and considerate, he was the lover of her fantasies brought to life and it really wasn't fair of fate to drop him in her lap and then in a moment of clarity make her realize that they were ill-suited.

She moaned and pummeled the pillow beside her, tucking it beneath the first one as if that might help her comfort level but it did nothing. Her discomfort was in her heart, not her bed.

Rising, she padded into the kitchen for a glass of water but stopped abruptly when she heard a soft whimper coming from Honey's room.

Flicking on the small bedside lamp, she went to Honey's crib and gasped at her daughter's flushed cheeks and blood-red lips. Pressing her palm lightly to Honey's forehead, she drew back in alarm at the heat radiating from Honey's small head. Moving quickly to the bathroom to retrieve the ear thermometer, she returned and gently took the baby's temperature.

A beep later, Annabelle nearly cried out in fear as the temperature gauge read 105. "Oh God, Honey," she said, plucking the baby's limp body from the crib. She rushed to the bathroom and wet a washcloth to hold against Honey's cheeks. Honey barely registered the cold cloth, the only movement a slight wrinkle in her brow. Don't panic, Annabelle told herself, continuing to wet the cloth and press it against Honey's heated skin. Babies got fevers all the time. Everything would be fine.

But another look at Honey's flushed skin had Annabelle practically running for the phone.

DEAN HEARD the phone, but the sound didn't register at first. Disoriented for a split second, his first thought when he came to his senses was that Brandon was in trouble, until he remembered that Brandon was asleep down the hall. The next thought was that calls in the middle of the night never boded well.

He picked up the phone and answered with his heart in his mouth, hoping it wasn't bad news.

"Dean?"

The fear in Annabelle's voice chased the sleep out of his brain and he sat up straight, tearing the bedsheets away from his body in one motion. "What's wrong?"

"It's Honey…she's sick. I don't know what to do. Her fever is really high and…I'm sorry, but I didn't know who else to call."

The fact that he was the first person she thought of when her best friend was a paramedic warmed him in a place that he'd thought long frozen over. But he didn't have time to consider the ramifications. His concern was for that sick baby girl. "I'll be there in five minutes," he promised.

Shoving his legs into the first pair of jeans he could find, and scribbling a short note to Brandon in case he woke up after Dean had left, he was out the door and on the road minutes later.

When he pulled into Annabelle's driveway, he saw Annabelle framed in the doorway, clutching her child to her chest, fear widening her gaze and making her mouth tremble.

"How high is her fever?" he asked, taking Honey gently from Annabelle's arms. She appeared grateful and he suspected she was about to collapse from the terror.

"A hundred and five."

Much too hot. "She needs to get to the hospital. She might have an infection," he said softly so as not to disturb Honey. He didn't wait for Annabelle's consensus and simply put Honey into her car seat inside his truck. "Let's go."

Annabelle didn't waste any time jumping into the seat. "Is she going to be okay?" she asked, needing to hear something to ease her mind, but Dean was afraid, too. Once Brandon had fallen and smacked his head on the sidewalk and they'd been afraid that he'd suffered a concussion. He and Beth had stood in the waiting room of the E.R., sharing the fear that their only son was terribly hurt. Annabelle was alone. Sliding his hand across the seat, he grasped her ice-cold fingers, telling her in the only way he could manage at the moment that she wasn't alone and it was going to be okay.

Dean carried Honey through the double bay doors of the E.R. and went straight to the nurse's desk. Annabelle followed close behind.

"We have a baby who's very sick. She's running a high temperature," he said to the nurse.

"How high?"

"A hundred and five," Annabelle answered anxiously. "Is she going to be okay?"

The nurse didn't answer and instead paged the doctor. She gestured toward an empty bed with two linen screens hanging to the side and said, "Put her on the bed. The doctor will be with you shortly."

Dean was half tempted to let the surly nurse know how he felt about her bedside manner, but he figured now was not the time. Annabelle looked ready to shatter from her tightly drawn nerves and he didn't want to compound the stress. Instead he gently laid Honey on the bed and tried not to worry. Honey's body was throwing off an impossible amount of heat; surely it wasn't good for a baby to radiate so much warmth. "Where's that doctor?" he muttered, glancing around the sterile E.R. He felt a hand on his shoulder and looked down to see Annabelle. Her presence calmed him and he pulled her against his side, needing her as much as she needed him.

A few minutes later a young doctor appeared wearing a weary but welcoming smile. "What do we have here? One sick little girl, I see," he noted as he turned to Annabelle and Dean. "Hi, I'm Dr. Grant. Are you the child's parents?"

Annabelle looked to Dean and answered, "I'm her mother. Dean is a family friend."

Dr. Grant took Honey's temperature, confirming the high fever, and then requested lab work from the nurse. Using an otoscope, he checked Honey's ears and frowned as he pulled away. "Well, her inner ear is inflamed, which leads me to believe she has an ear infection. Has she been pulling at her ear at all?"

Annabelle nodded. "A little. I noticed her doing that the other day. But she didn't seem sick."

"Babies don't always present their symptoms like adults. Often, symptoms don't show up until the fever gets pretty high. But don't worry, we'll bring that temperature down and start attacking that infection with some antibiotics."

Annabelle smiled her relief and clung to Dean. A shudder shook her frame and he pulled her tighter against him. The doctor left to talk with the nurse and soon another nurse—a much friendlier one—began administering the antibiotics.

"She's going to be all right?" Annabelle asked and Dean nodded. Annabelle exhaled in relief. "Thank God. I've never been so scared in my life. You know, some things you just take for granted until you're faced with a situation that makes you realize how fragile life is." She ducked her head. "I suppose you've already learned that lesson. With Beth."

"Yeah. That day changed a lot of my perceptions about life. What's important…what's not."

If Annabelle had a response it was quelled by the reappearance of the doctor. "As soon as we get her labs back, and providing we're not looking at anything more serious, you'll be given your discharge papers. Make sure to follow up with her regular pediatrician to ensure the infection has cleared. Ear infections can be tricky if you don't watch them."

"Thank you, doctor," Dean said, shaking the man's hand. Relief that Honey was going to be fine making him a little light-headed. "We'll do that."

Annabelle shot him a look but otherwise remained quiet until the doctor left the vicinity.

"I don't have a pediatrician," she said.

He smoothed the frown worrying her forehead. "Don't worry. I'll see if Brandon's old pediatrician is taking new patients. Dr. Barski is a little hard to understand at times but she's a great doctor."

"What do you mean she's hard to understand?"

"She's Russian or Czech, not sure which. Either way, she has a thick accent."

Annabelle looked tempted but, to his surprise, declined to have him call Dr. Barski.

"Why not?"

"I don't have insurance and I'm sure the office visit is expensive. There must be a free clinic somewhere in town. I'll have to take her there."

"A free clinic?" Dean balked. "Absolutely not. Honey needs—"

"She just needs someone to look in her ear to make sure the infection is gone. I'm sure the clinic physician's assistant is qualified to do that and many other medical things."

Dean wanted to argue, hating the idea of Honey being subjected to a free-clinic atmosphere, but Annabelle had a point. He supposed, provided the lab results were clean, that a PA could handle a simple ear infection. "Fine. We'll do it your way. But they'd better not miss anything. We're talking about Honey's health, not a Jiffy Lube."

In spite of the fatigue bracketing her eyes, Annabelle laughed. "A Jiffy Lube? How is that even a good comparison?"

"I don't know. It's all I could think of at the moment. The truck needs an oil change soon," he admitted with a short grin.

Annabelle sobered. "Thank you for coming. I probably should've called Dana—"

"You did the right thing," he broke in, not liking that she was backtracking. "You can always call me, Annabelle. Always."

She stared at him with wide, soft brown eyes and he resisted the urge to plant a kiss on her trembling lips, if only to sear into her brain that she could depend on him no matter what the circumstance, but he sensed she needed to absorb that concept on her own and merely waited.

She looked away, but not before Dean saw her waver. He wondered what was happening between them. It was irresponsible of him to encourage more, but it was almost as if he couldn't stop himself. He didn't merely want more—he *craved* more in such a way that he felt powerless to stop the train heading their way. And he had no doubt it was a freightliner. He could only hope that when it slammed into them, there were enough pieces to pick up and start again.

CHAPTER FIFTEEN

DEAN GAVE Annabelle the day off since they didn't get back from the hospital until nearly five in the morning and he wanted Honey to be able to rest in her own bed instead of the playpen at the office.

Annabelle had protested, but it was plain that she was just as eager to seek her bed when her eyelids drooped and a yawn escaped.

If he hadn't had a full schedule, he would've crawled into his own bed, but, instead, he downed a strong cup of coffee and headed out to his appointments.

At lunch, he ran into Brandon and Jessie as they left the local pizza place.

"What happened last night?" Brandon asked. "Your note was kind of hard to read."

"Honey was sick and needed to go to the hospital."

"And that's your problem how?"

Dean frowned. "You know someone tampered with Annabelle's car. She needed a ride."

Brandon shrugged. "Again, I don't see how that's your problem. Doesn't she have friends? How about a phone? She could've called 911."

Jessie scowled at Brandon and walked toward his car and Dean didn't blame her. His son was being an ass.

"We'll talk later. You need to get back to school," Dean said, moving past him to open the doors. Brandon said something under his breath and Dean looked at him sharply, but whatever Brandon had said he didn't feel the need to repeat. "Son," Dean warned. "You need an attitude adjustment. I suggest you get to work on it."

"Whatever, Dad."

Dean's temper flared, but Brandon had wisely chosen to keep walking. Annabelle's comment about Brandon returned to his memory, and he had to admit that his son seemed intent on making a liar out of him. Wonderful, he thought sourly. Just wonderful.

ANNABELLE CHECKED IN on Honey for quite possibly the tenth time in as many minutes, and once she was satisfied her daughter was sleeping soundly with a normal temperature, she let herself sink into the sofa with a weary groan.

She'd made an appointment with the free clinic and Honey was scheduled to go in tomorrow, but there was little to do today except let Honey sleep and recover while the antibiotics did the work. Although Dean had given her the day off, she continued to feel as if she should be at the office. Being home with nothing except her thoughts to keep her company led to dangerous musings.

Don't think about Dean, she commanded her thoughts as she grabbed a magazine and thumbed through it. What a man, though! She could imagine how Beth must've felt the moment she laid eyes on her future husband. Annabelle sighed, disturbed by the faint twinge of jealousy she felt toward a dead woman and dropped the magazine to the coffee table. Who was she kidding? Her eyes burned from fatigue. There was no way she was going to be able to read.

Settling deeper into the sofa, she grabbed the colorful afghan and tucked herself into it.

As sleep drifted closer, her mind conjured an odd assortment of images, some of which were comprised of last night's adventure at the hospital, others of her and Dean, but just as she dropped into deep slumber, a blue ceramic bowl filled her mind's eye, shattered into a million pieces.

DEAN ENTERED Annabelle's house after a short knock produced no results. He found her snoring lightly on the sofa, a long tendril of red hair curling along her jaw, and small breaths escaped from her parted lips. In peaceful repose, Annabelle's expression gentled, revealing a soft vulnerability that made her glow. The word *beautiful* was too trite, too clichéd and certainly didn't describe the vision he saw before him. But she certainly was that and so much more.

As if she sensed she wasn't alone, her eyelids fluttered open and then widened as she scrubbed the sleep away. "I didn't hear you come in," she said, scooting up and moving her feet so Dean could sit down. "How long have you been standing there?"

"Long enough to find out you snore." He smiled.

She scowled. "I do not."

"You do. And it's adorable."

Her displeasure melted into a shy grin. "You have odd criteria for what is considered adorable." She straightened, listening for Honey. "She's been sleeping for hours. Do you think that's normal?"

"Sick babies need lots of rest. Here, hold on, I'll check on her."

Annabelle murmured her thanks and Dean peeked in on the baby. Fast asleep. Dean backed out of the room and returned to Annabelle, who was folding the afghan she'd been sleeping under.

"She's fine," he said and she relaxed a little, but she still seemed a little bothered. "Everything okay? You seem tense."

"I'm not sure if taking a nap was the right thing to do. I feel a little muggy in the brain. Now I'll probably be up all night. Thanks for coming over to check on us. You don't have to do that, you know."

He shook his head. "I wouldn't have been able to go home without knowing Honey was on the mend. Did you make an appointment with the clinic?"

"I did. She has an appointment tomorrow." Before he could offer to take them, Annabelle added quickly, "Dana is going to take us, so we need to get the car seat out of your truck before you leave."

He nodded, but he wished Annabelle would let

him be there for her more. Since her outburst the other day he had a better understanding as to why she wouldn't allow him to help her with the car situation, but it didn't stop him from wanting to be there for her. Restless, he walked the living room and perused the windowsills. "Did you ever talk to your landlord about these windows? I see screens still haven't been installed."

"I did but the property manager told me exactly what I told you he'd say. The landlord isn't interested in spending more money on this place. Oh well. It's not a big deal. It's getting too cold to have open windows anyway."

Dean didn't comment further, knowing what Annabelle's reaction would be. Besides, his mind was made up. He was going to pay a visit to this property manager and find out who this scum-sucking slumlord was and have a nice chat with him about his rental practices. "Do you need anything from the store? Diapers? Milk? Anything?"

She shook her head and his mouth quirked knowingly. "You wouldn't tell me if you did, would you?"

"You're a smart man."

That was debatable. "All right, I'll take off. I'll leave the car seat in the kitchen."

"Thank you. I appreciate everything you've done. See you tomorrow after Honey's appointment."

"I wish you'd change your mind about the pediatrician," he grumbled, to which she simply smiled. "See you tomorrow."

He wanted to kiss her. More than anything. But he didn't know if he should, so he left, feeling he'd forgotten to do something or as if he'd left something unsaid that was important. In all, he left very dissatisfied.

DEAN WALKED into his house and couldn't stop the yawn that nearly cracked his jaw with its intensity. Damn, he was tired. The lost hours of sleep had finally caught up to him but he couldn't crawl into bed just yet. He and Brandon needed to have a talk.

"Brandon?" he called out, going from room to room until he found his son playing pool in the game room. "You got a minute? We need to talk."

"I'm a little busy," Brandon replied, taking a moment to chalk his cue stick but not to spare Dean a glance. "Maybe later."

Dean chuckled but there was no humor in the sound. In fact the smile he wore in response to Brandon's attitude was probably glacial. "Now, Junior. Or you're going to spend the rest of the year being home-schooled."

Turning on his heel, Dean didn't wait to see if Brandon followed. His son wasn't stupid and knew better than to push buttons that were bound to set off an atomic bomb.

Settling into his favorite chair, he watched as Brandon came into the room wearing a sulk. "What?"

"I think you know what this is about. We need to clear the air."

"Why? So you can just make promises you have no intention of keeping?"

Dean shifted. "Annabelle is a friend."

Brandon snorted. "Friend with benefits. Cut the crap, Dad. I know you're sleeping with her."

The urge to lie was strong, but his son was smarter than that and deserved better from him. Dean inhaled a deep breath and tackled the situation head-on. "First, I'd appreciate some respect. Second, you're right. Annabelle and I have become closer than I imagined we would have when I first hired her. But if you were to give her half a chance I think you'd like her."

"So it's like Mom never existed, huh?"

Dean stared at Brandon. "Watch your mouth. The love your mother and I shared isn't at stake here."

Brandon's mouth twisted. "No, just your need to get laid by a woman half your age. I'm sure Mom would be thrilled you've chosen a teenager to replace her."

Dean sprang from the chair and came to stand next to his son, barely keeping a hand on his rising temper. He hardly recognized this foul boy in front of him, but a part of him knew Brandon was lashing out from a place of pain and loss. Mentally counting to ten, he took a step away from Brandon before he spoke again. "Annabelle is younger, but she's more mature than most women her age. Son, you have an opportunity to learn a life lesson here. You shouldn't judge people. She's a good person and she deserves a second chance in life."

"A good person? How well do you know her? Do

you know anything about her past? Dad, you're one of the most eligible bachelors in town because you come with money and a stable job. She's a single mom without a dime to her name who can't even afford to get her car fixed. What does she come to the table with? A kid. And a whole lot of baggage from what I can see. Maybe you ought to try and get to know her better before you start inviting a stranger into our lives."

Dean's first reaction to Brandon's impassioned speech was anger, but some of what his son said made a certain amount of sense. It was true he knew little about Annabelle and whenever he asked anything personal, she changed the subject or became downright prickly. He vowed to dig a little deeper, but, in the meantime, he wanted Brandon to lighten up.

"I know she's a good person trying to make a life for herself and Honey. That's enough for now. Just try giving her a chance," he said, but Brandon's hard stare didn't bode well.

"Sorry, Dad. I'm not on the Annabelle bandwagon. I see her for what she truly is. A gold digger."

Dean saw red, but Brandon had wisely chosen to leave the room before his father's temper exploded.

IT WAS LATE but Annabelle's eyes popped open and her senses were on heightened alert. There was someone in her house.

Fear gripped her and she reached down to pick up

the baseball bat she kept under her bed. Gripping it with sweaty palms, she eased out of bed and tiptoed into the hallway. Darkness blanketed the living room, but she could hear someone in the kitchen, rummaging around in her cupboards and going through her drawers. She caught muffled voices but couldn't make out how many there were. Honey must've sensed something was wrong for she woke up and whimpered for Annabelle.

"There's a kid?" She heard a harsh whisper, and she flattened against the wall as footsteps headed her way.

Knowing it was now or never, Annabelle flipped on the living room light and managed to catch sight of three men dressed in black and wearing ski masks before one of them rushed her, taking her to the floor and tumbling into the lamp at the same time. Annabelle managed to scream as she fell, but her head connected with the corner of the small table the lamp had been sitting on, and everything turned to silence. Her last coherent thought was coated in total terror. Buddy had come for her and he was going to kill her.

DEAN DROVE like a madman straight to the hospital, his only thought to reach Annabelle.

He went through the double doors of the E.R., feeling a strong sense of déjà vu, and immediately he could hear Honey screaming inconsolably. He sprinted toward the sound and found Dana trying to soothe the red-faced toddler. The minute Honey saw

Dean, she twisted out of Dana's arms and straight into his. She hiccuped softly against his shoulder and he offered gentle words to calm her even as he silently asked Dana where Annabelle was.

"She's getting stitches," Dana answered, the worry evident in her expression. "She's got a pretty good gash in her head from hitting the table."

"What happened?" he asked, rubbing Honey on the back as he rocked her. "You said something about a break-in?"

"I don't know what happened. The neighbors called 911 when they heard her scream. Nobody saw anything. The police are waiting to talk to Annabelle when she's done."

"Thanks for calling," he said to Dana and she nodded.

"I'm just glad I was working tonight, otherwise neither one of us would've found out until tomorrow. I've told her over and over again to put me down as her emergency contact, but she never wants to be a bother to anyone."

"You were the paramedic on scene?"

"Yeah. Worst feeling of my life to see a call turn out to be someone I know, much less my best friend. She may have a mild concussion, too."

Dean swore. "Who would've done this? I'm starting to think someone is after her. First the car, now this… Seems too deliberate to be coincidental."

Dana looked as if she agreed, but there was confusion in her expression as well. "I don't know. I hate that she lives in that awful duplex. Although if it weren't for her neighbors…" She shook her head and was relieved of finishing her thought as the nurse appeared with Annabelle in a wheelchair. "Oh, ouch," Dana said, going to Annabelle and referencing the stitching around her wound. "That's going to leave a scar. Good thing your hair will cover most of it."

Dana's attempt to lighten the mood failed and the fear in Annabelle's eyes, despite her attempt to hide it by averting her gaze, struck at Dean's heart. "You're coming home with me tonight," he said firmly. "There's no way you or Honey are going back to that place. Don't even try to argue. Not tonight."

Annabelle gave a weak jerk of her head. "Let's go."

HER MIND wasn't functioning on a higher level. Fear had numbed her brain capacity until all she could think, see or hear were memories of that awful moment. She used to think she'd had more than enough bad moments to last a lifetime, but fate hadn't felt the same. Now she had one more to add to the library. Was she putting Dean at risk by agreeing to go home with him? And who the hell had been in her place? Her first thought had been Buddy, but now she wasn't so sure. But who else could it be? Was it random? It seemed highly coincidental when she thought of the incident with her car. Someone was targeting her. If not Buddy, who? The question weakened her knees and made her dizzy.

"I brought the playpen over from the office. I've

already got it set up in the bedroom with us," Dean said as he strode away from her with Honey asleep on his shoulder.

Annabelle stared after him, not quite sure what to make of his actions. On the one hand it was sweet of him to think ahead for Honey's needs; on the other hand, she didn't know if sleeping in his bed was the right decision.

As if sensing her distress, he turned. "If you prefer, I can take the couch. It's your call. I just didn't think you'd want to be alone after your ordeal. I'm not asking anything of you. I want to be there for you if you need me."

Tears crowded her sinuses and she jerked her head in a nod. "Thank you. I'd like you to stay with me, please."

"You're safe here, sweetheart. I promise."

Annabelle nodded, swallowing around the awful lump in her throat. She wanted to feel safe. If even for just one night.

After Honey was put to bed and Annabelle had changed into one of Dean's long T-shirts, she climbed under the covers and shut her eyes against the image of the three strangers in her house. A violent shudder racked her body just as Dean climbed in beside her and pulled her against him.

He wrapped his arms around her snugly, but she continued to shiver.

"Do you need more blankets? I have a quilt in the closet I could get."

"Please don't leave. Just hold me."

"I'm not going anywhere," he promised.

It was a long time before the quakes stopped, but Dean's hold never lessened. She felt safe and secure in his arms but tears leaked from her eyes.

"I was so scared," she managed to admit in the darkness. "All I could think of was Honey. Would they hurt her? She's just a baby. But there are bad people out there who don't care about babies and what if they were those types of bad people?" More tears leaked out. "And I couldn't do anything to stop them. I felt so helpless."

He shushed her with soft words and pressed a kiss to her crown, but she felt his body tense as if he were trying to control the impulse to do something rash. She swallowed and brushed the side of her face against the pillow beneath her head.

"Thank you for coming," she said again. "You didn't have to."

"I did."

That single statement meant the world to her, hitting a tender spot that she kept hidden from view, safe from prying eyes or sharp objects.

"I'm complicating things between us. I shouldn't do that. It isn't right," she murmured softly. Why couldn't matters of the heart be simpler? She wished she had the right to snuggle up to Dean every night, share their dreams, weather their challenges together like a normal couple. But nothing in Annabelle's life had ever been normal. Why should now be any different? She couldn't possibly drag Dean into her mess. He had Brandon to consider just as she had Honey and if she told him that a convicted felon might be after her, she doubted he'd appreciate that kind of complication in his life.

So, as she turned and wrapped her arms and legs around him, feeling desperately as if she were trying to imprint the feel of his body against hers, she knew she wouldn't involve Dean any longer. It just wasn't right. No matter how her heart felt.

Besides, it was readily apparent that Annabelle sucked in the judgment department.

CHAPTER SIXTEEN

DEAN FROWNED when Brandon dropped his spoon for the second time at the breakfast table as he tried putting sugar in his cereal.

"Sorry," Brandon muttered, avoiding eye contact with Annabelle.

Annabelle shot Dean a pained look, knowing exactly how much Brandon must hate sharing breakfast with her and Honey, but Dean sensed there was something else eating at his son. Each time he looked at Annabelle he winced, and something akin to guilt flashed in his expression. She did look a little rough. The stitches stood out against her pale skin and her eye had blackened from the blow she'd taken on the table, but he was surprised by Brandon's reaction.

"Did you see who did this to you?" Brandon asked, staring down into his cereal bowl as if her answer would suddenly come from the soggy flakes instead of Annabelle's mouth.

"No," Annabelle murmured. She cleared her throat. "It was too dark and then when I hit the light seconds later I was on the floor unconscious."

"Deputy Rodney will find out who did this, you can trust me on that," Dean said, anger returning at the thought of what Annabelle had gone through. "And whoever did this better hope to God I don't find them first."

Annabelle cracked a smile, but quickly grimaced as if the action had caused her pain, and Dean fought the urge to pull her into his arms. "No need for knight-in-shining-armor heroics. I'm sure they're long gone. I doubt they'd hang around. It was probably just bad luck," she said.

"Like your car?"

Annabelle swallowed, but nodded just the same, as if she didn't know for a fact that coincidence was not a factor in this case.

The sudden screech of Brandon's chair interrupted whatever direction Dean's thoughts had been traveling and he glanced at his son shouldering his backpack. "Catch you later," Brandon said, barely looking at Annabelle. He paused and turned only slightly, saying, "I'm sorry you got hurt."

Annabelle looked puzzled but accepted the sentiment. "Thank you, Brandon. I appreciate your concern."

"Right."

And then all semblance of an olive branch was withdrawn as Brandon disappeared out the front door.

Dean continued to stare after his son, not liking the ugly feeling brewing in his gut. His jaw tensed and he had to make a conscious effort to relax or else he'd worry Annabelle. Too late, he noted as she glanced at him anxiously.

"What's wrong?"

"Aside from the fact that someone out there wants to hurt you?"

Her expression froze, and any attempt she might've made at nonchalance failed miserably. *Good.* As much as he didn't want to see her hurt or scared, he didn't want her to evade his questions any longer and if fear was what finally unhinged her jaw, he was going to take it. Reaching across the table, he gently grasped her hand. The soft flesh was cold to the touch. "Do you need a robe or blanket?" he asked, to which she shook her head. "Annabelle, please tell me what's going on. No more lies or evasions. I need to know who might be after you before it's too late."

"I've never lied," she bristled.

"Every time you say it's nothing or that you're fine when you're plainly not and it isn't, you're lying."

"It's no one," she answered, standing abruptly to gather the dishes to take to the sink. "No one I want to talk about, anyway."

"Stop," he said tightly. "We've gone past the point where the runaround will work. You could've been killed. What about Honey? Last night you were thinking clearly. You were right to be afraid. You were lucky Honey wasn't hurt."

The stricken expression on her face was further confirmation that she knew exactly who was after her and it was enough to scare the living shit out of her.

He gentled his voice and came toward her. "Whoever it is, we'll face him together."

"Stop."

"Stop what?" he asked, perplexed.

"Stop pretending that we're some kind of couple. I'm no one to you and neither is Honey."

"That's not true. You're blind if you can't see how I feel about you and Honey. Why won't you let me help you?"

"Why?" she asked incredulously. "I think that's a fairly obvious answer." When Dean only stared, she slapped her thigh in aggravation. "Dean, c'mon, you're not a stupid man. You can figure this out on your own without needing me to spell it out."

"Humor me."

"I'm not in a humoring mood."

"Fine. Then let's cut the crap and worry about the relationship stuff later. Who's after you?"

Her eyes watered and she faltered on her feet. He would've wrapped her in his arms if it weren't for the hard look in her eyes. She dragged in a deep breath as if needing the strength and said, "I can't. It's not right to drag you into what is following me. You're right. The man who might be out there terrorizing me is dangerous. He put my mom in a wheelchair and I put him behind bars. But he was just paroled. So, he's out there and for the past handful of years I imagine what got him through his sentence was the hope that someday he'd get his revenge on the little bitch who put him there."

Stunned, he could only stare until he realized with a start that she was gathering Honey's things. "Where are you going?"

"I need to get back to my place and find out if anything was broken or stolen. Would you mind giving us a ride?"

"Of course not, but this conversation isn't over. I want to know exactly who this monster is, down to a physical description and where he's from."

"Dean…"

"No. There's one thing I can promise you. He's not going to come within ten feet of you without my knowledge because you're moving out of that crappy duplex and in with me."

ANNABELLE STARED, unable to comprehend what Dean had just offered until the words sank in a full minute later and she could only gape like a codfish. "That's not going to happen," she said, recovering with a shake of her head. "Absolutely not. If I won't accept the loan of a car I certainly won't move in with you. Are you kidding me? Why don't you just slap a big scarlet letter on my chest and be done with it? The town can start throwing rotten tomatoes at me as I pass in the street and whisper bad things about me when I go to the grocery store."

"A little melodramatic, don't you think? Why would anyone do that?"

"Because that's what happens to women like me when they're in these kinds of situations."

"Only in classic literary novels. Not in real life. Let's get serious. What are you afraid of? People talking? Who cares what a few busybodies might say? I don't, and no one who cares about you would even listen to anyone trying to run you down. And before you say anything else, there are a lot of people in this town who like you enough to defend you if the need arose."

"You don't know what it's like to be judged for something that's out of your control."

Confused, he said, "You think people will judge you for being attacked? Like it was your fault or something?"

"No. I was talking about when I was a kid. Those of us who lived on Bleeter Street were looked down on by the rest of the town. Called us trailer trash under their breath. It didn't matter that kids don't have a choice where they live. No one ever asked me if I wanted to live there. No one ever stopped to think that maybe I was a good kid living in a bad situation. They just judged me because of where I came from. And I swore I'd never let anyone judge me again."

"No one will judge you here."

"You don't know that, and I'm not about to take the chance. I have Honey to think of and I'm not ever going to put her in a position where she might feel the need to defend her mom because people don't have the decency to mind their mouths."

"Annabelle, you're not the only person who's ever felt vulnerable because of a situation," he said. "It's how you handle that situation that matters. I can't understand how you could possibly think for one second that anyone would think less of you for allowing me to help you out. For crying out loud, I'd make the offer to any friend who needed the help."

Her gaze narrowed. "Do you make it a habit to sleep with your friends?"

He sputtered. "Of course not."

"Then it's not the same at all because you and I both know that if I moved in here, even on the pretense of friendship, I'd end up in your bed in a short amount of time. And then what? We're not a couple. It's not like either one of us is comfortable with taking it to the next level. So what does that make us?" She paused, then continued with a firm shake of her head. "I can't stay with you. End of discussion."

"It's not safe," he ground out. "You're taking an unnecessary risk."

"No, I'm not. I'm going to start looking for a new place." He started to relax until she added, "Somewhere else. Out of Emmett's Mill."

BRANDON FELT ready to puke. Jessie nudged him and he glanced her way.

"What's wrong?"

"Nothing."

"Liar."

He looked away. "I don't want to talk about it."

"I heard that someone broke into Annabelle's place

last night," she remarked, a frown on her face. "That's so unusual for Emmett's Mill. I wonder who it was?"

"How'd you hear about that?" Brandon asked sharply, his fear gelling into a solid mass inside his stomach.

"My dad told me this morning."

Brandon almost smacked his forehead for his stupidity. Jessie's dad was a volunteer firefighter. He must've been on call last night. Sweat beaded his brow as he looked to his girl and wished he'd taken her advice and just let the whole situation drop. Now he'd royally screwed himself for a prank that went horribly wrong. No one was supposed to get hurt. Annabelle's sutured gash stood out in his memory as a garish reminder of how he'd messed up. Add to that Honey's frightened screams and his stomach nearly rebelled against the cereal he'd wolfed down at breakfast.

"You love me, right?" he asked suddenly, needing to hear some kind of positive affirmation. She looked at him oddly but nodded. He pressed even though he knew it made him look suspect. "Even if I did something stupid and possibly illegal?"

"What are you talking about?"

He swallowed and shook his head. "Nothing."

"Brandon Dean Halvorsen, don't treat me like an idiot. The last few weeks you've been a jerk over this thing with your dad, but I swear to God, if you've done something stupid that you can't take back I will kick your butt from here until tomorrow and then I'll leave your ass."

He cracked a smile, but it was weak at best. Still, he tried for some semblance of charm. "Calm down. Just checking in case I decided to forgo college and pursue a life of crime. I'm just kidding. Okay?"

She stared at him, not quite believing until bit by bit she let down her guard and shook her head. "You have a weird sense of humor. In the future…don't do that. It's a risky game."

Brandon agreed. He knew all about risky games and he really didn't want to play any more.

DEAN WALKED into the property management firm handling Annabelle's apartment, went straight to the woman behind the desk playing computer Solitaire, and wasted little time on pleasantries.

"I want to know who owns the duplexes on Morning Glory Road."

She blinked owlishly at him. "Why? Is there a problem? I'm authorized to handle certain things such as routine repair."

"I just need a name." He glanced down at her name badge and added, "Ms. Grafton."

She fumbled with her paperwork and stiffened a little. "If you'll just tell me—"

"We could do this all day but the outcome will be the same. I need a name and I'm not leaving until I get one. One of your client's tenants suffered a break-in last night and she was nearly killed because of the shoddy locks your client keeps on the doors. Not to mention there are no screens on the windows and no discernible heating that works. I believe that's against the law. If you'd like to take responsibility for your client's shortcomings as a landlord, then by all means, let's continue this pointless dance."

She swallowed. "Aaron Eagle."

His mouth formed a grim line. He should've known. Dean smiled, though he knew there was nothing warm and fuzzy about the action. "Thank you, Ms. Grafton. You've been very helpful. Have a good day."

Dean strode to his truck, his mind teeming with all the things he wanted to say to Aaron. His hands curled with the promise of violence, but he kept his temper cool for Annabelle's sake.

Driving straight to Aaron's latest construction site, he wasted little time with anyone else and within minutes he was in Aaron's face.

"What—"

"Shut up and listen, you slumlord piece of philandering shit," Dean interrupted, not interested in playing nice at this point. "Annabelle Nichols lives in one of your crappy duplexes on Morning Glory Road, and last night she was attacked because of the shoddy locks on the doors, not to mention the fact that you've consistently refused to replace the window screens throughout the place. I suspect if a county health inspector were to take a look at those duplexes he'd come away with a laundry list of health-code violations so I suggest you spend less time trying to weasel your ass into my jobs and more time on your properties before you lose all credibility in this town when people find out what kind of homes you're renting out."

To Dean's surprise Aaron just smiled. "Let's get serious, Dean. I have a good relationship with the health-code secretary, and I doubt your messages would even make it to Paul's desk so stop embarrassing yourself in front of my crew and get off my property. As for taking the jobs out from under you, why would I give up one of my favorite pastimes? I'm hoping one of these days your head explodes."

"Don't push me, Eagle."

"Yeah? Why not?" Aaron mocked, then his expression hardened.

Dean stepped closer. "Because I might do something I regret."

Aaron laughed. "Impress me."

"I didn't come here to waste my time playing games with you. Just take care of your rental property on Morning Glory Road and we won't have to spend another minute in each other's company. Sound good?"

"You know what sounds better? Kiss my ass and get off my property."

"Let's end this right now," Dean growled, his hands fisting.

"You'd like that, wouldn't you?"

"If this is personal, don't take it out on Annabelle."

If a moment of guilt passed across Aaron's face Dean couldn't tell, but then again he didn't expect much from a man who would pretend to be a friend and then move in on another man's territory.

"Look at you acting like the hero. How sweet—and complete bullshit. We both know if it weren't for you Beth would still be alive. Yeah, you heard me right. She's dead because you're a selfish jerk who only thinks of himself. I find it amusing that you've found your soft side with a woman half your age. What? Beth wasn't good enough for you?"

Dean felt the air leave his lungs. Bitter memories rose to gag him. *Had* he been responsible? Maybe if he hadn't insisted that Beth come home that night instead of the following morning… Maybe if he had truly forgiven her he wouldn't have been so unyielding.

"Truth hurts, doesn't it?" Aaron asked.

Pouring all of his hatred for Aaron into his stare, he nearly choked on all the bile he wanted to spew in Aaron's direction. If Dean was to blame for Beth's death, Aaron surely had had a hand, too.

Aaron waved him off, his features tight. "Get the hell out of here. I'm done talking with you."

He agreed. Talk was overrated. Dean reared back his fist and clocked Aaron straight in his smug, lying face. "That makes two of us, asshole," he gritted, coming to stand over Aaron with a menacing growl. "You're not fit to say her name much less pretend to champion her. She was *my* wife…not yours. Try to remember that fact."

As Dean walked away, he heard Aaron say as he spat the blood from his mouth, "What makes you think I've ever forgotten?"

ANNABELLE OPENED the front door cautiously, still on edge from the ordeal, but when she saw Dana she relaxed and stepped aside even though she knew what was coming.

Dana gingerly touched the area around Annabelle's stitching and compressed her lips tightly.

"It's not that bad. Hardly hurts anymore," Annabelle said, moving briskly into the living room to finish picking up the pieces of the shattered lamp.

"Tell me the truth…do you think Buddy did this?"

Annabelle averted her gaze. "I don't know. It doesn't seem like his style. He preferred to work alone but…who else could it be?"

Dana shook her head, confused as well. "So, did you tell Dean about Buddy?"

"Sort of."

"That's not an answer. What does that mean?"

Annabelle took the fragments to the trash, uncomfortable in her own skin as Dana's gaze gave no quarter and expected nothing less than fact. "I gave him the basic truth. I put a guy into prison for hurting my mom and now he might want to hurt me. That's about it in a nutshell anyway. Why elaborate when it's not necessary?"

Dana exploded. "Geez, AnnaB, get your head out of your ass for just a minute! There could be a seriously pissed-off dude after you and you decide to go all 'less is more' when Dean asked? Why don't you just save us all the trouble and give Buddy a call, tell him when and where you'll be and then strap on some stilettos and try to run through the forest for all your stupidity."

Annabelle exhaled loudly. "Oh, c'mon, don't get righteous on me. Have you been completely honest with Sammy about the parts of your past that you aren't proud of?"

"Totally different," Dana said stubbornly. "My secrets aren't going to show up and stab me while I sleep."

Two could play the stubborn game, Annabelle thought. "I can't drag him into my mess. It's not fair to him or Brandon. Besides, the kid hates me enough, why make it worse?"

"Could it get worse?"

Annabelle slanted a look Dana's way. "You and I know it can always get worse."

"Yeah, that's true so let me tell you how it gets worse in this scenario. You let a good man slip through your fingers because his whiny kid doesn't like you and you're going to let a violent felon chase you out of town instead of accepting the help that is offered and just might save your butt."

"How'd you know I was leaving?"

This time Dana was the one throwing the look. "Because I know you."

Annabelle sank into the sofa in a miserable heap and fought the tears that came from nowhere. "I can't take this anymore. I'm exhausted from being afraid, and Brandon's animosity is wearing on my nerves.

Normally, I'd just laugh it off, but I kinda feel bad for the kid."

"Why?"

"Because he lost his mom and he's afraid of losing his dad. I get that. I really do. I would've done anything to keep my mom from falling in love with Buddy when she did. I know how it feels to be helpless to stop something. If he's not interested in welcoming me into his family I'm not going to force myself. I can't do that to Dean, Brandon or Honey."

"C'mon, let's be honest. It's not really about the kids. You're scared."

Annabelle hated that with Dana she was practically transparent. She nodded. "I *am* scared. What if…" She stopped herself, not quite able to voice the fear bubbling inside.

Dana sat beside her, digesting Annabelle's statement for a long minute before saying quietly, "What about you, AnnaB? I know you're in love with him. Don't deny it. I can see it in your eyes and read it in your body language."

Annabelle's misery intensified. "I do love him. Damn it, Dana. I do. But I don't want to. I want to walk away from this town and every memory I've made so far. I'm a bad person, aren't I?"

Dana's expression melted with understanding. "You're a woman with her fair share of scars. I empathize with your need to run, but if you can fight that impulse and let this man love you, I think he has what it takes to heal those broken parts hiding inside you."

Annabelle uttered a watery sigh. "How do you know?"

"Because I went through the same feeling with Sammy. The hardest thing I ever did was to have the courage to stand and fight when all I wanted to do was run and hide. We're not kids anymore, Annabelle. There are no sofas or chairs to hide under or secret forts where we can huddle and lick our wounds."

"God, I'd give anything for a good fort right about now."

Dana smiled. "You have something better than a fort. You have Dean. That man is practically a fortress of reliability. Give him a chance."

"What about Beth?"

"Beth is dead." Dana shrugged. "Sorry, but it's true. She had her time with Dean and from what I know of her, she would've wanted him to be happy."

Annabelle sobered. "Yeah, I get that, too, but I don't want to compete forever with a ghost. I don't think I could ever measure up."

"Stop selling yourself short. Dean doesn't see Beth when he looks at you. I can promise you that."

Annabelle considered Dana's advice and a part of her wavered. Should she stay and fight as Dana suggested or should she cut her losses and start fresh elsewhere?

If she stayed she'd have to tell Dean exactly who Buddy King was and somehow try to make amends with Brandon. She didn't want the kid to feel the way she had when Buddy had moved in. Annabelle would never do that to a kid, no matter how much she loved the father.

She drew a deep breath and her gaze drifted to Honey's bedroom. Her daughter loved Dean with all her little heart. Annabelle sensed it with a certainty that was hard to explain. Dean was the father Honey had been waiting for.

Somehow that knowledge didn't make her decision easier but infinitely more difficult.

Annabelle turned to regard Dana and said reluctantly, "I'll give it until D-Day to decide, okay?"

"Wise choice," Dana said sagely, then ruined the whole effect by cracking a wide smile. "You wouldn't want to get on the bad side of your future mother-in-law by dropping out of your refreshment responsibilities at the last minute. Mary would *kill* you."

"You are incorrigible," Annabelle shrieked, bouncing a throw pillow off Dana's head. "And maybe a little deaf. I'm not marrying Dean anytime soon. Geesh, we can't even agree whether or not we're dating, much less going to the next level."

Dana giggled and tossed the pillow back. "We'll see…"

"Crazy woman," Annabelle muttered. "It must be nice to live in your own personal fairy tale."

Dana offered a dreamy sigh. "It most certainly is."

CHAPTER SEVENTEEN

ANNABELLE was dumbfounded when a window company arrived to put in double-paned security glass and screens throughout the duplex just before 8:00 a.m. Within the hour, a new door was delivered and installed and this one, she noted, was far more secure than the flimsy excuse that used to hang on the door frame.

Dean's truck rolled up shortly after. She handed him a cup of coffee as he walked past the laborers doing the installations and gave him a suspicious look.

"What did you do?" she asked, going straight to the point. "I know you had something to do with this so don't even try to feign ignorance."

He pulled her to him and pressed a tender kiss on her mouth. "Wouldn't dream of it. You're right. I did have something to do with it. A simple thank you is fine with me."

No fair stealing a woman's ability to breathe, she thought as a smile threatened to ruin the stern expression she was projecting. "I'll thank you when I don't get an eviction notice for your meddling," she retorted.

Even though she was quite comfortable up against him, she pulled away. "I ask again. What did you do?"

He shrugged. "I reasoned with the property owner. He and I came to an understanding. It was all quite civil. For the most part."

"Yeah, that's the part that worries me," Annabelle said.

"Well, don't. I'm a problem solver. We had a problem. You refuse to move and I refuse to let you live without safety precautions. Problem solved. I wish you'd take me up on my offer to move in, but I understand your reasons and I won't push."

Annabelle bit her lip and tried not to jump into his arms to rain kisses all over his face. She realized she was beaming and quickly dropped the smile. Dean chuckled.

"Can't let anyone know you like me, huh?"

"Something like that," she said. There was a polite knock at the front door and she was grateful for the interruption. The laborers were finished. One of the men handed her a set of keys, and then the small crew left.

Dean did a quick check of the work and once he proclaimed it sufficient, he surprised her by sweeping her off her feet.

"What are you doing?" she gasped, winding her arms around his neck.

"I'm going to make love to you," he answered, and her cheeks flared with excited heat even as she protested about Honey. A quick glance down the short hallway revealed Honey fast asleep. She licked her suddenly parched lips and felt wondrously dizzy. He pinned her with a look that made her feel like the sexiest woman alive.

She pretended to check her watch though her heart was beating painfully in her chest with anticipation. "I suppose we have time for a quickie…"

"Oh no," he said, shaking his head right before he tossed her gently to the bed. "There will be no quickies today. I'm going to take my time and slowly savor that luscious body of yours until you're wet, hot and ready for all the things I'm going to do to you."

Barely able to find her voice, her toes curling from the memory of what he could do with that teasing tongue of his, she said, "Which are?"

His mouth twisted in a sensual way. "A little dirty but a whole lot of fun. By the time I'm finished with you, you won't remember your own name."

She started to offer a witty comeback, but he'd already divested her of her capris and her panties. All she could manage was a quick inhale and then…*ohhhhh!*

Lord help her. She did so love a man serious about his work.

BRANDON LEANED against his truck and gritted his teeth as the raging headache made mush of his brains. He hadn't slept in days and it was starting to show.

"Dude, you need to relax. No one knows it was us. We're in the clear."

Brandon scrubbed his hand through his hair before slanting his friend Derek a dark look. "No one was supposed to get hurt. It turned into more than a prank. There was a sheriff's report taken."

Derek shrugged. "She spooked me. I reacted. Big deal," he said with a fair amount of annoyance in his voice. "What's your problem? You're the one who was all gung ho to scare her off. You're getting your wish. I doubt she'd stick around after—"

"Just shut up, okay?" The pulse behind Brandon's eyeball exploded in a riot of pain. Grinding the heel of his palm into his eye, he tried rubbing it out but the ache remained. "This whole thing has turned into a nightmare."

"Was her kid all right?" asked Nolan, his other friend and reluctant participant that night. "She sounded pretty freaked out."

"Yeah…she's okay. I guess she's been real sick and that's why she woke up. God, I wish I could take it back. I didn't think it would scare the baby like that."

"Quit whining about the kid. You said yourself she's fine, right?" Derek snorted and made an uncomplimentary remark about Brandon's balls when Brandon failed to say anything. "Listen, just because you're turning into a pussy over this, don't drag us down with you. If you keep your mouth shut, everything will blow over. If you start blabbing all over the place you're going to screw us all."

"I'm not going to say anything," Brandon growled, hating Derek at that moment. "Relax."

"Good. See that you don't. You're not the only one eyeing a scholarship for college. We get convicted of a felony over your stupid idea, the only place we're going is jail with a future of 'Would you like fries with that?' and I, for one, have bigger plans. You hear me?"

Brandon looked to Nolan. Whether he was searching for backup or confirmation that Nolan felt the same, Brandon wasn't sure. He said, "I hear you. You're right. It'll blow over and everything will be fine."

D-DAY BROKE sunny and warm despite the fall weather. Annabelle glanced up at the blue expanse of sky overhead and wondered if Mary Halvorsen had had a personal conversation with the Man upstairs to ensure that rain did not fall on the biggest day in Emmett's Mill's history.

Annabelle took great care in her wardrobe choice, selecting her favorite soft pink georgette-sleeved top and a matching skirt that she knew made the most of her legs and hips. A secret smile curved her lips as she imagined Dean's reaction. The man wouldn't know whether to stare or look away and would likely be torn by the impulse to do both. She giggled and, picking Honey from her crib, prepared for a long day.

Showered and properly prettied, she and Honey arrived at the designated place, and she was astounded by the bustle of activity. Annabelle drank in the sight of so many people working toward a single cause and her heart filled with a flood of emotion. There were booths set up with vendors of homemade crafts, including baked goods that Annabelle doubted came from a box, and fund-raising booths aimed to bolster the restoration effort.

Dana and Sammy found her just as she and Honey wandered over to a booth selling knitted baby blankets.

"Aren't they adorable?" Dana asked, eyeing the powder-blue blanket in Annabelle's hands with yearning, then turned to Sammy, saying, "We should buy one right now before they sell out."

Sammy chuckled. "Those hormones are working overtime, aren't they? Don't worry, by the time we put a bun in the oven, I'm sure we can get a custom-made blanket or two."

"All right," Dana said. "But if you're wrong I'm going to personally take it out of your hide, Halvorsen."

Of course, there was no real threat behind the words and Annabelle fought the urge to sigh at the love that flowed so easily between her best friend and Sammy. Her gaze strayed to the work site, surreptitiously looking for Dean. When she found him, her breathing quickened and she almost laughed at her reaction, silly as it was, for she was surely asking for heartache by the time this wild ride was over. And really, that was no laughing matter.

Mary bustled over to them, and before Annabelle knew it, Honey had been passed to one of the many teenage girls on babysitting detail and Annabelle was directed to the booth designated for refreshments.

"There's lemonade and iced tea and bottled water

for sale, but remember anyone on Dean's crew—
they'll be wearing the red armbands—gets free refreshments on account of they'll be working the
hardest. Any questions, dear?"

"No, I think I got it," Annabelle answered, amused
by Mary Halvorsen in drill-sergeant mode. "Will I
get helpers throughout the day?"

"Oh yes, we have students from the S Club who
will be helping out. I've assigned Jill, Michelle and
Brooke to your booth. Oh, and before I forget, here's
your walkie-talkie. Just press that side button when
you want to talk. Any problems, give me a buzz. I'll
make sure someone comes running. Got it?"

"Got it."

Mary smiled with appreciation. "Good. Now, I'm
off to check the status of the lunchbox raffle."

Annabelle swallowed the giggle that was too close
to the surface for safety and considered how different life in Emmett's Mill was compared to where she
grew up. Like night and day, really.

A lunchbox raffle? Annabelle had never even
heard of one until she'd joined the D-Day committee.

It was a simple concept. The ladies each created
a lunch and the men bid on them to raise money and
for the opportunity to enjoy a meal with the lady
who'd made the lunch. Annabelle had planned to
attempt a lunchbox in the hopes that Dean might bid
on hers but circumstances had thwarted her, so she
was going to have to watch as others tried to tempt
Dean with their culinary prowess.

Annabelle wasn't the jealous sort…until today. She hated the idea of Dean bidding on someone else's lunchbox.

Three giggly girls appeared and Annabelle straightened with a smile. "You must be my helpers."

"Yep. I'm Jill," said the blonde with the bouncy ponytail. She pointed to her two friends, nearly identical with their ash-blond hair and jaunty ponytails. "This is Brooke and this is Michelle. What do you want us to do first?"

Annabelle gave the girls instructions to take small cups of drinks to the men and women working within the mill, who were shoring up the structure after it had endured its trip from its original location to the museum. Annabelle felt another smile creeping toward her lips. She rubbed her mouth as if that might be enough to wipe away the impulse and busied herself with filling cups. Goodness, if this is what happened to a woman after a few bouts of good sex, she might be reduced to little more than a smiling idiot if she and Dean couldn't keep their hands to themselves.

The mill was in good shape in spite of its age and decades of disuse, but Annabelle was still impressed with how Dean's crew had the mill wheel repaired enough to actually turn, though there wasn't any water beneath it yet.

Taking a break, she left the booth in the girls' able hands and personally took Dean a drink.

"Looking good," she murmured as he guzzled the offered water.

"Thanks," he said, wiping the sweat from his brow. "It was crafted well. Sturdy. Looks like my ancestor knew what he was doing when he built this thing." He finished the water and handed Annabelle the empty bottle. "How's life in the refreshment booth?"

"Good. Busy." The musky, sharp scent of red-blooded American male tickled her senses and she had to remind herself that they were not alone. She drew a deep breath and tried to stick to neutral territory. "Are you going to bid at the lunchbox raffle?" she asked innocently.

"If I didn't my mom might tan my hide. She expects me to place a hefty price on her fried chicken basket."

"What about your dad? Doesn't he bid on her basket?"

"Nope. He said he's been buying Mom's chicken baskets for going on twenty-five years at various functions. He figures he can share the wealth."

"I take it lunchbox raffles are pretty popular for event fund-raisers?"

"They're a staple."

Annabelle grinned, warmed by the idea that Dean wouldn't be buying another woman's lunchbox. *Really, AnnaB, could you be more obvious?* "So, I suppose you're going to share lunch with your mom…"

Dean edged closer but didn't take her into his arms as she'd irrationally hoped. Instead, he simply said, "Wrong again. I'm eating with you and Honey. My mom packed enough for three."

Annabelle gasped. "She knew you were going to share with us?"

"Nothing gets past my mom. She's the matriarch of the Emmett's Mill grapevine of gossip."

Annabelle didn't like the sound of that. She worried her lip until Dean knuckled her jaw with a gentle motion. "She likes you. That's a compliment. My mom is hard to impress."

"But if she knows, then likely everyone else knows...."

Dean laughed, the sound low, deep and throaty and thoroughly arousing, and Annabelle forgot why she was freaked out. Until she saw Brandon walk by carrying a load of wood on his shoulders.

Sighing, she pulled away, but not before agreeing to meet Dean for lunch—that is, if he wasn't outbid on Mary's basket.

THE DAY ENDED with a resounding *Hurrah!* from the crowd and Annabelle could practically feel the community spirit coming off everyone in waves. Wrapping that precious feeling around herself and enjoying every minute, she finished cleaning up and tearing down the refreshment booth and then went to collect Honey. She found Dean already there with Honey riding his shoulders.

"Look at you, Honey-pie," she crooned to her giggling daughter. "What are you doing up there? You're taller than Mommy."

"Dada!"

Annabelle started and her cheeks flushed with embarrassment. She looked to Dean and rushed to apologize but Dean waved her away with a gruff chuckle. "She's just a baby. She doesn't understand. It's okay."

"I don't even know where she'd learn that word...."

"Babies are like sponges. She probably heard Brandon call me Dad." He gave her a reassuring grin. "It's fine."

But Annabelle didn't want to let it go. It was bad enough that her heart was entangled; she didn't want Honey to suffer as well. "No, sweetheart," she gently corrected. "Dean is our friend. Not Daddy."

Honey smiled the guileless, toothless grin of a baby, but somehow the expression in her blue eyes told a different story. Annabelle looked away, disturbed by how badly she yearned for a future that didn't belong to her. But the part of her that was desperate to cling to the possibility of a life with Dean sent a wild thought ricocheting through her brain. What if she confronted Buddy and somehow convinced him to leave her and Honey alone? Dana would say it was suicide. Annabelle—if she were thinking clearly—would agree. But right now, she just wanted the fear to go away so she could be free to dream of a bright future.

And that desire was stronger than her fear. In that moment, she resolved to pay an old acquaintance a visit.

"WILL YOU GO with me?" Annabelle asked Dana anxiously, knowing the request was a hard one. "I know

Bleeter Street is the last place on the planet you ever want to return to but I don't want to go alone."

Dana paused for a long moment, clearly debating her answer, then she said, "I think you should ask Dean."

Annabelle straightened, confused by Dana's answer. "What do you mean? Are you crazy? I don't want him to see that part of my life."

Dana nodded. "I know. But I think he's the one who should be with you when you face Buddy. Hear me out. Aside from the fact that I think you need him with you for emotional support, it would be smart to have a man with you simply for the Y-chromosome factor. If Buddy tries to blow up on you, chances are he'll think twice if you have a big, burly, scowly type man by your side."

Annabelle wanted to be angry with Dana for refusing, but there was a certain amount of logic in what she'd said. But logic wasn't the only issue.

"The first time he saw my duplex, I practically watched his lip curl. If he sees where I grew up and in what conditions, what will he think of me then?"

Dana shook her head. "Do you really think he cares about that stuff? Yeah, he probably didn't like the duplex, but neither did I, and it had nothing to do with judging you. It has everything to do with wanting you to have better. You *deserve* better. Please get that through your head before you ruin something great because of your insecurities."

Annabelle winced. "Harsh."

"But true."

She had to give her friend that. Still, she had other fears. "What if he says no?"

Dana's smile was reassuring. "He won't."

Annabelle inhaled a short breath. "We'll see."

CHAPTER EIGHTEEN

HER PALMS were sweating. The last time that had happened she was in high school. Wiping her hands quickly, she smiled as Dean entered The Grill and walked toward her.

"I have to admit I was surprised when you suggested lunch. I thought you didn't want people to see us together," Dean said as he took his seat.

"No, I said I didn't want to go to dinner. Lunch is perfectly acceptable because we work together and this could be a working lunch. Maybe we're talking shop. You know, cement, steel trusses, hammers?"

"Hammers?"

Annabelle blinked. "You guys use hammers. I've seen them."

He chuckled. "Yes, we use hammers, but there's really not much to discuss about them. So, not that this conversation isn't fascinating, but what's the real reason you called this little meeting?"

He wasn't one to beat around the bush. She could appreciate that if only she wasn't shaking in her boots over what she was going to ask him.

"I need to ask a favor, but part of the favor is that if you accept I don't want you to ask questions."

"Come again?"

"I need you to go with me to my hometown of Hinkley to…ah, see someone."

"Thad?"

"No."

"Who then?"

She wagged a finger at him. "Ahh-ahh, that's a question and you haven't even agreed to go. You're breaking the rules."

"Call me the rogue. Annabelle, seriously, what's going on?"

"Can't you just say yes without needing details?"

He gave her a look that said *not on your life,* and she sighed. It had been worth a shot. Her palms slicked again and she had to rub them down her thighs. "I can't believe how freaked out I am asking you to do this."

"Just ask. I'm sure you're making a bigger deal of it than you need to."

"I need to go to Hinkley."

"You already said that." He frowned in confusion. "What's the big deal? I can take you. I'll just put Paulo in charge of the job site and we'll make a day of it."

"It's not a fun day trip," she snapped, her nerves getting the best of her. He peered at her intently and she knew she was spinning her wheels in mud. She wet her lips and decided to be honest and hope it got her somewhere. "I need to go and see a man named Buddy King."

"And he is?"

"The man who…put my mom in a wheelchair."

Dean sucked in a breath. "Why would you want to see him?"

"I need to know if he's the one who's been giving me trouble. So far the incidents have been somewhat small, but if it's Buddy and he's the same way he used to be, I know it'll get worse. He's the only one who would want to make me miserable, but I want him to know that I'm not going to play his game by cowering in fear."

"You think he's been doing this stuff as payback?"

"Yeah. What else could it be?"

He thought for a second and then made a deal of his own. "I will take you, but I'd like to know what we're walking into. Is he violent? What kind of man is he? And, I want to know what happened to put your mom in that wheelchair."

She stiffened. "What difference does that make?"

"I need to know."

Annabelle hated going back to that night. She'd worked diligently to block out the screams and the smell of blood that seemed permanently etched in her memory. "I don't like to talk about it," she said, her voice tight. His strong and steady expression gave her an unexpected burst of courage and the words started to pour out in spite of her desire to keep what happened to herself. "It was raining and my mom had to work the late shift at the plant. Buddy had gotten home hours earlier. By the time Mom came home, he was pretty drunk. They got into an argument over potato chips. Buddy yelled that she was supposed to pick some up at the store when she got off, but my mom said she was too tired and just came straight home. He hit her. I tried to stop him. He put my head through a wall. I blacked out. When I came to my mom was making these awful gurgling noises and Buddy was standing over her screaming to her to get up. There was blood everywhere. He broke my mom's neck that night. The doctors might've been able to help her if Buddy hadn't dragged her out into the yard, causing irreparable damage. Buddy was arrested, and I testified against him in court. End of story."

Dean looked stricken by her story. "God, how awful."

"Yeah, not quite a bedtime fairy tale."

He reached across the table and slid his palm over the side of her jaw in a tender gesture. She inhaled sharply and her gaze flew to his. "You're an amazing woman," he said.

She crooked an unsure smile. "Why do you say that? I didn't save my mom that night. I was unconscious during the main event. Maybe if my head was made of harder stuff I might've been able to help her. All I did was call 911."

"Don't do that."

"What?"

"Sell yourself short."

She looked away, unable to hold his gaze. Tears stung her eyes. "She died from pneumonia complications. She drowned from the fluid in her lungs. I couldn't do anything to stop that, either."

"No, but you were there for her when she needed you. You helped put Buddy away so that he couldn't hurt her anymore. That took guts. I admire that strength. Whether you believe it or not, you *are* made of sterner stuff. And I would consider it an honor to stand by your side when you confront this man." He leaned forward, adding with a subtle menace, "And if he so much as raises a finger toward you in a way that's not friendly I'll teach him some manners."

She pressed her hand against her lips to prevent the sob from escaping. "Thank you," she whispered.

He shook his head. "No, Annabelle…thank you for trusting me with your painful past. It means a lot to me."

As they both absorbed the enormity of the moment, Annabelle realized Dana was something of a genius. But then, Annabelle had always known that. Anyone who could rise from the ashes of their past the way Dana had was a force to reckon with. Heart considerably lighter, Annabelle wiped the tears at the corners of her eyes and asked, "Where's our waitress? Soul-baring makes me hungry. Bring on the food."

ANNABELLE and Dean stood before the single-wide trailer parked in space twelve. She felt Dean's hand slip into hers and drew strength from the small gesture. Offering a brief smile in gratitude, she took a bold step forward and gave the aluminum door a hard knock. No one answered. She looked to Dean.

"Try again," he said softly, gesturing to the old beat-up Ford sedan parked in the carport. "Someone's home."

Annabelle knocked harder. Movement sounded inside the tin can of a residence and for a second a flash of debilitating fear almost sent her running. But when she looked to Dean she knew she had to have an answer.

The door opened and for the first time in years Annabelle saw the face of the man she had hoped never to see again.

Prison had not been kind to Buddy King. He squinted against the late-afternoon sun, and then asked in a feeble voice that she hardly recognized as that of the man who snarled and roared in her nightmares, "Who are you? What do you want? I paid my rent. Is there a problem?"

Annabelle was speechless. "Buddy?" she asked, finding her voice again, though it came out scratchy and rough as if her throat was rebelling against the very feel of his name on her vocal cords.

"Yeah? Who's asking?"

"Annabelle," she whispered.

"Annabelle?" he repeated in a gasp, his eyes glazing with a regretful memory that Annabelle knew they shared.

"Yeah. That Annabelle. Sadie's daughter."

Buddy's eyes cleared but his mouth tightened. "What do you want?"

"I want…" *my childhood back.* She swallowed, reminding herself that she wasn't here to ask for the impossible. She just wanted him to leave her alone. But as she stared at the man, his lip trembling as if he suffered from some kind of palsy and his eyes reflecting the soul of a man who'd long since forgotten how to feel joy, she knew with certainty that Buddy King was not the person trying to make her life miserable. She looked to Dean and knew he shared the same belief. Backing away, she shook her head, saying, "I'm sorry, I made a mistake in coming here."

Annabelle couldn't leave fast enough, but Buddy stopped her.

"I loved her, you know." His voice cracked. "I really did."

Annabelle squeezed her eyes shut, and slowly turned. "You don't know how to love."

He shook his head and his tremble increased. "I did. I'm sorry things ended so bad."

"*Bad* isn't the word for it."

He hung his head and jerked his head in a nod. "I know."

"Goodbye, Buddy." *I'm done with you. You're not in my dreams. You're not in my life.* "May you find forgiveness elsewhere because you won't find it from me."

THE RIDE HOME was silent, but Dean doubted the reason for Annabelle's silence was the same as his own. He had a bad feeling he couldn't shake. If Buddy wasn't responsible for the break-in or the sugar in Annabelle's car, who would go to such lengths to hurt her? Or to drive her away?

The answer that came to mind made him nauseous, and he refused to give it any weight. He was jumping to conclusions. Shifting, he moved to flick on the radio, if only to fill the cab with anything other than the noise in his head, but she stilled his hand.

"Please…no. I need to think."

He nodded, deciding to hit the question head-on. "Is there anyone else, maybe one of King's friends, who might have it in for you?"

"No. Buddy wasn't overly social. He pretty much kept to himself."

Dean fell silent, his mind working. "I'll see if the deputy has found any leads," he said, feeling the need to say something.

She smiled but remained quiet. Dean followed her lead, preferring the silence over the fear that was quickly building to a crescendo in his head.

ANNABELLE was perplexed. Had everything that happened to her been purely coincidence? Somehow, she couldn't buy that. Maybe her past experiences colored her thinking, but she just couldn't believe that everything had been the luck of the draw.

But who hated her so much that they'd—

Her thought was cut short as she saw a police cruiser parked in front of her duplex. She looked to Dean. His mouth was cut in a grim line. Her unease increased as they climbed from the truck. She wasn't psychic, but she was willing to bet she wasn't going to like whatever that deputy had come to tell her.

"Dean, Annabelle, perfect timing. I was just about to leave a message to call. I have information on your case."

"What have you found out?"

The deputy looked at Dean and seemed regretful as he answered. "Seems a few kids thought it would be funny to scare you."

Annabelle paled. "What kids?"

Dean swore. "It was Brandon, wasn't it?"

The deputy nodded and Annabelle gasped. "Are you sure?"

"Pretty sure. Some kids overheard the boys talking about it."

"Who else was involved?" Dean asked, jaw tensed.

"Derek Odgers and Nolan Thompson. Listen, I have to be honest, I don't think these boys meant to hurt anyone, but you're within your rights to press charges for breaking and entering and vandalism, seeing as they broke your lamp and gave you quite a scare. What do you want to do?"

Annabelle stared. What did she want to do? *I want to cry.*

The future she'd caught a glimpse of was simply a product of her overactive imagination. What a fool she'd been. If Brandon hated her enough to be so vicious and cruel, there was no way she was going to win him over. And frankly, she didn't want to try. She'd never ask Dean to choose between her love and his son's, which made her next decision painfully easy.

DEAN WANTED to follow Annabelle as she bolted inside the duplex, but he had to convince the deputy to give him some time to talk to her before the boys were taken down to the station. It took some doing as it went against procedure, but the deputy must've seen something in Dean's eyes for his son's involvement and taken pity on him.

"You get an hour, then we need a decision whether or not to proceed. Sorry about this, Dean."

Dean nodded and headed inside.

He expected to hear sobs but when he heard nothing, somehow the silence was worse.

"Annabelle?"

"Dean, you should go," came her quiet answer from the living room. He found her sitting on the sofa, curled with her feet tucked under her and the afghan wrapped around her shoulders. "Really. Just go."

"We need to talk about this."

Her laugh held no trace of amusement. She shook her head. "What's to talk about? We were living in a fantasy. This never would've worked on multiple levels. This is really just a wake-up call."

"I'll talk to Brandon."

"Please don't. I understand why he did it. Honestly, maybe if I'd turned to more drastic measures Buddy might've left before he had a chance to ruin my mom's life. Brandon was just looking out for his family. Please don't punish him over this."

"I can't let this slide. This went beyond a prank. It was malicious, and—God, I can't believe my son capable of something so mean. I'm just glad Beth's not here to see this. She would've been devastated."

Annabelle sighed and let her chin rest on the back of the sofa, her gaze drifting out the window. "I wish I could've met her. I can't say I agree with his methods, but for a son to love his mother so much that he'd do just about anything to protect her memory…it's touching."

Dean heard the trace of sarcasm in her tone and felt chilled. He was losing her. And he couldn't blame her. Worse, the guilt he felt over what Brandon had done—what he had driven Brandon to do—was making it hard to swallow.

"This is my fault," he said suddenly, pacing. "I promised Brandon I wouldn't see you romantically. I swore to him that I wasn't into you that way. I lied straight to his face, but I hated the fact that I was attracted to you. I didn't want to be."

"I seem to have that effect on people. I tend to make them do things they don't want to do. It was one of Buddy's favorite lines right after he hit my mother for my rebellion. I'd smart off and my mom would get one right across the chops. Nice, huh?"

"I'm sorry, that didn't come out right. You're not to blame. It's me. I should've stayed away, should've tried harder to find you another job, but you got under my skin and I liked it."

Dean knew he was rambling, but the fear of losing her was messing up his frontal lobe. Unfortunately, it wasn't just his love life that was going down the tubes. His son's life was on the line. He hated to bring it up. By rights, Brandon and his friends should be charged, but all three boys were up for scholarships and something like this going on their record would cripple their chances. Tears blinded him as he pressed his lips together. "Are you going to press charges?" he asked.

"No."

Her answer should've been a relief; instead, it made him feel sick to his stomach. It was a lose–lose for them both. He didn't foster any misguided ideas that they could return to how things were just because Annabelle was taking the high road on this situation. If things were reversed, Dean knew he'd run without wasting the energy to look back. He couldn't expect her to stay. And he wouldn't ask. He loved her too much.

"Thank you." His voice came out a harsh whisper.

She didn't respond. Sensing the invitation to remain both in her duplex and in her life had just been rescinded, Dean walked out, fairly certain he was leaving a piece of his heart behind with her.

He couldn't even think of Honey. He'd started thinking of the sunny-haired toddler as his own and it felt nearly as bad to walk away from her as well.

CHAPTER NINETEEN

DEAN WALKED into his house and saw that Brandon was waiting anxiously in the living room, flipping through channels on the television without really watching anything. The minute Dean appeared, he jumped up, his eyes scared.

"Dad? I'm so sorry—" he started to say in a rush, but Dean wasn't in the mood, and when he spoke his words came out an anguished roar.

"How could you?"

Brandon swallowed and his eyes watered. "I don't know. It's like I was possessed or something. I mean, I know that's no excuse, but I couldn't stand the thought of you being with her and I snapped."

Dean stared at his son, feeling as if he didn't know the boy at all. "You could've seriously hurt her or Honey. Did you stop to think about that at all before you broke into her house? Poured sugar in her gas tank?"

"No. I didn't," he answered honestly. "I wish I had. I wish I'd stopped when Jessie kept telling me to quit acting like such a jerk but I couldn't. I was so...I don't know...hurt." Brandon hung his head and a tear slipped down his cheek before he wiped it away angrily. "It was stupid. And reckless. I'm sorry."

Even as his heart broke for Brandon, Dean's pain and disappointment were still in control of his mouth. "For all your hatred for a woman who has never been anything but nice to you when you've been the exact opposite, she isn't going to press charges. Do you hear me? In spite of your despicable actions, she's going to let you and your friends walk. It makes me sick to my stomach that I'm relieved. I don't want your future jeopardized over this stunt, but you deserve punishment. If nothing else, you've lost my respect. I will always love you, but right now, I don't like you very much."

At that Brandon's tears increased, but he didn't seem to care. "Yeah? That makes two of us, Dad. You think I'm proud of myself? I hate what I've done. I haven't been able to eat or sleep since it happened, and I've been going out of my mind with guilt. I'd do anything to take it back."

Dean wished the same. "Why did you hate her so much?"

"She wasn't Mom."

"So, would you have been like this with anyone I dated? Are you saying I can't have a life any longer? Because if that's the case, you didn't know your mom very well."

"What do you mean?"

"Your mom was the kind of person who put her own happiness on the back burner for others. Why do you think she drove home that night instead of staying at her sister's like she'd planned? I called her. I needed her here for the contractor show and didn't want to wait for her to arrive the following morning. She cut her visit short because I asked her to. She shouldn't have even been on the road. I was wrong to ask just as you're wrong to ask me to stop living."

"Annabelle's just so different. It was hard for me to deal with. She came off like a gold digger and with the way she dressed, all the guys were always staring at her. I hated that. I didn't want you to get hurt."

At that Dean had to offer a weary smile. "You were trying to protect me?"

"Yeah…"

Going to Brandon, Dean pulled his son into his arms. "You can't judge a person by the way they dress. I loved your mother, deeply, but things weren't perfect. You have to know that, right?"

Brandon drew away and shrugged. "I guess."

Dean didn't want to go into detail. Children shouldn't know the full extent of their parents' sins but Brandon hadn't been too young to realize the last two years before Beth died were tense. They'd been trying to rebuild what they'd had before Aaron had wormed his way into their lives. In spite of the pain, they'd both wanted to fix things. Then she'd died.

Drawing a deep breath, he realized there was little else to say, except that Annabelle was leaving.

Brandon nodded, and Dean had to turn away before he saw anything that might be perceived as triumph in his son's eyes. He didn't want to believe Brandon could feel that way in light of the circumstances, but he didn't really know what was going through his son's head right now and he didn't want to chance it. Dean couldn't be sure how he'd react and thought it best to err on the safe side.

"Make sure to get your homework done. I'm going to bed."

But, hours later, as Dean rolled and tossed, sleep eluded him and his brain kept replaying Annabelle's stricken expression. Brandon had long since hit the sack so Dean padded softly into the kitchen for a glass of warm milk to soothe his nerves. No one but Beth knew of his secret love for warm milk during a crisis and as he swallowed the first mouthful, he couldn't help but think of how Beth would feel about the situation.

Brandon was right about Annabelle—she and Beth were nothing alike. Perhaps that's what had drawn him. Being able to make comparisons would've been distracting and painful. And unfair. But, even as different as they were, he suspected Beth would've liked Annabelle. Beth had always appreciated people with spirit and pride. Annabelle had those in spades.

But what did it matter? Not a whole helluva lot when Annabelle had every reason to leave and there wasn't much he could do about it.

All manner of guilt rose to curdle the milk in his gut but in spite of this, he downed the rest of the glass.

He'd let Beth down by failing their son, and he'd broken Annabelle's heart. He was worse than a deadbeat boyfriend.

And that didn't feel very good.

Worry replaced the guilt as his mind switched tracks. Where would Annabelle go? Did she have enough money to settle elsewhere? Would Honey have to go to daycare with a bunch of strangers? Would another man raise that sweet girl and reap the reward of her love? A physical ache followed the thought and he gritted his teeth against the very real urge just to jump in his truck and beg Annabelle to stay. But even as he turned to grab his keys the voice of reason chimed in, reminding him of what a mess things were.

Stay for what? His son hated her enough to mess with her life, and, although Annabelle didn't press charges, he doubted they'd ever feel comfortable around one another. So to ask her to stay was really just selfish. Better that he let her find true happiness elsewhere, he thought to himself.

Yeah, you're a noble son of a bitch.

Not really, but he loved Annabelle enough to let her go, and that, he realized, was something he'd never truly learned with Beth until it was too late.

THERE WAS a benefit to being dirt-poor, Annabelle thought as she finished packing boxes—not much to pack.

How sad that her life fitted so easily into a handful of boxes that barely filled the back end of a pickup truck. Honey had more things than Annabelle, certainly more clothes. She smiled as she grabbed a fresh box for Honey's meager keepsake items.

Honey played on the floor beside her as Annabelle rolled fragile items in newspaper in the hopes that they would survive the trip back to Hinkley. She hated going back but her mom had owned that rattrap mobile home and it would be a roof over their heads. She'd already informed the tenants that they'd have to move out, and they'd been accommodating despite the scant notice. Seems they'd found a better place to rent anyway so everyone was happy.

A knock at the door sent her heart hammering with ridiculous hope that Dean was on the other side with some plan to make everything better.

Right. Get real. She was well aware that things didn't happen like that in her world. With her luck, it was likely a traveling salesman who would spend the next fifteen minutes trying to sell her something she couldn't afford, but, hey, everyone's gotta eat, so she wouldn't begrudge him the time.

But it wasn't a salesman nor was it Dean.

It was Aaron Eagle.

"Can I help you?" she asked, feeling very conscious of the stitching in her forehead and the bruising still healing on her face.

"I know I haven't given you much face time, but I'm actually your landlord. Thought I'd come by and chat a little."

Annabelle frowned with concern. "I know I

signed a lease but due to the circumstances, I thought you might be accommodating…."

"May I come in?"

She nodded reluctantly and, after picking up Honey from the bedroom, met Aaron in the living room.

"This isn't about the lease," he started.

"Then what's it about?" It was then she noticed the bruising around his lip, and she exclaimed, "Oh my goodness, what happened to you?"

He grimaced and pressed the pads of his fingers gently against the flesh under his eye. "Just two guys getting a few things straight. Nothing to worry about."

"Dean did that, didn't he?"

Aaron met her apprehension straight on. "Yes."

It was good thing she was moving out because she had a feeling Aaron had come personally to throw her out for Dean's barbaric action.

"Why'd he do that? If you don't mind my asking."

Aaron chuckled and his gaze went to the new windows. Instead of answering, he went to survey the handiwork. "Not bad for illegal immigrants who shouldn't even be in the country, huh?"

Annabelle remained quiet. Dean didn't like Aaron for a multitude of reasons and she wasn't privy to them all, but she knew for a fact Dean hated that Aaron hired illegals.

Aaron sighed and shook his head as if unable to believe what he was about to say. "Listen, a part of me wants you to walk away from this place and leave Dean's heart in pieces when you go, but I guess there's also a part of me that wouldn't want another man to feel as I did when I lost the woman I loved."

Annabelle couldn't help but stare. She was caught between really uncomfortable and intensely curious over Aaron's revealing statement, but couldn't quite decide which emotion was stronger. "I don't know what you're talking about," she ventured, hoping he'd continue. She got her wish.

"Not everyone marries their soul mate," Aaron said quietly, then met her gaze. "Sometimes you don't meet that person until you're *both* married with families. And even though you both know that you're meant to be together it's just not the right timing for either of you. And that's when it really sucks."

Annabelle already knew the answer but had to ask anyway. "Who do you think was your soul mate?"

His mouth quirked. "Her husband is the one who clocked me the other day at my own job site in front of my crew for saying something I shouldn't have."

"I'm sorry."

"Don't be. It was a wake-up call. I realized something. Beth made me want to be a better man. The way I've been acting since she died…it's an insult to her memory. I know Dean loved her and Beth loved him, but there are different types of love, Annabelle. What Dean feels for you…is how I felt about Beth. And if you leave, Dean will lose an important part of himself. As much as I hate the lucky bastard, he's a good man, and he doesn't deserve to go through that kind of pain."

Annabelle digested the startling information and

then said in a slow moment of clarity, "But aren't you still married? With a new baby? What about your wife?"

A rare spasm of pain crossed his features and Annabelle wondered if it was laced with regret or heavy resignation.

"We've got a few things to work out. She's a good woman. She deserves better than me, but if she'll keep me, I aim to be a better husband."

"I don't know what to say...."

"Don't say anything, particularly to Dean, about this conversation. I'll just deny it if you do."

"What happened to your declaration of becoming a better man?"

His smile returned. "I didn't say I was turning into a saint."

She met his smile with a slow one of her own. "I think there's hope for you, Aaron Eagle."

"From your mouth to God's ear... We'll see, right? Old habits are hard to break and all that."

"If Beth believed in you, there must be something worth believing in. From what I've heard, she was an amazing woman."

"That she was. She would've liked you."

"Maybe."

"No maybe. Absolutely. Now, quit acting like such a baby and go after your man. Don't let that kid of his run you off. You're made of sterner stuff, right?"

"Hell, yes," she retorted, thinking of her recent anticlimactic showdown with Buddy. "And then some."

"That's my girl."

"No," she corrected firmly. "I'm Dean's girl."

"Then go get him."

What a fabulous idea. Why hadn't she thought of that herself?

CHAPTER TWENTY

DEAN WAS startled to see his parents' car pull into the driveway. Brandon peered over his shoulder and reacted with surprise as well.

"What're Nana and Pops doing here? Isn't today their golf day?"

Yeah, it was, but by the determined step in Mary Halvorsen's stride and his father's grim expression, he had a feeling Sammy had told them the dirt. Dean didn't want to be in Brandon's shoes right about now.

The door opened and before Brandon could say hello Mary launched into him with the force of a gale wind that Dean certainly remembered from his childhood.

"Brandon Dean Halvorsen, I'm appalled at your behavior!"

"Nana," Brandon started but Mary wasn't hearing it. She waved him silent and gestured imperiously that he take a seat. Brandon shot Dean a look that plainly begged *Help me*, but Dean wasn't going to lift a finger. Brandon deserved it. By the time Mary was finished with him, Brandon might wish he'd just served time.

"Of all the brain-dead, juvenile, despicable stunts you could pull, this takes the cake. I expect better from you, young man. You hear me, better!"

"I know, Nana," Brandon said meekly. "I've already said I'm sorry."

"To whom? Did you apologize to the woman you terrorized with your pigheaded bullying?"

He hung his head. "No. I don't think she wants to see me."

"I don't blame her one bit. I don't want to see you, either, but you're my favorite grandson and I don't have a choice." Dean smothered a grin, remembering that Mary used to use this tactic with her sons as well. They were each her favorite. She drew herself up to her full matronly height and huffed a short breath. "So, let's be a part of the solution, shall we? Brian, you're up."

Dean's father stepped forward with a tight jaw. Brian Halvorsen was never one to blabber on, preferring to say only what needed to be said in most situations, but they were a formidable team, his mother and father.

"First off, you and your friends are going to pay for the damages to Annabelle's car." When Brandon started to protest, Dean gave him a warning look that said *Take your licks,* and Brandon wisely shut his trap. "Second, you and your friends are also going to pay for her hospital bill."

"No one was supposed to get hurt," Brandon said, a tad sullenly, and Brian snapped.

"Well, I'd say you weren't supposed to be breaking and entering, either, but what's done is done and now you have to clean up your damn mess!"

"Yes, sir. Anything else?"

"Yes, one more thing, you're going to apologize to Annabelle and Honey for being such an ass and embarrassing this family." Brian turned to Dean. "Does that sound about right to you?"

Dean nodded.

Tears sprang to Brandon's eyes. "I really am sorry."

"Then prove it, boy. Words are cheap but no one is buying. You hear me?"

Brian stalked from the room and Mary went to follow but as she got to the door, she turned, her eyes warming a little as she patted Brandon's cheek. "You're a good boy," she said. "But if you pull another stunt like this…"

"I won't. Believe me."

She smiled. "I do."

Turning to Dean, she said, "You're not off the hook, either."

Dean started. "What?"

"You're to blame for some of this, too. You should've been open about your feelings with everyone, including Annabelle. It's not too late to fix things. So, fix it."

"Mom, it's not that simple."

"It is if you make it so. That woman loves you. What more do you need? Don't let her walk away over something that can be repaired."

"That's just it, Mom. I don't know that this *can* be repaired. Annabelle's been through a lot. It's not fair to ask her to stay and deal with the aftermath."

Mary sighed and gave Dean a light slap on the cheek that left a painful zing.

"Ow, Ma," he exclaimed, rubbing at the spot. "What did you do that for?"

"Because for all your smarts, you can be pretty damn stupid when it suits you. Stop overthinking things. Just go after her. Show her how much you love her and that baby. You'd be amazed how simple things become. Trust me." Her eyes sparkled. "I'm your mother. Would I lie to my favorite son?"

Wisely, he chose to keep his mouth shut.

"She's at your brother's house. Don't let her get away."

UNDER NORMAL circumstances, Annabelle had an excruciatingly precise memory, but after Dean showed up at Sammy and Dana's house with a determined look in his eye, Annabelle could only recall one ridiculous detail.

Dana nearly pushing Annabelle out the door and slamming it behind her.

Some friend, she'd thought.

Dean bounded up the stairs and stood before her, and for a second there was an odd sense of awkwardness that stretched between them until a muffled yell from behind the front door prodded them into speech.

"Don't blow it!"

"Stop eavesdropping," Annabelle yelled back and a grumbled "Fine" resounded. She returned to Dean, who seemed to have gotten closer than before. "I'd have dropped off your office key," she said, not wanting to jump to conclusions.

"I'm not here for the key."

"Oh?"

An annoyed groan followed and Annabelle kicked the front door with the flat of her boot. "I said stop listening."

The door cracked open and Dana glowered. "What's to listen to? You're not saying anything." Annabelle returned Dana's look with a glower of her own. "Fine. I'll leave you to your awkward and stilted conversation about nothing important. Get to the good stuff," she hissed, before slamming the door.

Annabelle looked to Dean and couldn't help the smile. "She and I have a difference in opinion on what my next zip code should be."

"Then I agree with Dana."

"You do?"

"Yeah. Stay."

"Stay?"

"Yeah."

A mournful sigh escaped her. "And if I did? What then? There's still major problems. Brandon…"

"Brandon and I had a heart-to-heart. He's going to make amends."

Annabelle shook her head. "Only because you're making him."

"No, he's been killing himself over this. The guilt has been eating him alive. Brandon is a good kid. In time, if you'll let him, he'll show you."

She wanted to believe him. God, she wanted to believe that there was a happy ending in her future but she couldn't shake the fear that she was being a fool.

"Aaron came by to see me," she said, needing to switch subjects so she could catch her breath.

Dean's eyes narrowed. "What did he want?"

"You wouldn't believe me if I told you, and he flat-out said he'd deny it if I brought it up. I know about him and Beth."

"That man needs a quick-dry cement sandwich," Dean said with a healthy dose of malice. "Or cement shoes. Either will do."

Annabelle didn't want to admit that hearing about Beth's affair had somehow lessened her fear of measuring up to the woman but it had. It was nice to know Beth hadn't been perfect, and that probably made Annabelle seem a little short on the sympathetic side but she couldn't help it. She had her issues and was well aware of them.

"Yet you stayed married?"

He backed away, putting space between them, and Annabelle fought the urge to follow. "It's an ugly chapter that I prefer to forget. I had eighteen wonderful years with Beth. I prefer to remember our marriage that way instead of the two terrible years we suffered at the end."

"Tell me about the night she died."

"Why?"

Annabelle bit her lip, wondering herself. She wasn't a fan of sharing but this seemed important. Maybe more so for Dean. That was the key, she realized with sudden clarity. If he was willing to open up about the most painful part of his own past, maybe they actually had something worth fighting for. But if he shined her on, she'd know in her heart that he'd never truly let her into the space previously owned by another woman. Steeling herself, she shrugged for effect and said, "I'm a good listener."

"Well, I'm not much of a talker. And I don't want to talk about that night *or* my wife's affair with another man."

"And I didn't want to talk about the night that a man nearly killed my mother but you dragged it out of me. Turnabout is fair play, right?"

"That was different."

"How so?" she asked, putting her hands on her hips, annoyed.

"Because my dead wife isn't trying to sabotage my life. If it had been Buddy doing all those things, don't you think I should've known the details?"

"I suppose. But on the flip side, don't you think that it's time to let some things go?"

"Such as?" His voice turned chilly.

"Such as the fact that even though your wife and Aaron made a mistake you need to put it behind you and move on. Stop putting her on a pedestal and admit it takes two to tango. Aaron has his faults, granted, but I saw a different side of the man. A side that you refuse to see because of what happened between him and Beth."

Dean's gaze sharpened to flinty points and Annabelle knew she'd just marched into dangerous territory, but she had a feeling these were things that had to be said if they had any chance. "Don't waste your time championing Aaron to me. He slept with my wife."

"And your wife slept with him," she countered evenly. "I'm not saying it was right, but you can't make her out to be an angel and Aaron the devil. They both had parts to play and choices to make."

"You don't know anything about that situation so I'd suggest you shut your mouth. Aaron pretended to be my friend and then moved in on my wife. He wrecked two marriages with his actions and didn't care about the mess he left behind."

"Beth did the same."

Dean's face flushed with anger and his lips compressed to a fine line as if he were trying to hold back something ugly. After a long moment, he said in a low voice, "I came here to ask you to stay, but after this conversation I've realized this would never work. Take care, Annabelle."

And then, he was gone.

IN HINDSIGHT it was probably a good thing she wasn't quite sure what went wrong that day. She tried not to think of what was happening because she didn't relish the idea of breaking down and sobbing like a baby for something she'd never really had in the first place.

She still had loose ends to take care of, such as her car, and loading up Sammy's truck with her meager belongings. Dana had said something about not being able to do the move until Friday because of her shift and since Annabelle was leaning on Dana for help she really couldn't argue about the schedule. And, if the truth were dragged out of her she'd have to admit she wasn't in a hurry to return to Hinkley. The very thought made her eyesight swim—with tears or nausea, she wasn't sure. Either way it wasn't pleasant.

A knock at the door surprised her and she fairly ran to answer it in the hope that it was Dean. *Stupid, I know,* she thought, but flung the door open anyway.

Brandon stood there looking about as miserable as a person could be. Perplexed and a little wary, she said, "Are you lost? Or did you forget something the first time around?" Okay, that part was probably uncalled for, but she wasn't feeling overly warm and fuzzy toward the kid.

Shoving his hands into his jeans pockets, Brandon shuffled before answering, his voice dripping with shame and regret so much that even Annabelle couldn't help but feel sorry for him. "I wanted to apologize."

At first her heart leaped at his admission but then she realized he'd no doubt been coerced into playing remorseful. Still, even if he'd been forced, it was the thought that counted, right? She fingered the bumpy scab on her forehead and thought, *Not really*.

"Thanks." If there were any less feeling in her tone she'd be made of stone. "Consider yourself redeemed. You can go, Brandon."

His pained expression made her want to throw up her hands in exasperation. What more did he want from her? She couldn't make it all better for him. If he was suffering from a staggering load of guilt—good. He deserved it.

"I screwed up big-time." He surprised her by breaking the silence. "I don't know what came over me. I'm so sorry things got out of hand."

"Yeah, well, what's done is done. Just don't do it again to your dad's next…ah, office manager."

"I don't think he'll hire anyone else after you."

She looked at Brandon sharply. "Why do you say that?"

"C'mon, Annabelle, he's got it bad for you. He's in love with you."

"He doesn't love me," she assured him, though it hurt just to admit it. "He cares for me as a friend. That's it. You have nothing to worry about."

"I know," he said. "I never did. I was just too freaked out to pay attention to what was really happening."

She slanted a suspicious look at him. "Which was?"

"My dad's second chance at happiness."

"Whoa, hold on there. Before you go all Hall-mark channel on me, I have to tell you that whatever you think you know, you're wrong. Okay? Let's leave it at that, because frankly, this conversation only serves to remind me how everything has fallen to crap in a very short time. And, while you certainly didn't help things with your little foray into felony, you weren't the cause of...*this*." She gestured to the piles of boxes stacked against the walls. "Emmett's Mill isn't the place for me."

And Dean isn't the man for me. But she couldn't actually manage to say that aloud, for all her bravado. Her lips pressed together in an effort to keep the tears from starting, but they came anyway. "Shit," she muttered, turning away from Brandon so she could wipe away the moisture without having an audience. She turned back to him, her voice tight. "Are we done here?"

"Yeah, just one more thing," he said, reaching into his pocket to pull out a folded yellow invoice. He handed it to her as she stared in confusion. He gestured as he explained, "Your car is paid for and finished. I'm sorry, Annabelle. We all are."

Annabelle stared at the slip of paper in her hand as tears of disbelief blurred her vision but even as she tried wiping them away they kept coming. Brandon didn't turn as he walked away and climbed into his truck, giving her the privacy and the space to bawl as her heart demanded for his integrity and the realization that she desperately wanted to remain in Emmett's Mill to watch him turn into a man.

She wanted the privilege of being a part of his family forever. But she wasn't one to crash a party she wasn't invited to.

CHAPTER TWENTY-ONE

DEAN FELT a growl deep in his chest but tried to keep it contained. Annabelle was gone. And he'd let her leave. Worse, he'd walked away. He was the lowest kind of hypocrite. He'd made Annabelle tell him about that night with Buddy and her mother, yet he couldn't open up about Beth.

Swearing, he tried returning to the pile of work on his desk, but he couldn't care less about bid sheets when his heart was beating a rhythm that practically spelled Annabelle's name. He should've opened up, just let Annabelle know the measure of his pain, but for the past two years he'd worked at creating a rock-hard scab over that wound and he didn't relish the idea of ripping it off.

He didn't think he could stomach what he'd find underneath after all this time.

Beth hadn't been perfect; he wasn't perfect. It stood to reason, then, that their marriage hadn't been perfect, but it was nicer to preserve the illusion.

Everyone liked it that way—him included.

The house was dark, the only light illuminating

his desk. Outside, hoot owls and crickets sang their individual medleys until finally their sounds caused his eyelids to droop. Gathering his paperwork in a messy pile for tomorrow, he dragged his body to bed and tried to tell himself that this was best. Annabelle deserved better than a man who was emotionally unavailable.

Wasn't that what Beth had called him? Sounded about right.

But damn, it felt like shit.

THE NEXT MORNING at breakfast, Brandon and Dean kept to their cereal bowls with a silent agreement not to mention Annabelle's name. But Brandon broke the rule first.

"She's leaving today. Jonas released her car. There's nothing holding her here anymore," he said, as if Dean needed to know.

Dean made a noncommittal noise and returned to his cereal. A new start was a good thing. He wished her the best. A cereal flake caught in his throat and his eyes bugged as he choked it out. Brandon continued as if his father hadn't just spat a wad of masticated Frosted Flakes into a napkin.

"She's going back to that rathole of a trailer park in Hinkley. You know, the one where that guy lives? Yeah. I bet she's looking forward to that."

Dean wiped at his mouth and stared at his son. "How do you know all this?"

"Uncle Sammy told me. They're using the truck to haul her stuff." He stopped, a frown wrinkling his forehead. "I don't know if a trailer park like that is the best place for Honey. She's just a baby. Is there a park there for her to play? Or a yard, maybe? It's just such a bummer for that poor kid."

"Annabelle is doing what she thinks is best for the situation," Dean said, with less conviction than before, hating the idea of Honey not being able to run around the way every child on this planet deserved. He tried not to, but he thought of their own giant backyard and how a new swing set would fit perfectly. He pushed his bowl away and eyed Brandon with suspicion. "What's with the sudden change of heart about Honey? You used to practically spit nails every time you came into contact with her."

Brandon shrugged. "I think we've already established I was being a jerk. Don't rub it in, okay, Dad? Listen, I'm just saying, maybe you have a chance to make it better for everyone. Honey included. But, whatever. It's your life."

Dean smothered the flare of anger that followed as his son took his cereal bowl to the sink and disappeared into his room to get his stuff for school.

His life. It didn't feel like his life. It felt as if he were living someone else's life.

And that person was a jackass because he couldn't bring himself just to go after the woman he loved and beg her to give him a chance.

Slamming out the door, he gunned the engine of his truck and spewed dirt and gravel as he took his frustration out on the driveway.

As he drove, the last conversation he'd had with Annabelle haunted him. He hated to admit she'd hit a nerve. A raw and painful one that made him howl and run the other way at the thought of touching it again. But she'd been right about a few things, which only made him more miserable.

Pulling into his parking lot, he slowed to a stop and a scowl pulled at his face when he realized Aaron was standing there waiting for him.

He exited the truck and the two men stared each other down like two alpha dogs circling each other, waiting to see who was going to make the first move.

"What do you want, Aaron?"

Aaron pushed off his truck, his arms folded across his chest. "I came to tell you that I've dropped out of the bid process for the Laraby project."

"Why?"

"Because my reasons for wanting it didn't make good business sense."

"That's it?" Dean didn't believe him for a second. Aaron had only bid on it because he'd heard Dean was going after it. Aaron surprised him with his honest answer.

"No." Aaron leaned back against his truck, looking away, and for a split second Dean almost thought he read regret in the man's eyes, but he didn't get the chance to see it again. Aaron continued, keeping his gaze on the treeline above Dean's office instead of looking him in the eye as he said, "I'm not going after you anymore. It's time to stop." Dean was so shocked, he could only stare. Aaron didn't seem to notice; he was too set on saying what he'd come to get off his chest. Aaron met Dean's gaze and it was pained. "We have to let her go."

"Who?" Dean knew the answer and thought it was surreal that he was having this conversation with the man he hated most, but there was something about it that made him pause, too. He couldn't have left if he'd wanted to. His feet wouldn't have obeyed.

"Beth." Heavy silence hung between them for a long moment. Aaron sighed. "I can't make a go of my marriage to Gina if I'm nursing a hatred against you for keeping Beth from me and you can't move on with your life with her ghost hanging around."

"Why do you care about my love life?"

"I don't know. Maybe because I know Beth would've. She was a good woman and she made me want to be a better man even if she and I didn't go about things the right way. And for the past two years I've been so pissed at you *and* Beth—you for having all those years with her that I thought should've been mine, and her for choosing to stay with you instead of me—that I've been sacrificing everything in my desire to see you go down." He inhaled a deep breath. "It's over, Dean. I want to be the man Beth saw in me. Not the man you believe me to be. That's it. Take it however you want." Aaron turned and climbed into his truck. He didn't try to wave goodbye as if they were suddenly buds with water under the bridge, but at least from Aaron's standpoint the fight was over.

And Dean felt the truth of it. Aaron wouldn't continue to stalk Dean's contracting prospects nor would he trash-talk him around town to subcontractors. Dean didn't know what to think. For so long he'd poured all his energy into hating Aaron, and now, his enemy wasn't interested in playing anymore.

Relief. Odd under the circumstances, but there it was, lifting his shoulders and loosening his chest. And with relief came clarity.

Startling, blinding clarity as if the biggest lightbulb in the world had suddenly blazed above his head.

Aaron had been right about one thing. It was time to let the *illusion* of Beth go. Time to admit she'd had faults, that she wasn't the paragon he liked to remember her as. That he'd loved her *because* of her faults, not because she'd been perfect.

And that was okay. A slow smile spread across his face. It was more than okay. It was right.

ANNABELLE, with Honey on her hip, walked into the musty trailer and fought the urge to walk right back out. The look on Sammy's and Dana's faces said it all, but she wasn't going to let them see her crumble. She'd already turned down their offer—again—to bunk with them for a while and she didn't want to give them more fuel for their argument. She smiled through the haze. "It seems smaller. Cozy even."

Dana's eyes were glazed and Annabelle knew she was fighting her own memories of this place. Swallowing the lump in her throat, Annabelle tried lightening the mood around them. "Boy, this place makes the duplex look like a palace, huh?"

Dana burst into tears and bolted down the rickety stairs before Annabelle could stop her. She started after her friend, but Sammy stopped her. "Let's just get you unpacked. Dana's having a hard time. She doesn't want to leave you here. Frankly, neither do I. I'm sorry, Annabelle, this place sucks."

Tears filled her eyes. "I know, but it's what I have, and I own this piece of crap, small as it is, and I'm going to make the best of it for now."

Sammy nodded, but his mouth was set in a grim line, which on Sammy seemed downright unnatural. Annabelle set Honey down gingerly, privately wailing at the dismal conditions but forcing herself to put on a brave face. "Things have been worse. It'll be fine."

"You're a trouper, Annabelle, but there's a time for pride and a time to accept help when it's offered. It's not too late. Let's get out of here."

"And do what, Sammy? Watch as Dean falls in love with someone else? I can't do that. God, I can't do that. He made his feelings clear. I'm not the one. Maybe Beth really was the only woman for him. And that's okay. In a way, it's beautiful." She wiped at a tear snaking its way down her cheek. "I'm such a closet romantic that a true love story gets me every time. What a sap, huh?"

Sammy pulled her into a hug. "Knock that off. You're going to give us real saps a bad rap." She drew away and he pinned her with a serious look. "I mean it, just say the word and we're back in the truck and you never have to look at this place again."

So tempting. She closed her eyes against the very real desire to scream *yes* and damn the consequences, but she knew herself too well. Watching Dean with someone else would kill the one place in her heart that was still untouched. She shook her head and declined.

Sammy sighed. "All right. Let's get this stuff moved."

They managed to get Annabelle's car and Sammy and Dana's truck unloaded within the hour. Then, after much hugging and fervent promises to keep in touch, Dana and Sammy drove away.

It wasn't until later that night, as Annabelle tried to find the bedding, that she let the tears come. Curling into a ball, she sobbed as if her heart were breaking because it really was. She imagined that useless lump inside her chest cracking in two from the pressure and bleeding out from the open wound. She wept like a baby for the pain her mother must've endured for every broken heart she'd suffered throughout her life to her own sad and pathetic denouement. The curtain had closed on her pitiful play and no one had come for the show. How much better would it have been for Annabelle to walk away from Dean that day in the restaurant, refusing to play along for the sake of his pride. She might've been spared this awful rending.

But then again, she might not have known how wonderful and kind he was, what a wonderful father he was, how he was everything she ever wanted in a man but didn't know how to find.

Oh, stop it, already! Look at yourself, blubbering on like a whiny kid. Life sucks and you get over it.

Grinding at the tears still leaking from her eyes, she found her mother's afghan and folded Honey and herself into it, deciding it was good enough for the night. She just wanted to sleep. Everything would look better in the morning.

DEAN WANTED to surprise Annabelle with some grand gesture that would communicate more clearly than his own bumbling mouth ever could how sorry he was and what an idiot he'd been. But in the end, all he could focus on was getting to Annabelle and fixing everything he'd royally screwed up.

So, armed with a blueberry muffin he bought at a roadside gas station for Honey, he found Annabelle's trailer and made his way up the wobbly stairs to the front door and knocked with his heart in his throat.

There was no immediate answer so he tried the door. To his consternation, it opened. This wasn't the kind of neighborhood where one could safely leave doors unlocked. Worry followed him as he went inside.

"Annabelle?" he ventured cautiously, peering around the boxes filling the cramped space that smelled of years of cigarette smoke and despair. "Honey?"

Honey squealed, "Dada!" and little chubby legs propelled her small body straight into his arms.

Inhaling her sweet smell, he held her tightly and knew without a doubt that somewhere along the way, she'd become his daughter and there was no turning back. "Where's your mama, Honey-girl?"

Honey pointed toward the doorway off the living room and Dean followed. He found Annabelle curled on her side, clutching the afghan to her chest as if it were a lifeline and Dean's heart contracted at the pain she couldn't hide from in her sleep. He'd done this. He'd fix it.

"Annabelle," he whispered, pressing a tender kiss against her temple. Her eyelids fluttered in alarm until the sleep cleared from her eyes and she saw Dean kneeling beside the bed with Honey. "Good morning, beautiful."

She rolled slowly to her back, wary confusion in her eyes. "What are you doing here?"

"What I should've done two weeks ago."

Her throat worked as if she might say something, but she held back. He took that as the silent invitation he needed. Rising, he gently pulled her with him and straight into his arms. He felt her body tremble. "If you want to know about my life with Beth, I'll tell you everything…from the good times to the bad. Just give me the word and I'll start talking. My pride cost me a lot with Beth. I don't want to make the same mistake with you. I love you, Annabelle."

The red around her eyes told him she'd spent the night crying, and it killed him that she'd spent a minute wasting her tears when they had a lifetime of laughter to create. "If you'll have me, would you make me the luckiest man in Emmett's Mill and marry my stubborn butt?"

She gasped and her hand flew to her mouth. "Dean, don't toy with my heart like that. I can't take it."

"No playing around. The last time I met a woman at the altar I was pretty damn serious about that 'for better or worse' line. That part about me hasn't changed. I can't imagine my life without you and Honey in it. Please don't make me try."

"Are you sure?"

"I have no doubts."

A slow, tentative smile spread across her face like sunshine after a summer rain and Dean felt his heart thump painfully. "Well?" he asked anxiously. "What's your answer?"

Wrapping her arms around his neck, she pulled him down to her lips, answering him with all the love she felt in her soul as she murmured her response against his mouth. "Absolutely."

His body tightened with joy and he took a brief moment to deepen the kiss with a promise of more to come, but then pulled away, intent on getting them out of there.

"You're never setting foot in this place again," he vowed. "Ever." He expected her to agree but an odd expression flitted across her face. "What's wrong?" he asked, shifting Honey on his lap.

"It was my mother's home," Annabelle said softly,

"It was all she had. At one time it made her proud—you know, before the bad boyfriends and Buddy."

He corrected her gently. "Wrong. She had you. And that's worth more than you could ever imagine. More than any old trailer."

Her eyes watered anew. "If you keep this up I might just marry you before we get out of Hinkley."

The idea of a quickie wedding on the front steps of the first courthouse they could find certainly held some measure of appeal, but Dean wanted to do things right.

"No way," he said. "You deserve the best, from the ring to the wedding, to the life we're going to have together." Nuzzling her neck, reveling in her soft skin and the intoxicating scent that was unique to Annabelle, he added, "And I'm going to enjoy every minute I spend pampering you and giving Honey the best life I can offer."

Annabelle tipped her head back and murmured with pleasure, "Then by all means, what are we waiting for? Let's get the hell out of here. I'm ready for whatever you are."

Dean looked at Honey and then back at Annabelle, his eyebrow raising in playful question. "Even if it means adding to the family?"

Annabelle laughed, full and throaty. "Bring it on, Halvorsen. I'm made of pretty strong stuff, I'm told. I think I can take it. Now—" she gazed up at him "—are we going to sit here all day or are you ready to take us *home*?"

Seconds later Dean had her on her feet and in the truck with Honey strapped in her car seat. *Home.* On her lips…the sweetest word ever.

* * * * *

Turn the page for a sneak preview of
AFTERSHOCK, *a new anthology*
featuring New York Times
bestselling author Sharon Sala.

Available October 2008.

n◆cturne™

Dramatic and sensual tales
of paranormal romance.

Chapter 1

October
New York City

Nicole Masters was sitting cross-legged on her sofa while a cold autumn rain peppered the windows of her fourth-floor apartment. She was poking at the ice cream in her bowl and trying not to be in a mood.

Six weeks ago, a simple trip to her neighborhood pharmacy had turned into a nightmare. She'd walked into the middle of a robbery. She never even saw the man who shot her in the head and left her for dead. She'd survived, but some of her senses had not. She was dealing with short-term memory loss and a tendency to stagger. Even though she'd been told the problems were most likely temporary, she waged a daily battle with depression.

Her parents had been killed in a car wreck when she was twenty-one. And except for a few friends— and most recently her boyfriend, Dominic Tucci, who lived in the apartment right above hers, she was alone. Her doctor kept reminding her that she should be grateful to be alive, and on one level she knew he was right. But he wasn't living in her shoes.

If she'd been anywhere else but at that pharmacy when the robbery happened, she wouldn't have died twice on the way to the hospital. Instead of being grateful that she'd survived, she couldn't stop thinking of what she'd lost.

But that wasn't the end of her troubles. On top of everything else, something strange was happening inside her head. She'd begun to hear odd things: sounds, not voices—at least, she didn't think it was voices. It was more like the distant noise of rapids— a rush of wind and water inside her head that, when it came, blocked out everything around her. It didn't happen often, but when it did, it was frightening, and it was driving her crazy.

The blank moments, which is what she called them, even had a rhythm. First there came that sound, then a cold sweat, then panic with no reason. Part of her feared it was the beginning of an emotional breakdown. And part of her feared it wasn't—that it was going to turn out to be a permanent souvenir of her resurrection.

Frustrated with herself and the situation as it stood, she upped the sound on the TV remote. But instead of *Wheel of Fortune,* an announcer broke in with a special bulletin.

"This just in. Police are on the scene of a kid-napping that occurred only hours ago at The Dakota. Molly Dane, the six-year-old daughter of one of Hollywood's blockbuster stars, Lyla Dane, was taken by force from the family apartment. At this time they have yet to receive a ransom demand. The housekeeper was seriously injured during the abduction, and is, at the present time, in surgery. Police are hoping to be able to talk to her once she regains consciousness. In the meantime, we are going now to a press conference with Lyla Dane."

Horrified, Nicole stilled as the cameras went live to where the actress was speaking before a bank of microphones. The shock and terror in Lyla Dane's voice were physically painful to watch. But even though Nicole kept upping the volume, the sound continued to fade.

Just when she was beginning to think something was wrong with her set, the broadcast suddenly switched from the Dane press conference to what appeared to be footage of the kidnapping, beginning with footage from inside the apartment.

When the front door suddenly flew back against the wall and four men rushed in, Nicole gasped. Horrified, she quickly realized that this must have been caught on a security camera inside the Dane apartment.

As Nicole continued to watch, a small Asian woman, who she guessed was the maid, rushed forward in an effort to keep them out. When one of the men hit her in the face with his gun, Nicole moaned. The violence was too reminiscent of what she'd lived through. Sick to her stomach, she fisted her hands against her belly, wishing it was over, but unable to tear her gaze away.

When the maid dropped to the carpet, the same man followed with a vicious kick to the little woman's midsection that lifted her off the floor.

"Oh, my God," Nicole said. When blood began to pool beneath the maid's head, she started to cry.

As the tape played on, the four men split up in different directions. The camera caught one running down a long marble hallway, then disappearing into a room. Moments later he reappeared, carrying a little girl, who Nicole assumed was Molly Dane. The child was wearing a pair of red pants and a white turtleneck sweater, and her hair was partially blocking her abductor's face as he carried her down the hall. She was kicking and screaming in his arms, and when he slapped her, it elicited an agonized scream that brought the other three running. Nicole watched in horror as one of them ran up and put his hand over Molly's face. Seconds later, she went limp.

One moment they were in the foyer, then they were gone.

Nicole jumped to her feet, then staggered drunkenly. The bowl of ice cream she'd absentmindedly placed in her lap shattered at her feet, splattering glass and melting ice cream everywhere.

The picture on the screen abruptly switched from

the kidnapping to what Nicole assumed was a rerun of Lyla Dane's plea for her daughter's safe return, but she was numb.

Before she could think what to do next, the doorbell rang. Startled by the unexpected sound, she shakily swiped at the tears and took a step forward. She didn't feel the glass shards piercing her feet until she took the second step. At that point, sharp pains shot through her foot. She gasped, then looked down in confusion. Her legs looked as if she'd been running through mud, and she was standing in broken glass and ice cream, while a thin ribbon of blood seeped out from beneath her toes.

"Oh, no," Nicole mumbled, then stifled a second moan of pain.

The doorbell rang again. She shivered, then clutched her head in confusion.

"Just a minute!" she yelled, then tried to sidestep the rest of the debris as she hobbled to the door.

When she looked through the peephole in the door, she didn't know whether to be relieved or regretful.

It was Dominic, and as usual, she was a mess.

Nicole smiled a little self-consciously as she opened the door to let him in. "I just don't know what's happening to me. I think I'm losing my mind."

"Hey, don't talk about my woman like that."

Nicole rode the surge of delight his words brought. "So I'm still your woman?"

Dominic lowered his head.

Their lips met.

The kiss proceeded.
Slowly.
Thoroughly.

* * * * *

Be sure to look for the
AFTERSHOCK
anthology next month, as well as
other exciting paranormal stories
from Silhouette Nocturne.
Available in October wherever books are sold.

REQUEST YOUR FREE BOOKS!

2 FREE NOVELS PLUS 2 FREE GIFTS!

HARLEQUIN®

Super Romance®

Exciting, emotional, unexpected!

YES! Please send me 2 FREE Harlequin Superromance® novels and my 2 FREE gifts (gifts are worth about $10). After receiving them, if I don't wish to receive any more books, I can return the shipping statement marked "cancel." If I don't cancel, I will receive 6 brand-new novels every month and be billed just $4.69 per book in the U.S. or $5.24 per book in Canada, plus 25¢ shipping and handling per book and applicable taxes, if any*. That's a savings of close to 15% off the cover price! I understand that accepting the 2 free books and gifts places me under no obligation to buy anything. I can always return a shipment and cancel at any time. Even if I never buy another book from Harlequin, the two free books and gifts are mine to keep forever.

135 HDN EEX7   336 HDN EEYK

Name	(PLEASE PRINT)	
Address		Apt. #
City	State/Prov.	Zip/Postal Code

Signature (if under 18, a parent or guardian must sign)

Mail to the **Harlequin Reader Service**:
IN U.S.A.: P.O. Box 1867, Buffalo, NY 14240-1867
IN CANADA: P.O. Box 609, Fort Erie, Ontario L2A 5X3

Not valid to current subscribers of Harlequin Superromance books.

Want to try two free books from another line?
Call 1-800-873-8635 or visit www.morefreebooks.com.

* Terms and prices subject to change without notice. N.Y. residents add applicable sales tax. Canadian residents will be charged applicable provincial taxes and GST. Offer not valid in Quebec. This offer is limited to one order per household. All orders subject to approval. Credit or debit balances in a customer's account(s) may be offset by any other outstanding balance owed by or to the customer. Please allow 4 to 6 weeks for delivery. Offer available while quantities last.

Your Privacy: Harlequin is committed to protecting your privacy. Our Privacy Policy is available online at www.eHarlequin.com or upon request from the Reader Service. From time to time we make our lists of customers available to reputable third parties who may have a product or service of interest to you. If you would prefer we not share your name and address, please check here. ☐

HSR08R

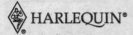

HARLEQUIN

SuperRomance

COMING NEXT MONTH

HSRCNM0908

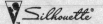

SPECIAL EDITION™

Tanner Bravo and Crystal Cerise had it bad
for each other, though they couldn't be more
different. Tanner was the type to settle down;
free-spirited Crystal wouldn't hear of it.
Now that Crystal was pregnant, would
Tanner have his way after all?

Look for

HAVING
TANNER BRAVO'S
BABY

by *USA TODAY* bestselling author
CHRISTINE RIMMER

Available in October wherever books are sold.

Mindful thoughts for
CYCLISTS

First published in the UK and North America in 2017 by

Leaping Hare Press

An imprint of The Quarto Group
The Old Brewery, 6 Blundell Street
London N7 9BH, United Kingdom
T (0)20 7700 6700 **F** (0)20 7700 8066
www.QuartoKnows.com

© 2017 Quarto Publishing plc

British Library Cataloguing-in-Publication Data
A catalogue record for this book is available from the British Library

ISBN: 978-1-78240-483-5

This book was conceived, designed and produced by

Leaping Hare Press

58 West Street, Brighton BN1 2RA, UK

Publisher: *Susan Kelly*
Creative Director: *Michael Whitehead*
Editorial Director: *Tom Kitch*
Art Director: *James Lawrence*
Commissioning Editor: *Monica Perdoni*
Editor: *Jenni Davis*
Assistant Editor: *Jenny Campbell*
Designer: *Tina Smith*
Illustrator: *Lehel Kovacs*

Printed in China

5 7 9 10 8 6

Mindful thoughts for
CYCLISTS

Finding balance on two wheels

Nick Moore

Leaping Hare Press

Contents

A Journey of
Discovery

A family friend, sadly no longer with us, once said: 'If you want to know about something, write a book about it.'

Let me begin with a disclaimer. This is not a how-to guide, or in any way definitive on cycling or mindfulness. Nor is it a manifesto, polemic or call to arms. What it does offer, I hope, is an alternative to the slew of books that exhort us to do more, achieve more, be more. These are thoughts; reflections on finding a mindful balance in cycling – and, perhaps, in life itself. They are very much like the rides that inspired them: short, circular, with no end other than pleasure in mind.

The last decade has seen a massive resurgence in cycling's popularity in Britain and the US (it never went away in Europe) and it's a joy to see so many taking to the road for the first time, or coming back to bike-riding after what is often many years away. And in many respects, there's never been a better time to be a cyclist. The problem is that cycling, like almost everything else in life, is now highly commoditized and skilfully marketed. These thoughts are intended to help you maintain a sense of balance and proportion amid the endless temptations, illusions and distractions. As I hope they show, cycling is replete with richness, diversity, pleasure and wisdom if we are truly present, and focus on what *is*.

If you're new to cycling, I hope this book will help you cultivate a healthy, balanced relationship with your bike from the get-go. For more experienced riders, it may resonate with your own search for a new direction, or bring something extra to your regular routine. There will probably be things you disagree with, or find simply don't work for you, but my hope is that you'll find something, somewhere, in these thoughts that enables you to develop a deeper awareness as you're riding, and be fully present in the moment. It could be learning to embrace the heat, the cold, the rain. Dealing with punctures or getting lost. Noticing and appreciating the natural world. Getting up hills. Or simply being conscious of how your body and bike are working together as a single, beautiful, biomechanical entity.

I spent my thirties as a fairly typical Middle-aged Man In Lycra (MAMIL), but was forced to rethink my approach when, aged 40, I developed osteoarthritis in my knees. Suddenly, I could no longer concentrate solely on going faster and 'getting the miles in'. I had to think about every pedal stroke, be minutely aware of gradients, gearing, my position on the bike, the pressure on my knee. I had to be fully aware of everything, every moment, otherwise things started to hurt. I didn't go looking for mindfulness. It found me.

After 20 years I've started to learn what cycling truly means to me. I don't know, and would never presume to guess, what it might mean to you. That's for you, and your bicycle, to find out – mindfully – together. Enjoy the ride.

Wheels
within
Wheels

Cycling is a game played out in circles: some concentric, some interlinked like a Venn diagram. The first and smallest is described by something you can't actually see: the spindle in the bottom bracket to which the crank arms are attached. The frame is usually held to be the 'heart' of the bicycle, but in some respects, this humble metal rod is a closer analogue. Year after year, mile after mile, it works out of sight and out of mind, calmly keeping the rest of the mechanism in motion. We don't pay it any attention until it gives us trouble, and when it does, everything comes to a halt. Sometimes, it can be fixed; sometimes, the only option is to replace it. And the day will surely come when it fails altogether.

Equally vital, and similarly unsung, are the hubs. A mechanic friend of mine once told me the surest test of a hub is to put the bike in a work-stand, spin the wheel with your hand, then go and make a cup of coffee. If the wheel's still turning when you come back, it's a keeper.

ON THE SUBJECT OF PEDALLING

The next circle is concentric to the bottom bracket: the rotation of the pedals. The key to riding efficiently, in addition to correct gear selection, is a smooth, fluid pedalling action – spinning, or what the French call *la souplesse*. So important is this circle that a tired, out-of-form or just plain inept rider is said, equally vividly, to be 'pedalling squares'.

Racers aim to maintain a pedalling speed, or cadence, of about 80–90 revolutions per minute. That's about 5,000 an hour; and a typical pro will put in four to five hours a day, 200 days a year. Call it five million pedal

strokes a year, over a career that might last a decade
or more. Even at the more modest cadences we mortals
can manage, it can soon add up over a lifetime of riding.
Hence the mindful cyclist is always listening to their
hips, knees and ankles: any 'twinges in the hinges'
should never be ignored.

THE TURN OF THE WHEEL

Further out still, the rims and tyres are in orbit
around the hubs, with the valve whizzing by like a
little geostationary satellite. Laced together with their
intricate tracery of spokes, they make up the whole wheel.
Seamless and never-ending, containing everything and
nothing, the wheel has long exerted a powerful hold
on our psyche. In Buddhism, the dharmachakra has
represented Gautama Buddha's teaching of the path
to nirvana since ancient times. Interpretations vary,
and fill whole books by themselves, but in essence, the
wheel's circular shape symbolizes the perfection of
the Buddha's teachings. The rim represents meditative

concentration and mindfulness – it's often shown with sharp spokes protruding beyond it, signifying penetrating insights – while the hub at the centre stands for moral discipline.

In the Celtic tradition, and in modern-day paganism, the year is viewed as a wheel, revolving through the active and dormant states of nature, man and agriculture. The winter and summer solstices, and vernal and autumnal equinoxes, are marked by the solar festivals of Yule, Litha, Ostara and Mabon. Between them come the fire festivals of Imbolc, Beltane, Lughnasa and Samhain, marking significant farming events. These live on in our modern calendar as Candlemas, May Day, Lammas and All Hallows' Eve, or Hallowe'en.

THE BIG LOOP

On a road bike, every turn of the wheels takes you a about seven feet (a little over two metres); call it 750 revolutions per mile. Think how many hoops we bowl through the air, even when we just pop down to the shops. And each of these little circles described by the bicycle itself are encompassed within larger ones.

Because every ride is, ultimately, circular. Even the mightiest of them all, the Tour de France, is colloquially referred to simply as *la grande boucle* – 'the big loop'. To make these circles right through the year is to see, feel and connect with the slow roll of the seasons. There's nothing wrong with confining your cycling to warm summer days, but for true understanding we must know cold, not just heat, and embrace the dark as well as the light.

The very act of tracing these circles can help keep us intimately connected to the present moment. Only a fraction of the wheel, a few square millimetres of rubber tyre, is in contact with the ground at any given time. If that tiny patch of Earth is free of thorns, nails, spilled oil or other hazards, we remain upright, moving, and all is well. In that pure state of living entirely in the here and now, all other things forgotten, we can enjoy the full freedom, magic and sense of possibility the bicycle bestows.

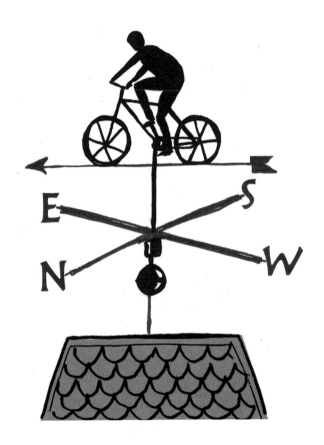

The
Wind

The ancient Greeks believed that air was one of the four elements from which the whole of creation was composed. Aristotle placed it between fire and water in his model of the universe, since he maintained it to be both hot and wet; had he ridden a bike in a climate like Britain's, he'd have known he was only half right. What's indisputable, however, is that for cyclists, the wind is a fundamental part of life: not Shakespeare's 'incorporeal air', but a substantial entity with weight, texture, energy, motion and moods all of its own.

As cyclists, we enjoy a special, complex relationship with the wind. Like sailors and pilots, with whom we have more in common than might be supposed, we are intimately affected by its power, direction and caprices. It's a relationship that, as so often in cycling, has an objective basis in physics, and an entirely subjective one rooted in our experience at any given moment. Put simply, we all love a tailwind, while a headwind poses very particular challenges.

THE INVISIBLE HILL

It is self-evidently more difficult to ride against the wind than to have it at your back: not for nothing, the headwind has been known to generations of cyclists as 'the invisible hill'. And the faster you go, the harder it gets, because, as cyclists, we're subject to one of nature's more inequitable laws, which states that every time your speed doubles, air resistance increases fourfold.

Unkinder still, a pitiless concatenation also means that to go twice as fast means your legs have to produce eight times as much power. If your sole focus is on reaching a destination, or crossing a finishing line, it's easy to regard the wind as an enemy to be beaten – or at least cheated.

But when we ride mindfully, wholly immersed in the journey itself, it's no longer a competition. Indeed, we might usefully see the physical tolls racers pay as the universe telling us it's OK to take things easy.

Because the wind is not an opponent, or some malevolent force out to spoil our fun. It is simply the movement of air between areas of higher and lower pressure. It has no agenda or intent, bears us no ill will. It merely obeys the higher laws of energy and motion: we cannot control it or (whatever the marketing people might tell us) conquer it through clever kit or clothing. What we can do instead is feel it, embrace it and learn from it, as a natural, ever-present part of the ride. In *The Man Who Loved Bicycles*, Daniel Behrman writes: 'You never have the wind with you: either it is against you or you're having a good day.'

MINDFUL OF THE WIND

The mindful cyclist is, nonetheless, a careful student of the wind. Flagpoles, church weathervanes, banks of cloud, the flight of birds and smoke from bonfire and chimney all have much to tell us about its strength and bearing. Routes may be planned so that you ride out into it, when the legs are fresh and the spirit bold, and home with it behind you, to reward and flatter weary limbs with speed conjured literally out of the air. On blustery days, I avoid the main roads with their dangerously unpredictable crosswinds, and explore narrow, sunken lanes, whose high, tree-topped banks provide welcome shelter, just as they did for drovers and other travellers down the centuries. Even the humble hedgerow becomes a battlement to hide behind and gain respite from the onslaught, but mindfulness also means being ready for the sneaky broadside as you pass a drive or gateway.

For now, perhaps, the wind is in your face. It makes you feel as though you're towing a sack of wet sand behind the bike, or a giant is stiff-arming you with his hand against your forehead. Flat roads become hills, hills become mountains, mountains become walls.

All you can do is keep going. You cannot outrun it, reason with it, or make it stop blowing. It knows its own strength, and never grows tired.

Be patient. Turn a corner, and it will swing behind you. In that moment, the whole world is altered. All that thick, treacly air and the elemental forces you've been fighting with now become your allies and friends. You are like a kite cut loose from its string, free to fly, all effort and struggle forgotten, able to savour and revel in your own, miraculous speed.

The Rain it
Raineth

The redoubtable Alfred Wainwright opened the eyes of millions of people – including me – to the glories of England's Lake District through his exquisitely illustrated, handwritten guidebooks. That this beautiful part of the country experiences rain on around 200 days a year was not, in his view, an obstacle to enjoying his beloved hills and footpaths. 'There is no such thing as bad weather,' he famously declared, 'only unsuitable clothing.'

Given the astonishing plethora of waterproof, windproof and thermal kit available now, one might think having 'unsuitable clothing' would no longer be an issue, if not actually impossible, for the cyclist. But like the smiles of Fortune, even today's exotic fibres, fabrics and surface treatments can still flatter to deceive. One soon learns to regard manufacturers' claims for their products with due caution, if not outright scepticism.

In short, no foul-weather gear is without its limitations. For the mindful cyclist, then, this means accepting that part of you (if not most of you) is going to get wet, cold, and probably both, at some stage. Coming to terms with this truth can transform the way you think about the rain. It is no longer something to be avoided or bemoaned, but part of the natural order – and perhaps, in time, something to be actively embraced, even enjoyed.

CAUGHT IN THE RAIN

There are basically two types of wet ride. The first is when we get caught in the rain part way through, having set out in the dry. This is a misfortune that can befall most of us living in temperate climates on almost any day of the year. But it need not be a problem. If we are fully present in the moment, tuned in to the wind, the temperature, the movements of the clouds, smoke from chimneys and the telltale ripples on roadside puddles, we should see it coming. Such observations and awareness connect us once again with the world. They also help us decide what to do next.

The instinctive response, inculcated from childhood, is to get under cover, or put on a coat. It's almost as though we fear getting wet, in case we – what? Rust? Dissolve? Soak up the water like sponges? There is the issue of becoming cold, of course, but on the bike, you can generate your own heat. What we are really grappling with here is not the weather but our own desire – our not-unnatural wish to be dry, warm and, above all, comfortable.

Paradoxically, our attempts to satisfy this desire can have the opposite effect. Trying to avoid or outrun the weather – or simply to get closer to home before it strikes – can involve long detours and/or some hard riding. Put on a jacket too soon, and you can end up wetter from exertion than you would have been from the rain.

Constantly stopping to put on and take off waterproofs adds further time, effort and frustration to the equation. And since getting wet is probably inevitable anyway, it is often better simply to keep going and endure.

CHOOSING THE RAIN

The second, more glorious, kind of wet ride is the one we deliberately set out to do when it's bucketing down already. This, in my view, is to be truly mindful: dressing up and getting on your bike, fully aware of what you're doing and what awaits you, and accepting whatever happens next for itself.

For there is something magnificent, uplifting and empowering about being out in weather that we could easily have chosen to observe from indoors. Riding in a biblical downpour is not especially pleasant, or pleasurable. Neither is it fun in any conventional sense. But it is deeply, viscerally *real*.

On the bike, you're completely encompassed – from above by the rain falling on you, from below by the spray fountaining up from the wheels, and from all sides by the slipstream of passing vehicles. There comes a point – usually fairly swiftly, in my experience – where you physically can't get any wetter. To give in to this, to accept it and embrace it, brings its own kind of pleasure: a physical and mental unshackling from deep-seated inhibitions, fears and prejudices. You are truly at one with the weather, fierce and indomitable, a force of nature in your own right. Any lingering feelings of misery or dejection are banished. You are self-sufficient, truly alive and discovering the true, perhaps unexpected, extent of your own physical and mental resilience.

By accepting whatever the elements throw at us, we grow as cyclists, and as people. It also helps us forge a deeper bond with the bicycle – as true partners, not just fair-weather friends.

On Ascending . . . and
Descending

Appealing and logical as it might seem, avoiding hills is a bit like going out only on sunny days: there's nothing wrong with it, but it is to miss out on a crucial dimension of cycling, and life. Hills are the crucibles where we're melted down, refined and forged anew. Plus, unless you happen to live somewhere unusually flat, any road you take will tilt you skywards somewhere along the way.

While hilly terrain is obviously more physically demanding than flat roads, it brings its own joys to the ride. There is real pleasure in exertion, in feeling your muscles working, the air racing in and out of your lungs, your heart beating, your blood surging round. And when you reach the top, there is that opportunity for stillness and reflection, to sense your body settling itself down from its highly charged state, and to gain the perspective that comes with a view from a high place.

Mindful climbing is about concentrating wholly on the here and now. In *Zen and the Art of Motorcycle Maintenance*, Robert M. Pirsig suggests that mountains (or hills, for those in less extreme landscapes) 'should be climbed with as little effort as possible and without desire'. We're conditioned to see hills as obstacles, objects of conquest, and to believe that reaching the top (as fast as possible) is all that really matters. Our goal is external, separate, somewhere up ahead in time and space. We are not truly 'here' because all our energy and focus is 'there'. Is there any state less mindful than that? No wonder it's so physically tiring, and mentally draining.

A CLIMBING MEDITATION

Mindfulness requires us to tune in to one thing – usually our breathing. Happily, this is also the key to riding uphill, so every climb can truly become a meditation.

Regulate your breathing and the legs will find their own rhythm. Feel your diaphragm rising and falling, steady and powerful. Try consciously 'inhaling' the road, physically pulling it towards you with each in-breath, then use the out-breath to push yourself forward. Be aware of the wheels rotating: all must be smooth and circular, without edges or angles.

As in yoga, maintaining a steady, focused gaze ahead aids concentration. Fix your eyes on a spot on the road about a bike's-length ahead, and what lies beyond ceases to exist, or matter.

A long, slow climb is also an opportunity to appreciate nature on her own level, and at her own pace. In spring, the steep banks that line many of my local lanes are overflowing with bluebells, stitchwort, celandines, windflowers, cow parsley, jack-by-the-hedge, orchids – a veritable Titania's bower. There are sandstone outcrops, too, craggy as canyons in a Western, roped with the exposed, knotted roots of oak, ash and beech trees, and dotted with rabbit warrens like the portholes in a wooden ship. As Pirsig also points out: 'It's the sides of the mountain that sustain life, not the top.'

And sometimes, the best and most comfortable way to reach the top is simply to take the bike for a walk instead. Even the professionals would agree.

GLORY IN DESCENDING

To every action there is an equal and opposite reaction – what goes up must come down, and there is a special glory in descending. The sheer delight of all that free, effortless speed is matched only by the delicious thrill of being on the edge of control and common sense, which captivated us in childhood and never really leaves us. We may still fall short of flying, but the bike can bring us closer to it than almost anything else.

Yet even in this exquisite state of grace, focus is required – nay, essential. As speed rises, so the margins of error contract. To descend mindfully is to cross the magical threshold from simply riding the road to reading it; not only knowing precisely where you are, but also sensing and predicting what might be coming next. Conscious thought is too slow and laborious. At 25 miles per hour, one second's pondering takes you 40 feet further down the road.

But to ride fast down a smooth, twisting road you know well is a transcendent experience. Slashing through a corner in a seamless, fluid movement is cycling's equivalent of hitting the high note or a hole-in-one. String a series of such corners together, and bike and rider flow down the hill like a raindrop on a windowpane.

To spend time in the hills or mountains is an exquisite mix of effort and exhilaration, steady progress and glorious speed. It is a mirror to the human condition – and the very essence of what it means to ride a bike.

Finding **the Upside** of Punctures

Few things are more dispiriting for the cyclist than a puncture – especially in the back wheel. A sudden, spongy vagueness in the handling is swiftly followed by the soul-sapping burble of metal rim and flaccid rubber on pavement, which sounds suspiciously like deep, mocking laughter. At best, you're looking at lost time and some strenuous, messy alfresco toil; at worst, a long walk, or the ignominy of having to be rescued.

To observe and accept this turn of events without judgement demands a singular effort of will, the more so if it's raining. (For me, acceptance comes after an involuntary exclamation of shock and disappointment, and a few good, deep breaths.) However, I've slowly learned that a flat can be a kind of meditation, and bring new and positive insights into the cycling life.

For instance, consider how amazingly frequently punctures don't happen. In a typical year, I'll get about three; an average of one every 90 rides or so. I'll take those odds. A few millimetres of rubber stand between the precious, pressurized air that makes cycling possible, and the numberless sharp objects trying to rob us of it. That these often unseen enemies succeed so rarely is almost miraculous – yet we take our tyres' ability to repel them almost entirely for granted.

MEDITATION ON A PUNCTURE

Prevention is, of course, vastly preferable to cure. We must be aware of, then avoid where possible, the flints, thorns, nails, potholes, raised edges, bits of glass and other agents of woe that await us. It's to hear the distant whine and clang of the farmer's rotary flail hedge cutter, and seek another way; to run good tyres, properly inflated, and change them if they're cut, cracked or threadbare. Above all, it's to ride with eyes and ears wide open. And when (not if) the dreaded moment arrives, framing what follows as a meditation can draw at least some of the sting.

Removing a wheel is a chance to reacquaint ourselves with a bike's vital components, which meld simplicity and robustness with intricacy and precision so elegantly that one can almost forgive them their grease and grime. It also reveals otherwise hidden parts of the frame; an ideal moment to inspect for damage or accumulated dirt to address at greater leisure. Plus, we can appreciate anew the wheel itself – in engineering terms, the strongest structure ever invented, able to support more than 100 times its own weight, and resist huge lateral and torsional forces generated in accelerating, braking and turning.

RESTORING SELF-SUFFICIENCY

Perhaps most importantly, dealing with a puncture restores a sense of self-reliance and self-sufficiency we're rapidly losing in today's hi-tech world. Any automotive problem more serious than a flat battery usually means a trip to the local garage: similarly, if something shuts down or goes haywire in your phone, computer or washing-machine, it almost inevitably requires professional intervention.

A puncture is one thing we're still able to fix ourselves, using basic tools and inexpensive parts we can carry with us. Sore thumbs, oil-stains and arriving home a bit later than planned are a small price to pay for the warm sense of self-sufficiency that comes from getting yourself and your faithful companion back on the road. From disaster, triumph; from defeat, victory; from despair, hope and faith renewed.

THE KINDNESS OF STRANGERS

But not all of us have the tools, strength, aptitude or inclination to be our own mechanic. I dread flats on my vintage bike, since removing a wheel means entirely disconnecting, then reconnecting, the brakes (the hub gear too, if it's the rear) and requires three separate spanners in three different sizes. And most long-haul cyclists (myself included) can ruefully recall the day they suffered three punctures, having set off cheerfully thinking two spare inner-tubes would be plenty…

On such occasions, the bicycle prompts us to reach out to family and friends – or to trust in the kindness of strangers. In the time I spent waiting for my father to arrive with car and bike rack after a recent puncture on my vintage machine (thanks, Dad), two riders pulled over and offered their help. Any cyclist worthy of the name will do the same, even if it's just to hold your bike, pass you things and provide moral support while you put in the hard graft. Even in the cauldron of professional racing, riders will wait and allow a rival to rejoin the fray after a crash, flat or mechanical incident. As cyclists, we are all part of a family of millions – and are also keenly aware that the situation may be reversed one day.

Punctures are an inevitable, if unwelcome, part of cycling. But regarded mindfully, they are opportunities for learning and growth, keeping us – literally – grounded, and in touch with the realities of cycling life.

The Weight
of the World

Archimedes claimed that given a lever long enough
and a fulcrum on which to place it, he would move the
world. What a shame he was born a couple of millennia
too soon to ride a bike. Because with our simple machine
(of which I think he would most wholeheartedly
approve), we cyclists boldly engage with the most
powerful, fundamental forces on Earth.

Every bike ride, taken mindfully, is a direct, hands-on
physics lesson. Had I understood this when I was
younger, I might have stuck with the subject. Now, in
adulthood, the abstract concepts and tangled formulae
I tried (and largely failed) to grasp in those far-off dusty
classrooms have become very real indeed. The bicycle,

which provides such a feeling of freedom, is subject to laws so ironclad and immutable they govern every moving object there is, and has ever been. Behind its art and poetry lies the rigid legislation of classical mechanics, codified by Sir Isaac Newton, and under whose stern jurisdiction we still labour.

LAWS OF PHYSICS

Take inertia, for instance. From the Latin *iners*, meaning idle or sluggish, it's the resistance of a physical object to any change in its state of motion. It is inertia you must first overcome to set your stationary bicycle moving, by applying a force to it: the heavier the bike and rider, the harder it is to get going.

And we all know, instinctively and unconsciously, what gravity is. As long as dropped objects fall unerringly to the floor, and we don't find ourselves floating off into the blue, we don't afford it a moment's thought. Get on a bike, however, and we are suddenly only too aware of gravity's absolute hold over us. On the flat, it's relatively benign, and goes pretty much unnoticed. But when the road tilts, it drops the whole weight of the world into your back pocket.

The same goes for air resistance, or aerodynamic drag. Most of the time, it doesn't affect us because we're either moving too slowly (as pedestrians) or letting machinery deal with it (as drivers or passengers). Again, the bike reveals just how wide of the mark Shakespeare was when he gave us the phrase 'thin air'.

Trundling along at 10 miles an hour, the effect of air resistance on your forward progress is almost imperceptible, since it's equal to other forces such as friction between your tyres and the road. But once you reach 20 miles an hour and above, overcoming air resistance will account for between 70 and 90 per cent of your effort. What's more, the faster you go, the more reluctant it is to let you through.

In fact, there's barely a line in Newton's canon that doesn't apply to bike and rider. It may not feel like it, but you're not losing energy as you go along: you're converting it from one form into another, neither creating nor destroying it. To the action of pedalling uphill there's the equal and opposite reaction of gravity trying to drag you back down again. And as you work, you produce heat. To arrive home dripping with sweat and legs like jelly is merely a mark of fealty to the laws of thermodynamics. And thanks to Sir Isaac, the traffic isn't all one way: he also grants us the effortless speed of a long plunge downhill, and the glorious relief of turning a corner and finding the wind's behind us at last. Physics giveth, as well as taketh away.

CONNECT WITH THE FORCES

But while we are inevitably, inextricably tied to these great laws, the bicycle ensures we aren't wholly enslaved by them. Though we may never escape them, we may find freedom within them.

Ernest Hemingway, who knew a thing or two about titanic struggles, wrote: 'It is by riding a bicycle that you learn the contours of a country best, since you have to sweat up the hills and coast down them.' Ride a road you habitually drive, and you'll find it's nowhere near as flat as you thought. With our cars, aircraft and other vehicles, we've become disconnected from the forces that govern our world. The bicycle reminds us of their presence, and gives us a deeper sense of our place in the universe, in terms of our insignificance, and our oneness with everything around us. And to challenge the physical laws is to gain a new perspective on the human powers and constructs that often weigh on us so heavily.

Feel the weight of the world as you turn it beneath your wheels. It will bring new appreciation for forces we learned about in school and have taken for granted (assuming we've thought about them) ever since. And for this moment at least, everything else will seem easy.

Cleaning
the Bike

When it comes to my car, I faithfully attend to the basic, common-sense, safety-critical stuff: regular servicing, maintaining correct tyre pressures and fluid levels, replacing worn wiper blades, that kind of thing. Cosmetically, though, good enough is good enough.

The same applies to my bikes. They're not pristine: they are, after all, high-mileage machines that work outside in all weathers. They are not ornaments, or precious works of art meant only to be looked at. A bike without a mark on it hasn't seen much of the world, and to my mind, a bicycle that isn't ridden is as melancholy as an unread book, or a Stradivarius kept locked up in a bank vault.

But while I don't – and, realistically, can't – keep them in showroom condition, I get distracted and jumpy if they're really filthy. This is partly because I can see a direct connection between cleanliness and safety when it comes to the bike, whose brakes, transmission and major bearings are all exposed to the elements. Plus, I know of no component manufacturer that deliberately designs its products to squeak, grate, grind or crunch.

THE HORSE THAT NEEDS NO HAY

It's also partly due to principles I learned in my teenage years, when I was fortunate enough to ride horses as well as bikes. Among the many rules drummed into me by a succession of formidable instructors was that you owed it to your horse to be properly turned out. It was, I was sternly informed, a serious faux pas to turn up to ride with muddy boots, or leave the yard with bits of straw from the stable still stuck in your horse's tail. Such oversights, though seemingly trivial, were deemed to show a lack of care and respect for your equine partner, and hinted darkly at a deeper negligence. Today, I feel the same lurking shame about a grimy chain or greasy thumbprint.

In similar vein, I was also taught that after a ride, you always take care of your horse first, then yourself; never mind that it's dark, freezing cold, pouring with rain, and the last thing you ate was a slice of toast 15 hours ago. So thoroughly inculcated was this honourable and selfless ideal that I still apply it to my bikes today. Before going indoors, I'll give the whole thing a quick wipe down and re-lube, even when my shoes are full of water and my fingers have gone numb. And if this throwback to my equestrian past appears fanciful, it's worth noting that early marketing campaigns in rural France promoted the bicycle as 'the horse that needs no hay'.

LITTLE AND OFTEN

Everyone has their own idea of what constitutes an acceptable state of cleanliness. Cosmetic considerations aside, cleaning the bike affords a valuable opportunity to check for damage and wear and tear. It needn't be a full-scale, take-everything-apart clean, either. A frayed cable, cut or threadbare tyres, a loose spoke, brake pads worn to wafers, a stretched chain, play in the hubs or headset – all can be revealed in the course of a quick once-over. Five minutes with a rag and a can of water-displacing spray at the end of the ride today could save a long walk home tomorrow.

Cleaning a bike is a bit like cleaning a bathroom. Do it every day, and it's a quick, simple, painless job: do it every couple of months and it's a whole different prospect. I have to confess I don't enjoy cleaning bikes enough to want to spend hours on it, so the little-and-often approach works for me. That said, I find there's something truly meditative in doing a thorough, deep clean now and again. Getting into all the bike's myriad nooks and crannies requires dexterity and patience. It also fosters a deeper understanding of how the machine is put together, and the interplay of its parts and systems – an intimacy that deepens and enriches the relationship. It is the path to 'a' bike becoming 'your' bike.

For me, though, the clincher is that a bike that's clean and running quietly just feels smoother, more 'together' somehow. The effect is purely psychological, of course, but no less real and potent for that. In fact, so much of cycling is in the mind that we should never underestimate the power of these little illusions. Wheeling out a shiny bicycle is like putting on a crisp new shirt, or stepping out of the front door on a sharp spring morning. Everything is bright. Anything is possible.

Adventures
by Night

Not everyone has a choice about riding in the dark. For regular commuters in higher latitudes, it's a fact of life for large portions of the year; for those of us with day jobs, going out at night is the only way to get a ride in during the working week in winter.

I put in many a moonlit mile when my daughter was small. By the time I'd finished work, bathed her and read innumerable bedtime stories, the day was long over, and I had no option but to take to the lanes tooled up with halogen lights and high-vis clothing. My brother-in-law, 10 years or so behind me, is now doing the same, heading out into the woods on his mountain bike when my nephews and niece are (finally) tucked up in bed.

To ride at night without these imperatives, however, seems contrary. Even in broad daylight, as cyclists we often seem to be invisible to drivers – and potholes, thorns and other puncture hazards aren't always easy to avoid, even when you can see them coming. So the jeopardy is vastly multiplied in darkness, especially on unfamiliar roads. I once rode a 400 kilometre event that involved riding through the night in territory I'd never previously visited. The experience of plunging down a steep, winding lane by the fitful light of a single 150-candlepower bulb still haunts me years later.

THE HOURS OF DARKNESS

As any Victorian novel or TV costume drama attests, our ancestors lived in a much darker world than we do. We're permanently bathed in our streetlights, car headlamps and omnipresent glowing screens, so much so that those of us who live in towns suffer from light pollution, and have almost forgotten what the night sky really looks like. We may have shaken off our irrational fears of ghosts and other things that go bump in the night, but we are also less attuned to and comfortable with the darkness than we once were.

As a result, we still place a block between ourselves and a large part of our world, and our lives. We see the hours of darkness as limiting, restrictive – even useless. In so doing, we voluntarily reduce both our cycling time, and our connection with a side of the human experience that has shaped us and our thinking since the beginning of time.

CAUGHT BETWEEN WORLDS

To ride in the dark is to find ourselves between worlds, crossing a strange hinterland that's neither entirely part of today, nor wholly belonging to tomorrow. The day is done, darkness is telling us to stop, rest and sleep – yet here we are, fully awake and alert as owls in a demi-monde full of excitement, intrigue and possibility. We can rediscover the sense of excitement and freedom we had as children when we took to the streets after

dark to go trick-or-treating or carol-singing. And in its
very irrationality and contrariness, there is also a sense
of rebellion and empowerment, of reclaiming something
we've learned (or been told) is no longer ours.

In this space, out of time and mind, the imagination
can go to work. Riding through a tunnel of trees on
a windy night under a full moon, I feel like the
highwayman Dick Turpin on his epic flight to York,
a messenger rushing urgent dispatches to a fretful HQ,
or the Scarlet Pimpernel galloping out of revolutionary
Paris, leaving his baffled, frustrated pursuers cursing far
behind. Others have described it as like being in an
incredibly immersive video game. To each their own.

A MINDFUL ESCAPADE

But to balance these fantastical allusions, night-riding
also calls for awareness of an especially high order.
The first focus must be on preparations: high-visibility
clothing, the bike lit up like a pinball machine, and
brakes, tyres and everything else in good working order.

Once under way, let your attention be on the road surface itself. Good lights, and sticking to roads you know well, are the best guarantees of avoiding sharps and potholes.

With our vision reduced, our other senses become keener at night. We tune in to the texture of the air, more like a clear, refreshing fluid than the day's mere assembly of vapours – colder, denser and filled with scents: damp grass, wood smoke, approaching rain. The sound of the wind is magnified, roaring in the trees like a big surf: when it drops, you can catch distant church bells and passing trains, the hoot of an owl, the vixen's shriek.

A mindful escapade by night has a power and magic all of its own. It is a meditative state, in which the world shrinks down to the cone of light in front of you: peripheral sights and distractions are almost entirely eliminated. The sensation of speed is also magnified enormously. It's as though gravity has been turned down a notch; everything, including the mind, feels lighter, freer, more fluid. It is a ticket to another world.

So, what are you doing tonight?

Birds and Beasts

I love cycling above almost everything else. Nothing, save sheet ice, serious illness or an immovable deadline, will keep me from it. Yet I will stop mid-ride to watch a bird or animal that catches my eye. In that moment, cycling comes second.

Although I'm not a naturalist, to encounter 'the wild' unlooked-for in the course of its normal daily round is precious to me, and the perfect mindful state. The world stops. Time ceases to have any measure or meaning. I can truly forget where, and even

who, I am. All other thought and sensory awareness is suspended. And when the event is over, I have a very real sense of coming back from somewhere distant, beautiful – and, I think, better.

TRULY IN NATURE

The bike connects us to the natural world almost as intimately as walking – with the added bonus that it enables us to see more of it in a given time. On the bike, we're part of the landscape, not merely passing through it; we have full use of senses we're deprived of in the car. We are truly in nature, not insulated from it. It's almost as though animals and birds understand that we pose no threat to them, and therefore accept us into their world. And since our approach is silent, we can get much closer to them before they realize we're there.

I've had some magical animal encounters where we've simply sat (or stood) and considered one another, without fear or prejudice, across the chasm between our species and universes. Riding between high banks, I've glanced

up and looked a stoat or snake straight in the eye;
on quiet lanes, I've stopped to hold lengthy, wordless
conferences with foxes. Reynard's reputation is for
cunning, but I admire him for his insouciance and
boldness: a brazen, careless fellow in his rich red coat.

HARMONY WITH BIRDS OF PREY

Of all the wild creatures I encounter on the road, the
birds of prey are my favourites. I see buzzards regularly
when I'm cycling; it thrills me to have these large,
yellow-eyed, razor-taloned raptors with their five-foot
wingspan, living so close to me. The kestrel is another
familiar sight, hovering over the fields, while glimpses
of his reclusive brother, the sparrowhawk, and their
transient, mysterious cousins, the merlin and hobby,
are rare, exquisite treats. I find their economy, focus
and purity of purpose truly exhilarating. I love their
swiftness and efficiency, the way they slice soundlessly
and almost invisibly through the countryside – much
as we cyclists do.

My ultimate prize, however, is the barn owl. The sight of this pale ghost patrolling the meadows at dusk will, quite literally, stop me in my tracks. On a couple of privileged occasions, I've even found myself riding along with this silent, spectral predator cruising just above and ahead of me, holding formation for a hundred yards or more. Such moments are uplifting and humbling, impossible to arrange and never to be forgotten.

NATURE'S REWARDS

It is uncanny how often nature rewards me for taking a longer, harder route, going out at an odd time, or braving poor weather, with a sight I would not otherwise have seen. On consecutive days, spontaneous detours recently presented me with a big brown hare running across a field of young wheat, and the first pair of red kites I've ever seen in this part of the world. Such meetings justify the extra time and effort a hundredfold.

For the mindful cyclist, being aware of wildlife is part of creating and maintaining a connection with the world and the seasons. Migrant birds tell me more surely than any calendar that the seasons are shifting: some arrive as harbingers of winter, while others bring summer with them from distant lands, and take it away again when they depart.

We are privileged to share their space and freedom, breathe their air, feel their sun and rain, and savour stolen glimpses of their hidden lives. They remind us that we are all part of the same living world, and finding our own way through it.

Riding in
Traffic

Paying attention is one of the underlying themes of mindfulness; focusing on the present moment – the here and now – is the hook on which the practice ultimately hangs. And it is never more critical than when you're riding in traffic.

Any time that cars and bicycles meet, absolutely the last thing you need is your mind wandering. Cycling mindfully in traffic is precisely the opposite of detaching from the world. It's about engaging eyes, ears and instincts – the conscious part of your brain can deal with the inflow of sensory information, but it is your unconscious that will get you through a gap that, if you stopped to think about it, would literally not be there.

And what about those inevitable occasions where a driver doesn't give you enough room? When they pass you six inches from your elbow, into the path of an oncoming bus, halfway round a blind corner, or on a narrow country road? This is when your state of mindfulness can, quite literally, save your life.

ACCEPTING THE MOMENT

In these moments (and I've had many of them), I feel the universe, and life itself, shrink down. Everything I am, know and feel is compressed into a space just a few inches wide and a million miles long, outside which nothing else exists. It is a fragment of time in which everything can change, or nothing. The margins are so small it's impossible to think about them: in the time it took to frame them, it might already be too late. All I can do is focus my attention on where I am and what I'm doing. In this minutely focused state, the brain shifts into warp drive, analysing data, running through scenarios, formulating and discarding options at fantastic speed. I've sometimes returned to the scene of a terrifying near-death experience, which seemed at the time to extend over leagues and aeons, and almost missed it because I blinked.

Mindfulness is about accepting the moment without prejudice: what is, is, and nothing more. Riding in traffic requires an acceptance, however hard it seems, that even if we do everything right, every time, one day that might not be enough. It is, perhaps, the hardest lesson the bike has to teach us.

But acceptance is not the same as fatalism, and awareness need not become paranoia. They give us a framework in which to operate, and freedom to choose how we respond. If you believe in divine protection, you may wish to invoke it. Most deities, however, would also point out that they have granted us enough intelligence to take steps to protect ourselves. I venture no opinion on the wearing of helmets, but I strongly advocate wearing bright colours in all conditions, and being lit up like a Christmas tree when venturing out after dark.

SIXTH SENSE

I apologize if this seems a very technical, functional kind of mindfulness. It's urgent, steely, imperative, rather than relaxing or meditative.

But it is mindfulness nonetheless. It's about paying attention to your position on the road, for example. The mindful cyclist does not hug the gutter, and knows – indeed, expects – that the door of the next parked car could open right in front of them. Remaining non-judgemental after being forced into the kerb by an eighteen-wheeler or carved up by a speeding SUV is extraordinarily hard, yet it is just a moment. A horrible one, to be sure, but that's all it is. (Unless there is real malice, in which case get their number.) The impulse to yell and scream and want to hit back is perfectly natural: adrenaline and cortisol are only obeying orders. This, too, will – and must – pass.

Over time, this awareness can develop into a kind of sixth sense. After more than 20 years on the road, I can generally tell not only what kind of vehicle is approaching me from behind but also whether it will give me ample, enough, too little or no room as it passes, just by its sound. Intuition and experience are good friends to have along for the ride.

For most of us, dealing with traffic and all its many challenges forms an inevitable part of the cycling life. As cyclists, we are part of the solution, but we still have a long way to go. For now, we must be constantly aware, embrace the realities of the roads as a shared space – and be the change we wish to see in the world.

The Road Goes Ever
On and **On**

The number 100 has a strange fascination about it – a certain 'rightness' or completeness. To reach 100 years of age, for example, is a universal landmark, whether for an individual or an organization. And for cyclists, there is a powerful mystique about the ride of 100 miles or kilometres, known as the 'century'.

To complete that first century is a rite of passage: the moment when one crosses an invisible threshold and becomes a cyclist, rather than someone who merely rides a bike. It's a qualification that can never be taken away – in the same way that a rider who finishes the Tour de France, even if he's flat dead last, can forever call himself 'a Giant of the Road'.

The century is a talisman because it's a simple, identifiable and unarguable measure, even to non-cyclists. What constitutes a 'long ride' is far more subjective. Fifty miles sounds reasonably daunting, yet as countless charity events prove, it's well within most people's compass, even if the bike remains untouched the other 364 days a year. By the same token, most of us would balk at riding 190 miles in one day, yet that's exactly what the pros do in the classic race from Milan to San Remo – and in seven hours or less.

QUALITY, NOT QUANTITY

Distance rarely tells the whole story of a ride. The ascent of Alpe d'Huez, in France, is less than nine miles long; Mont Ventoux is just over 13. The Arenberg Forest sector of Paris–Roubaix is a trifling mile-and-a-half. All routinely leave hardened pros openly shattered in body and mind.

Hence racers always measure their rides in duration (usually hours), not distance. They'll also confirm that the toughest challenge in cycling – if not all of sport – is the Hour Record. Uniquely, it's not about who can cover a set distance the fastest, but who can ride furthest in a fixed time. The Belgian racer Eddy Merckx, who broke the record in 1972, swore it was the hardest thing he ever did on a bike, and reckoned it took four years off his life expectancy.

What we're really talking about is relativity. Einstein famously summed it up thus: 'Put your hand on a hot stove for a minute, and it seems like an hour. Sit with a pretty girl for an hour, and it seems like a minute.' Or: ride a century with your best friend on a summer's day and it feels like a spin round the block. Ride round the block alone in a hailstorm and get three punctures, and it feels like 100 miles.

So we should seek always to define our rides in terms of quality, not quantity. To focus on distance is to project ourselves to some unseen point down the road, rather than being fully aware of the road we're travelling right now. Fixating on the fact that you still have however-many miles to go won't help you get up this hill, round that tricky corner. The other danger is that if you set out to cover a certain mileage and don't manage it, you perceive the ride (and possibly yourself, too) as a failure.

EVER MINDFUL

To remain mindful on a long trip, especially alone, can be desperately hard. A niggling noise or slight discomfort can become all-consuming. It is made much easier by ensuring the bike is in good order, and that both it and you are properly equipped. Fifty miles in the rain is hard enough without leaving your waterproofs or pump at home.

The mindful cyclist is also keenly aware of what the body is telling him or her, and refuels regularly. A long ride burns up the body's glycogen stores, which provide energy to the muscles. Once these reserves are gone, they're running on empty. The result is a sudden, spectacular implosion known rather quaintly to

Anglophone cyclists as the 'hunger knock' or the 'bonk', and to our French colleagues as, somewhat fancifully, 'the witch with green teeth' or, rather more graphically, 'meeting the man with the hammer'. Not an acquaintance you want to make, believe me.

To have nothing to do but ride the bike, and all day to do it, is a pleasure to be savoured. If that's your happy lot today, take the sounds, sights, smells and sensations and store them up like bright golden pennies against shorter, duller days to come. Set yourself no targets for speed or distance. It is quality, not quantity, that counts.

Riding Together...
and Alone

Cycling is one of those rare sports for which you don't need teammates, a partner or an opponent. The basic activity and equipment are the same whether you're taking to the road solo, or with thousands of others on a charity ride. The choice to go alone or in company is thus entirely yours to make, according to your mood and ambitions. But from a mindfulness perspective, there are some important differences.

At any given point in my cycling career, I've always been lucky enough to have one good riding partner. And there's a lot to be said for finding someone compatible with whom to share experiences, knowledge, new roads and good times.

When you're both strong, you can push each other to go further and faster than you would alone. You take turns riding at the front in the wind, and fixing a flat or mechanical problem becomes a shared endeavour. Etiquette and common sense require you to go at the pace of the slowest, so you must be aware of your partner's state of mind and being, as well as your own. You tune in to each other's strengths and weaknesses, matching your efforts to mutual benefit. It encourages a kind of collective, corporate mindfulness: a wider, more encompassing awareness, not focusing solely on oneself.

POWER IN NUMBERS

This becomes even more crucial when riding in a group. You must be constantly, acutely aware of your position relative to your companions: a touch of wheels, elbows or handlebars can bring everyone down in a whirling tangle of bodies, limbs and unyielding hardware. You must also judge the pace correctly, neither slowing the group down nor shelling people off the back – and, of course, take your turns in the wind. It's tight, concentrated, fast and fluid, and takes time and nerve to perfect.

The rewards can be stunning. Riding in someone's slipstream, known as drafting, reduces your required effort by around a quarter, allowing groups to sustain much higher speeds over much longer distances than soloists. For a while, I rode with an informal team, and experienced the amazing potential of aggregated effort. On one memorable day, with a tailwind and everyone working seamlessly together, I looked down at my bike computer and saw we were flying along at almost 40 miles per hour. All you could hear was the low, hollow roar of hard racing tyres on tarmac, the whirr of chains and the hiss of stiff aluminium rims through the air. A magical, inspirational sound: the music of motion and human power.

ALONE, BUT NOT LONELY

Riding solo, by contrast, we can set our own pace, find our own rhythm. There's no slowing or waiting, no trying to keep up, no comments or conversation to divert and distract the attention. We can concentrate fully on what we're doing, and the moment as we perceive it. This, to me, is liberty in its purest and sweetest form.

I remember vividly the day when, aged about eight, I was permitted to ride round the block on my own for the first time. It was a heady cocktail of excitement, anticipation, nervousness and resolve. I was completely alone – yet I wasn't lonely; instead, I positively revelled in my new-found solitude and freedom. For me, that was a moment of liberation and infinite possibility, when I suddenly became aware that once you were on the road, you could keep going more or less forever. Forty years later, I still get the same feeling every time I go out.

The bike is one of the few places where, if we wish, we can be left alone. Even at home, the phone rings, people come to the door, and partners, children and pets demand our attention, while unpaid bills and undone chores eye us accusingly. When we ride, these things can come with us only if we invite them.

On the road alone, we are our sole source of motivation and inspiration. There's no one to encourage us as we toil up that hill, cheer us as we speed down the other side, or pat us on the back when we return. We have complete control over our own destiny, but to exercise it, we must be constantly aware of ourselves. Riding mindfully means sensing when it's time to head home, then doing so – or that you've still got gas in the tank, and the will to burn it. And whoever you ride with, the bike is always there, as an enabler, partner and extension of yourself. Which means you'll never be left to fend entirely for yourself.

Mental Strength
and Physical Power

Cycling is hard work – at least, if you plan to go any distance, at any speed, in any terrain that isn't as flat as a table. So physical strength and fitness are obviously important. They're also among the main reasons many of us start, and stick with, cycling in the first place.

Very often, cycling is reduced to a knock-down, drag-out contest between ourselves and the forces of nature – gravity, inertia, friction, air resistance and rolling resistance. To an extent, this is true. The basic technique is simple, and the laws of physics mean the more power you can produce, the faster you can go. But the beauty of cycling is that it's not solely dependent on brute strength. It's also a mind game.

PLAY THE LONG GAME

Getting fitter and stronger is, in itself, a good thing. Apart from the health benefits, it broadens our range and expands our horizons. For me, it's about being confident I can tackle any terrain I might encounter, and not having to avoid a given route because of a particular hill. And if, perchance, I wake up with a fancy to put in 50 hard miles today, I know it's within my compass.

But riding well, and ensuring you're still doing so years from now, is less about the raw power you can expend and more about how efficiently you can use it. As cyclists, we must play the long game. That means being attuned to how much effort we're putting in. In search of a 'good workout', many of us end up riding a bit too hard, most of the time (guilty as charged). Ironically, this can leave us stuck on a plateau, never getting any stronger or faster. We become like an elastic band kept permanently at full stretch: when we need to extend ourselves just a little further – to make it over a particularly steep climb, or put in an extra-long day – there's nothing left.

TUNE IN TO YOUR LEGS

We need to let go of the 'no pain, no gain' mantra
that pervades life, not just sport – the deathly notion
that, somehow, if it doesn't hurt, you're not trying hard
enough, and won't see the best results. As long as you
can get up that hill somehow – even if it means walking
part of the way – that's all that counts. How fast you do
it is utterly unimportant (unless you're racing, of course).

Yet we must also be aware that *some* effort is required.
Our muscles enlarge and strengthen only when we ask
them to do more than they're currently capable of. Not
Nietzsche's 'that which does not kill us makes us stronger',
exactly, but we must break them down (carefully) in order
to build them up. So tune in to your legs as you ride.
Focus on your perceived effort – how hard you feel you're
working. Could you sustain this effort all day? Recognize
when you're asking your body for extra power – on a hill,
for example – and how easily it can provide it (or not).

The great Italian *campione* of the 1960s and '70s,
Felice Gimondi, said: 'Basic physical strength is

necessary. But you need to have a little imagination, to be intelligent and calm. You need mental control. It is self-control.' And, he might have added, you need to be fully in the moment, not worrying about what could happen, or might lie ahead.

OBSERVE AND ACCEPT

One of cycling's most oft-quoted truisms is that whether you think you can, or you think you can't, you'll be right. In other words, the moment the head starts questioning whether you can get up this hill/maintain this pace/ manage another five miles against this headwind, the legs lose all their impetus, and you're suddenly struggling.

This is emphatically not a manifesto for positive thinking. As anyone who's ever tried to quit smoking, lose weight or do anything else requiring self-inflicted physical deprivation will testify, willpower is unreliable and overrated. The challenge is to not think about whether we can or can't, and merely observe and accept the moment as and for what it is.

On the bike, our psychological strength is constantly assayed and refined. A long, steep climb (or even a short, steep one), a relentless headwind, the cold, the heat, the rain: all can be as mentally demoralizing as they are physically exhausting. In fact, it's often the will that gives up first.

But cycling trains the mind, as well as the body, making it stronger and more resilient. Overcoming hills, bad weather, mechanical problems, close encounters with cars – all require us to draw on our reserves of fortitude, patience, hardiness and courage. Just as exceeding our muscles' capacity makes them stronger, so stretching our mental resources helps them grow in size and power – a training that equips us for life itself.

Riding
Off-road

These days, it's easy to forget that at one time, *all* cyclists were off-roaders, since there were no roads to be on. (It's another overlooked fact that in both Britain and America, it was cyclists, not motorists, who first lobbied their governments to make improving the highways a national priority.) But with traffic volumes ever increasing, the appeal of leaving the tarmac behind is obvious, and technology now allows mountain bikes and their intrepid riders to reach places even goats would think twice about.

Riding on the road generally requires us to be entirely immersed in what the traffic is doing: it's difficult, and hazardous, to give our attention to much else. Heading

off-road allows us to refocus completely. With no
cars to consider, we can be fully attuned to ourselves,
our surroundings, the sounds and textures of the trail,
birdsong, sunshine, the scent and quality of the air.
We're also free to revel in the workings of our limbs,
lungs and heart – and if it's wet, indulge in the childhood
pleasure of playing in the mud and getting filthy under
the sensible, grown-up guise of sport and exercise.
As the English Romantic poet William Blake puts it:
'Great things are done when men and mountains meet.'

And Blake's use of the verb 'meet' is pivotal here. We
apply it in the context of friends, colleagues and minds
– and also of targets, objectives and opponents. So it's
important that we approach the mountain (or hill, or
forest, or anywhere else) in the appropriate state of mind.

GUESTS OF NATURE

At a dedicated trail centre, with its purpose-built,
graded runs, to view our meeting as a squaring-up,
staring-down kind of encounter is OK. The challenges

we face here – jumps, berms, boardwalks, drop-offs
– are the products of human imagination: artifice built
on natural foundations with the deliberate intent of
testing our skills and nerve. Nature is generous, and
will join us in our games with grace and good humour,
allowing herself to be wrestled and overthrown like a
large, affectionate dog romping with a boisterous child.

But in the mountains, hills, forests and byways, we
are her guests. Though we are vastly less intrusive than
anything with an engine, we still bring alien wheels,
metals and mechanisms into her domain. We should
approach this meeting, then, with a degree of reverence
and humility. If we hammer through the country without
seeing, hearing, thinking or feeling, we are not visitors
but intruders, and risk missing – or even destroying –
the very things we came out here to find.

We are also unlikely to be the only people nature is
entertaining today. Although the road is nominally a
shared space where everyone has equal status, it certainly
doesn't feel that way to most cyclists. The outdoors,

though, emphatically is. In my part of the world, we coexist with walkers of the serious-long-distance, Sunday-afternoon and dog-accompanying variety, picnickers, families, birdwatchers, hang gliders, kite-fliers, runners and horse riders – to say nothing of the resident livestock and wildlife. They must be part of our awareness and acceptance too – just as we would wish to be part of theirs.

BE IN AND WITH NATURE

With their sophisticated suspension, braking and transmission systems, mountain bikes allow us to tackle almost any terrain. They enable us to go further, faster, and to more extreme locations. But they also, to some degree, insulate us from the rough surfaces, steep gradients and natural hazards that make off-road riding what it is. Too much technology can make us little more than operators, while creating a sense of invincibility and entitlement that detaches us from the moment. If we are too focused on doing our own 'great things', we are not in and with nature; we're seeking to control and co-opt her for our own ends. The desire to explore new territory is a primal human urge that riding off-road allows us to satisfy in ourselves. But we must also be alive to our equally hardwired instincts to possess, exploit and conquer what we find.

Going off-road provides a sanctuary from the frenetic pace of life, and the crush of traffic. The bike is an enabler, taking us further than our feet alone. It connects us to the earth, air and sky, and can, depending on the surface, literally shake us into a deeper awareness of ourselves. And even if, like me, you live hundreds of miles from the nearest mountain, there are great things to be done when we meet nature, whatever form she takes, on the right terms, and with due respect.

Shift in Focus

When we were kids, how many gears your bike had was an important bragging right. More was obviously better – a notion that tends to stay with us, and in more aspects of life than just cycling. As adults, many of us are inclined to make gears something of a fetish. Today, you can buy a bike with anything up to 33 gears (3 chain-rings up front, 11 sprockets behind): if you have the means, you can run pro-grade kit with carbon fibre and titanium parts to save weight, ceramic bearings for smoothness and durability, and electric shifters that operate wirelessly. Even more modest offerings are robust, reliable, easy to adjust and so intuitive a child can master them in five minutes flat.

All of which probably has Henri Desgrange, who in 1903 created the Tour de France to promote his *L'Auto* newspaper, turning in his grave. Irascible and dictatorial, as well as publicity hungry, Desgrange deliberately set out to make his race as inhumanly demanding as possible. To this end, he resolutely forbade the use of derailleurs at the Tour until 1937. 'I still feel that variable gears are only for people over 45,' he famously trumpeted. 'Isn't it better to triumph by the strength of your muscles than by the artifice of a derailleur?' His uncompromising stance condemned the riders to such punishing labours that in 1924, journalist Albert Londres dubbed them *les forçats de la route* – the convicts of the road.

BE MINDFUL OF YOUR GEARS

Happily, we're not bound by Desgrange's strictures, and for the vast majority of us, gears simply make sense. But we must always be aware of what they're actually for. They're not there to make cycling easier per se (although they undoubtedly can). Gears are designed to make our human engine as efficient a source of power as possible. They achieve this by allowing us to sustain the optimum pedalling speed (or cadence), regardless of gradient or terrain.

Racers have lots of gears, closely spaced, so they can adjust their cadence precisely, conserving energy and maximizing output. That kind of detail matters when you're riding immense distances at high speed for money, and when a 200-kilometre race can be decided in the final 100-metre sprint, and won or lost by the width of a tyre. For we mere mortals, though, such a bewildering multiplicity can actually be a distraction. I love the simplicity of the three-speed Sturmey-Archer hub gears on my vintage bike, and the mere 10 speeds I have on my mountain bike. One shifter, one chain-ring, limited options. As any artist will confirm, it is when we have to work within constraints that creativity truly thrives.

Over time, most riders find that a version of the Pareto principle applies, and that 80 per cent of their riding is accounted for by 20 per cent of their available gears. So as you ride today, tune in to how many of your gears you actually use. It probably won't be all of them – and may not be as many as you thought.

LESS IS MORE

When we ride with awareness, we effectively create our own gears. Modern indexed gear systems make shifting so easy it can become a reflex action. But instead of automatically changing down at the slightest rise, simply applying a little more pressure with the legs first is often enough. If it isn't, *then* shift. Similarly, once the gradient slackens, just pedalling faster is often more efficient, and easier, than immediately changing up. If your legs can sustain the required cadence, you're in the right gear. It doesn't matter what number it is. When we're fully aware of the road, legs, heart and lungs, we ride more smoothly, powerfully and efficiently than the rider who relies on gears alone.

We're constantly exhorted to push ourselves, told that working hard – or at least, appearing to – is a virtue

in itself, regardless of whether it's truly productive.
As a result, we can often find ourselves, metaphorically,
straining to turn gears that are much too high, or
spinning madly in gears that are far too low. Either
way, we expend unnecessary effort and, ironically,
end up going slower. The bike provides direct, tangible
lessons in the relationship between input and output.
It teaches us to be aware of when we're overworking
or cruising comfortably, when all we need to do is apply
a little more effort, and when it's time to make a shift.
Gears also remind us that simply having more doesn't
necessarily make things easier. As with so much in life,
it ain't what you've got, but how you use it.

The Cyclist as
Passenger
and Engine

The Olympic cyclist John Howard once said that 'the bicycle is a curious vehicle: its passenger is its engine'. His observation is now one of the sport's most famous aphorisms, and for the mindful cyclist, it goes to the very heart of our relationship with the machine.

To paraphrase the dictionary definition, a passenger is someone who rides in (or on) a conveyance or vehicle that is driven or powered by someone (or something) else. On that basis, you could argue that as cyclists, we're not really passengers at all. We're not, and can't be, passive. We can't simply sit idly in the saddle while the bike takes us where we want to go, since the bike can't steer itself, and produces no power of its own. Even an electric bike requires a human hand to start and stop it. The only time we can realistically call ourselves passengers is when we're going downhill, but even then, it's gravity, not the machine, that provides the motivating force.

DO THE LOCOMOTION

Strictly speaking, we're not passengers when we're behind the wheel of a car, either. The crucial difference between the motorist and the cyclist is, of course, that the former is merely controlling and applying power produced by the engine. As cyclists, we have to produce the power ourselves; we must be the engine.

The word 'engine' comes to us, via Middle English and Old French, from the Latin *ingenium* meaning 'talent' or 'device' – as in our other modern word, ingenious. Racers still make this linguistic connection. In their world, a rider's 'talent' relates to strength, power and endurance, rather than technique (which is, after all, essentially the same for everyone, including us mere mortals). By the same token, they'll talk of a strong rider as having 'a big engine': they'll also refer to one capable of sitting at the front and hauling the bunch along in their slipstream as 'a locomotive'.

A UNIQUE RELATIONSHIP

But as cyclists, are we really engines? The human body technically qualifies on the basis that it converts energy (the potential energy stored in food) into work, such as moving and lifting. However, up to 75 per cent of the calories we take in are required by basic metabolic processes, which are essential to keep our system running even when we're at rest. To convert food energy into kinetic energy – the energy of movement – we need machines. And in our entire span of history, we've never come up with a better one than the bicycle. As the French writer Paul Fournel puts it in *Need for the Bike*: 'The bike is a brilliant device that permits a seated person by the force of just his or her own muscles to go twice as far and twice as fast as a person on foot. Thanks to the bike, there is a faster man.'

In this respect, then, the divide between ourselves and the bike becomes blurred. We provide the basic power, but it's the bike that converts it into motion. Together, we comprise a single, biomechanical entity, in a partnership based on interdependence and mutual benefit. Without our power, the bike simply stands still (or falls over). Without the bike, we're limited to the speed and range imposed by our own limbs, genes and metabolism.

HALF MAN, HALF BIKE

The Irish novelist Flann O'Brien took this symbiotic relationship to its logical (or, rather, surreal) conclusion in *The Third Policeman*, where 'people who spend most of their natural lives riding iron bicycles over the rocky roadsteads…get their personalities mixed up with the personalities of their bicycle as a result of the interchanging of the atoms of each of them'. Author and cycling journalist William Fotheringham picked up on the same theme when he gave his biography of Eddy Merckx the title *Half Man, Half Bike*. (Merckx's devotion to his craft was so all-consuming that his wife, Claudine, once joked that her husband had been 'inoculated with a bicycle spoke'.)

For the mindful cyclist, the unique, intimate relationship we have with the bike is something to be conscious of, cherished and nurtured. As Fournel says: 'When you get on a bike, it's not to forget a machine but, on the contrary, to connect with it.' Riding mindfully, we can marvel at this simple contrivance that enables us to travel across town or around the world with no fuel but food and water, and rewards our labours with liberty and speed. It enlarges, emboldens, enables us to do the impossible. It makes us, in a word, superhuman.

Mindful
Preparations

Getting ready for a ride is its own meditation. It has ritual moves – putting on cycling shoes and gloves, adjusting eyewear and headgear, stowing things in bags and jersey pockets – that switch us unconsciously from civilian to cyclist. It's a shift of mental gears, a transition from one energy state to another: from the potential to the kinetic. Call it a mantra, or simply running through a mental checklist to make sure you've got all you need, the effect is the same. Those few minutes of preparation form a cordon sanitaire around the ride, protecting its purity from contamination by the outside world. On a more pragmatic level, it's a chance to adjust anything that's rubbing, scratching, twisted or pinching, and it reduces the likelihood of getting half a mile down the road and having to come back for a pump, phone or other crucial item you've forgotten.

Checking the bike is an important part of this meditation, too. Like us, it's about to undergo a transformation, from inanimate object to one half of a biomechanical entity; unlike us, it can't devise its own mantra, so we have to supply one, in the form of looking over tyres, chain, brakes and other critical systems. Apart from the practical and safety considerations, performing some basic pre-flight checks reconnects us physically and spiritually, elevating the bike from passive, servile machine to equal partner in the coming enterprise.

OPENNESS TO POSITIVE EXPERIENCES

So what does the mindful cyclist take on a ride? When I first started cycling, I knew literally nothing, so for the first couple of years that was what I carried, not even a pump – and never suffered a single problem. Make of that what you will. I soon wised up, but then, mortified at my former insouciance, I overcompensated by toting enough tools and spares with me to reactivate a grounded 747.

Now, sage and seasoned, I feel I've struck a reasonable balance. Each bike has its own pump attached to its frame, and tyre levers, adhesive patches, a spare inner tube and spanners and hex keys in the appropriate sizes stowed in a seat-pack. When the weather is uncertain, I'll have a packable gilet or waterproof jacket stuffed in my jersey pocket. If I'm going long, I'll take water bottles and cereal bars; nothing for rides under two hours. And that's it.

Carrying a few basics is about being responsible, present and open to positive experiences. Even if you don't know how to use these things yourself, chances are another rider who does will come along at just the right moment. Over the years, I've lent pumps, tools, extra hands and elbow grease, donated inner tubes, energy bars and time, and received similar beneficence in return. Happily for us all, the golden rule of 'do as you would be done by' is still largely respected on the road.

WHAT IS ESSENTIAL?

But the question of what to take and what to leave behind goes beyond the purely practical. Most of us who ride a bike for pleasure do so for the unique sense of freedom it brings. That sense is magnified when we strip everything back, and go out into the world carrying with us only what is truly essential, and no more. To encumber ourselves with extraneous baggage does more than burden the machine: it adds clutter to our already over-freighted minds. And in every sense, it weighs us down, slows us up, and holds us back.

As the years and miles pass, so our definition of 'essential' changes. The one thing I did remember to take with me as a novice was a few coins for a payphone. Today, I carry a mobile phone because it seems silly and contrary not to (and in contemporary rural England, telephone booths are about as common as unicorns). At the same time, I see no necessity to have it switched on. I've also learned the hard way that basic eye protection isn't a luxury or an affectation.

DIVESTING OURSELVES OF STUFF

Paradoxically, perhaps, touring cyclists provide excellent models for economy and forethought. Though freighted with panniers front and rear, they carry not a gram more than they absolutely have to. Stories abound of long-distance riders sawing handles off toothbrushes, drilling holes in cutlery, and painfully writing diaries with pencils an inch long. Straws, camels' backs and all that.

To consciously divest ourselves of stuff seems counterintuitive in today's society. We feel vulnerable, half-dressed, irresponsible, if we go anywhere or do anything without preparing for every eventuality. But there's also something deliciously liberating, even subversive, about it. Like freedom, unpredictability is a fundamental part of cycling's essence and appeal. Mindfulness means being reasonably prepared, while accepting there are still some things there isn't an app for. And long may that continue.

Getting
Lost

Having ridden my local lanes daily for almost two
decades, I can safely say I know my way around.
In fact, you could drop me blindfold pretty much
anywhere within a 30-mile radius of home and, when
you uncovered my eyes, I could tell you immediately
where I was, and how to get back again. Such intimate
acquaintance with the country helps me avoid the
busiest roads, trickiest junctions and crossings, worst
traffic snarls and most intimidating hills. This is
pleasant and comfortable and has much to commend
it, and I can honestly say I never get bored. Yet I also
have to be wary. It is but a short step from comfort
to complacency, familiarity to fear of the unknown.

Hence one of life's simple treats is to take the bike somewhere new – preferably in France, which is my cycling heaven-on-Earth – and get lost.

A RELATIVE TERM

Of course, in this context, 'lost' is a relative term. When riding on roads, one is unlikely to be genuinely so; a few minutes' riding in more or less any direction will produce a signpost, settlement or friendly local who can set you back on the right route. So to be mindful is to accept the situation for what it truly is, which is that one is simply somewhere unknown, unfamiliar or unintended. It is neither a failure, nor some great cosmic conspiracy: a straightforward navigational error, a moment's inattention or a wilfully misleading road sign is all it takes. As any mindful gardener will attest, a weed is merely a flower in the wrong place. So the cyclist who appears or thinks themselves lost is in fact an explorer. And to be an explorer is, essentially, to set off with the deliberate intention of getting lost; to see and learn for oneself whether here, in truth, be dragons. If you're not stepping off the edge of the map, you're merely following others, and that is not true discovery.

The lure of terra incognita is among our most ancient and potent instincts, yet we've dulled it with our sat navs and handheld GPS. Going the wrong way on a bike ride is a low-risk adventure, a respectful nod to our wandering ancestors, and a small rebellion against technologies that, when we arrive in a new place, make us feel we've already been there.

PARTNERS IN A ROAD MOVIE

Getting lost also deepens our appreciation of and affection for the bike. It didn't get us into this fix; we did. More importantly, it's the only way we're going to get out of it. We have to be partners, the lead characters in our own road movie, where we find out exactly what kind of stuff we're made of.

Once we've extricated ourselves, there is more than just relief. There is the same deep satisfaction, the same upwelling of self-belief and respect, that we can get from fixing a puncture on the roadside. It comes from being thrown on our own resources and not found wanting. Anyone can find themselves in a tricky situation: growth lies in how we respond to and resolve it. (For my fellow men in particular, it can thus also be a powerful exercise in humility, if we're left with no alternative but to ask directions…)

THE JOY OF SERENDIPITY

The process of disentangling ourselves, when undertaken mindfully, leaves us open to new discoveries and serendipities. A missed turn can force us to make a hitherto unknown connection between familiar points, and open up a new route that may be ridden with joyful intent in future. Even the simple loss-cutting expedient of turning around and retracing our steps shows us new things, since the road looks entirely different when viewed from the opposite direction. By being present, seeing where we are and not where we thought we should be, we redraw portions of our mental map, filling in blanks and joining up dots. To extend our physical boundaries, even if unwittingly, is to enlarge our inner world.

It is good, and important, to become disorientated and disconnected in an age that compels us to be certain – and inform everybody else – where we are and what we're doing every moment of the day. The corollary of not knowing your exact whereabouts is that no one else does, either. For some, this can be worrying. But seen mindfully, it is truly liberating. Sometimes, getting lost is the only way to find ourselves again. Because at that moment, we are all we have.

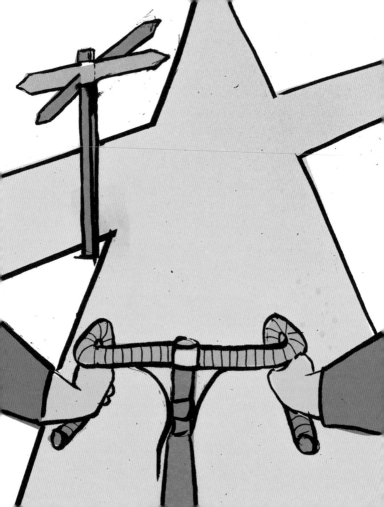

Riding without
Technology

To measure things is a profound human instinct. Whether it's distance or duration, weight or wealth, height or happiness, talent or time, we can't help recording, comparing and analysing everything around us. From this blizzard of statistics – some trivial, some transformative – we assemble a picture of the world and an understanding of our place in it, both literally and metaphorically.

This urge to know begins in infancy and lasts all our lives. Like many kids, I had a simple mechanical odometer, like the ones cars used to have, on my bicycle fork. A metal peg attached to one spoke flicked a cog each time it passed, advancing the numbered rotors inside. Even when it worked, it wasn't accurate; and when one day the bracket bent so every spoke struck the cog, it was suddenly 37 noisy, hilarious miles to my friend's house in the next street.

Twenty years later, my friends and I all had wireless LCD bike computers that calculated trip and total distances, current, average and maximum speeds, cadence and elapsed time. Then we started using heart-rate monitors too, with sensors strapped to our chests sending data to chunky watches on our wrists. Whenever we stopped at a road junction, a chorus of electronic bleeping and twittering broke out as our various devices switched to standby mode. Another decade on and it's GPS units, smartphones, headcams and power meters providing the soundtrack.

IN PURSUIT OF A NEW HIGH SCORE

All this technology is not, in itself, a bad thing. If you're preparing for an event, it's only sensible to track your progress – and all but essential if you're racing. Used judiciously, these devices can add to our enjoyment, by giving us the information we're hardwired to gather, in all the detail we could wish for. That millions of people choose to use GPS-linked apps to track their performance and compare it with others' stats worldwide tells its own tale.

But if we're not careful, we can become fixated on these gadgets and their endless flow of data. If we're looking at a screen, we're less aware of our surroundings, instincts and selves. We rely on facts, not feel; we're literally riding by numbers. (Incidentally, I trust that the follies of listening to a music player while cycling are sufficiently self-evident to make further discussion unnecessary.) At worst, we risk turning our cycling into a real-life videogame, in which we're merely characters in endless pursuit of a new high score.

As many of us are finding with computers, smartphones and other technology, the demarcation between who's in charge of whom can become blurred. Over time, my bike computer morphed from passive recorder into punitive taskmaster. I could see at a glance if my pace was slackening, my cadence slowing or the mileage falling short of the daily target. The heart-rate monitor, too, became a stern, implacable overseer, as I focused all my attention and efforts on keeping my pulse within the strict parameters it imposed. Their numbers didn't lie, and left me nowhere to hide. A poor set of figures and I'd not only let myself down, I'd let them down, too. I'm only grateful I saw the light before GPS and power meters became commonplace (not that I could have afforded them anyway).

JUST YOU AND THE BIKE

Today when I ride, I don't even wear a watch. But all those years of careful calculations left their mark. When we got back from a ride, my cycling buddy used to ask me how far I thought we'd been. It was a long-running joke that, without consulting a computer, I'd usually know to within a quarter of a mile. If he tried me now, I'd be guessing, and almost certainly wrong.

This, to me, represents tangible progress towards a more mindful approach. Because while I'm hazy on the distance, I can remember precisely where I went, what I saw, how the bike performed and how I felt pretty much all the way round. I also know when I've done enough, and when I've got a few more miles left in the tank, but it's my legs, heart and brain that tell me, not a piece of hardware.

Gadgets can have a useful, legitimate place in our cycling life, and satisfy a deep human need. But today, try going without the GPS, leave the computer behind, forget about your King of the Mountains points on Strava. Make it about just you and the bike. See if you notice, feel and remember any more about the ride – or enjoy it any less.

Light Enough,
Fast Enough

I have owned numerous bikes in my 20-plus years of cycling. Beginning with ancient second-hand 10-speeds, I progressed through unlovely steel hybrids and aluminium road bikes to carbon-fibre and titanium exotica worth more than my car.

In my desire to go further and faster – not, in themselves, bad things – I became fixated on finding the perfect machine, and the bike industry was only too happy to indulge me. In accordance with their orthodoxy, each bike I acquired was lighter, stiffer, more technically advanced and more uncompromising in its pursuit of speed than its predecessor. It was only after 10 years, too many bikes and far too much money that

I realized I was caught up in cycling's own insidious arms race (or should that be legs race?) and that, to quote cult 1980s movie *War Games*, 'the only winning move is not to play'.

LOVE THE BIKE YOU'RE WITH

The French writer Paul Fournel says: 'The desire to have a beautiful bike is shared by everyone. Some cultivate it, others repress it, but it's always there.' Mindfulness is recognizing when this natural, innocent and entirely wholesome desire is in danger of being subverted. Then, the bike is no longer a means but becomes an end in itself, and cycling quickly loses much of its simple joy.

I have learned, the hard way, that mindfulness means riding the bike you're riding, with all its imperfections – unless, of course, they're potentially dangerous or causing you actual physical discomfort. It means letting go of the mythical perfect bicycle in our heads that will magically transform us from *lanterne rouge* to *maillot jaune* overnight. According to Robert M. Pirsig: 'The test of the machine is the satisfaction it gives you. If it produces tranquility, it's right. If it disturbs you it's wrong until either the machine or your mind is changed.'

In any case, trying to buy our way to greater speed is ultimately doomed, since we ourselves are the engine. However sophisticated the machine, sooner or later we will always come up against our own physical limitations. You can have what is, on paper, the best bike in the world, but where it matters – on the road – it's only as good as you are. The one sure way to get faster, and/or make cycling easier, is to get as fit and strong as time, motivation and genetics permit. As the greatest racer of all time, Eddy Merckx, succinctly advised: 'Don't buy upgrades: ride up grades.'

A GOOD BIKE

Today, my fleet comprises a vintage bike based on a design from the 1930s and a mountain bike with no suspension and only 10 gears. They're heavy, old-school and possess not a single strand of carbon fibre between them. In terms of their technology, performance and 'seriousness', they belong in another age.

But to me, each meets, in its own way, the essential criteria for being A Good Bike. They run exactly as I want them to, and they make me happy when I look at them. Their little dings and scuffs aren't flaws or wounds but battle honours and (sometimes painful) reminders – the ink stains on the writer's fingers, the names carved into an old school desk. I know my bikes so intimately I'd instantly notice an unfamiliar sound from the transmission, or if the saddle height were altered by a fraction of an inch, or that the brakes no longer bit at precisely the right point, or that the tyre pressures were down by 10 psi.

So today, take a fresh look at your bicycle. See it not as a static object but a living thing: a repository of experiences and memories, and a true extension of yourself. A bike like this cannot be bought: it's made – transformed from shop-floor-shiny to its present state by the road, necessity, communion and time. It's so one and only, so completely yours, you'd know it at a hundred paces. Someone could build another, using identical components down to the smallest bolt, and it just wouldn't be the same.

We all have our own idea of what makes a good bike. You may define it as the latest, lightest and fastest, made from moon dust, spider silk and starlight. Or it could be the budget gas-pipe clunker that fell out of the ugly tree and hit every branch on the way down, but has never failed you yet. In the end, a good bike is the bike you're glad you took today, and want to ride again tomorrow. And chances are that, whatever the marketing people try to tell you, you've already got one.

Riding in the **Heat...** and the **Cold**

Like the rain, the cold is often regarded as an enemy, a malevolent force to be feared and conquered, wrapped up against, shut out and kept at bay wherever possible. Consider how we use 'cold' as an adjective in our idioms. It's almost always negative or pejorative: we give someone we dislike the cold shoulder or leave them out in the cold; at best they can expect a cold greeting (or frosty reception); at worst we might murder them in cold blood. We pour cold water on ideas, offer cold comfort, and lament others' cold-heartedness. No wonder we balk at cycling in it.

But, as with venturing forth in the rain, there's a kind of steely joy in braving that which others shy from, or assume is beyond their capacity to endure. The hard man's hard man, Sean Kelly, once said: 'You can never tell how cold it is from looking out a kitchen window. You have to dress up, get out training and when you come back, you then know how cold it is.'

TOUGHER THAN WE THINK

Even if you can't muster Kelly's fearsome brand of resolute indifference, riding in the cold can be highly invigorating, given the right preparation and attitude. Tempting as it is to put on the warmest clothes you can still move in, we must be aware of the difference between standing around or even walking in the cold, and riding a bike in it. If you set off feeling toasty, chances are that after 10 minutes you'll be perspiring profusely. Much better to start out feeling slightly underdressed, and let the bike warm you up.

It's the extremities that suffer most, so that's where our focus tends naturally to fall. But since even the best gloves and socks are of limited aid, we must consciously shift that attention elsewhere. Think about how your body's core – that is, from neck to waist – is doing. This is where all the vital organs are, so we must be attentive to draughts and cold spots. (Your arms and legs generate their own heat through the working of your muscles and can take care of themselves.) As long as your core is warm and reasonably comfortable, all is well. Now consider your hands. Again, provided they're not so cold and stiff you can't operate the brakes safely, there's no need for concern.

THE MARK OF THE TRUE CYCLIST

The cold reconnects us with the world our forebears knew, and restores some of the resilience and self-reliance that our warm houses, heated cars and insulated clothing take away.

And as it hardens us, so the heat reforges and tempers us.

On a hot day, our instinct is to seek shade, stay cool. On the bike, there's nowhere to hide. It's another grounding, reconnecting experience – this time, with our ancestors who longed for the sun that ripened their crops, then toiled in its heat to bring the harvest in. To ride for hours on broiling tarmac is to labour indeed. And on such a day, the long flight downhill, or the sudden darkness of a line of trees, is like plunging into clear, cool water. Luxuriate in it, let it wash over you. It is a blessing unknown to those who now just sit in a chair, or choose to stay indoors.

Feel the heat on your skin. See how your wrists glisten, and how the sun gives special attention to your upper forearm and above your knees. Then, back at home, roll up your sleeves and take pride in the kind of tan everyone else spends all summer trying to avoid. Tan-lines are the indelible mark of the true cyclist, the uniform we can never take off.

WE'RE GROWN-UPS NOW

From childhood, we're told both to 'wrap up warm' and 'stay out of the sun'. Deliberately doing neither is a great way to tell our inner parent we're grown-ups now, and can make our own choices. And when so much of modern life is dedicated to eliminating discomfort, it also reminds us just how physically resilient we are. I've ridden at -8°C (17°F) in winter and at 37°C (100°F) in summer, and apparently survived both. It is temperament, not temperature, that is ultimately important on the bike. Acknowledge the cold and heat, respect and accept them, but do not fear them. They are transient – literally here today, gone tomorrow. In summer, you'll forget you were ever cold; come winter, you'll wonder if you'll ever be warm again. So they will pass. And you can take them both.

As Easy as
Riding a Bike?

We all begin our cycling lives in the same way: with a miracle. Even if we no longer remember it, we all had that moment where the training wheels were removed, the adult hand came off the back of the saddle, and we were suddenly, gloriously, free. The falls and frustrations, tedium and tantrums were left in the dust, the voice inside that told us we'd never do it abruptly and permanently silenced. For many of us, learning to ride a bike is one of the first great triumphs of our lives – and, proverbially, one of the few things we never forget how to do.

Having mastered the basic technique, all things become possible. We can bowl along on the flat, climb hills and mountains, and descend at speeds that set our

eyes and (though not in my case) hair streaming in the
wind. We can pop to the shops or roll around the globe,
ride to compete, commute or contemplate, surround
ourselves with company or head out alone. And all the
while we can talk, sing, gaze at the scenery, meditate,
compose music and poetry, eat, drink, solve problems,
meet people and be at one with the world. No wonder
the bicycle has been hailed as the greatest invention
of the last two hundred years.

AN ORDINARY, EVERYDAY MIRACLE

But we rarely stop to consider just what an extraordinary
skill we've acquired, or how casually we use 'riding a
bike' as a simile for anything simple. Which it is, until
you try explaining it to someone who's never tried it (or
even to yourself) or watch a child trying to learn. We've
all seen it: the wobbling start, the front wheel suddenly
veering off course, the wild over-corrections, and the
inevitable tumble and tears. Now ask yourself: when
did I last fall off my bike while riding along (as opposed

to a crash)? It almost never happens. In more than 20 years, I've had just two 'offs', both caused by black ice.

When, aged 40, I learned I had osteoarthritis in my knee, I found myself consciously thinking, for the first time since early childhood, about the physical act of riding a bike. I had to tune in to the mechanics of pedalling: the angles formed by my knees, hips and ankles through each stroke; the exact position of my foot on the pedal; the antagonistic interplay of my quads and hamstrings. Focusing on this repetitive, seemingly simple yet highly intricate action became a form of meditation – and set me on the path to becoming a mindful cyclist.

LIFE IS NON-LINEAR

We all know that riding a bike depends on balance. But since it's impossible to sit perfectly still, or apply precisely the same amount of power with both legs throughout the pedal stroke, the bike is fundamentally out of balance the moment we climb aboard. And that's before you add the influence of the wind, irregularities in the road surface, wheels slightly out of true, and so on. Next time you find a puddle on a dry road, ride through it, then hold the straightest line you possibly can. Look back at your trail, and you'll see not one tyre print, but two, braided together like a length of fine rope.

Thus on the bike, as in life, the idea that we can maintain a smooth, uninterrupted trajectory is illusory. Those intertwining tyre tracks are visible proof of the constant, tiny adjustments we make as we weave our way forwards, compensating for the forces we exert, and that act upon us. Bike-riding reminds us that life is non-linear. Even if we arrive at our intended destination, we do so via a series of zigzags and subtle course corrections.

BE MINDFUL OF THE ROAD

Speed is important, too. Go too slowly, and we can find ourselves weaving erratically, going more side to side than forwards, as we struggle with forces barely within our control. Too fast, and the tolerances and margins for error shrink dramatically. You can lean a bike surprisingly hard to maintain speed through a corner, but go a fraction of a degree past the centre of mass and there's no recovering. And just as a tiny patch of spilled diesel is enough to reduce your tyres' grip instantly, disastrously, to zero, so we must be aware of our own limits of adhesion.

We're constantly exhorted to focus on the road ahead. To be mindful is to identify, accept and understand what's under our wheels right now. It is also to recapture the magic we knew and believed in as children. And how many things in our busy, rational lives can promise us a miracle like that?

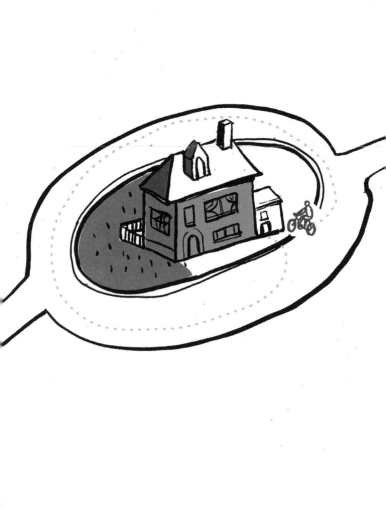

No Ride is
Too Short

My daughter plays the violin (really rather well, as it happens), so concerts are a regular, and welcome, feature of our lives. I'm always amazed, though, at how many parents watch their offspring's entire performance through the screen of a digital camera, tablet or mobile phone. Are they really listening to them, I wonder? Are they actually 'present' at all? And does all this filming spring from a simple, understandable desire to capture a special moment, or signify something deeper: that somehow they need something they can show and share with others to make the event 'real'? As the taunting internet slang has it: POIDH – Pics Or It Didn't Happen.

This need to record and share everything has become a pervasive force in our lives. It's as though the moment itself isn't enough – which is, of course, the very opposite of mindfulness. The dreaded multitasking is another symptom: that to be doing only one thing within a given moment isn't enough, either. So is the inexorable rise of brands over products. We are not content simply to buy something: we need to buy *into* a story, experience or lifestyle to feel complete.

MERE PEOPLE ON BIKES

In cycling, this sense of insufficiency manifests itself in the plethora of multi-day charity rides and the ever-growing number and popularity of sportives – amateur, mass-start, single-day events, usually over a choice of distances from about 30 to 100 miles-plus. The *grand-père* of them all is the Étape du Tour, first held in 1993, which every July sees 15,000 masochists tackle a full Tour de France mountain stage through the Alps or Pyrenees.

Such events are popular because they turn a bike ride into an experience, giving it an identity, and thus greater validity. When you go into work on Monday and co-workers ask about your weekend, you can say you did The Dragon Ride or The Beast, and give them chapter and verse on your time, average speed and vertical feet of ascent. Sounds so much more serious and purposeful than 'I went out on my bike'. Because in the prevailing world view, that is no longer enough.

This gnawing dissatisfaction and insecurity also stokes cycling's arms race. It persuades us that our current frame, wheels, gears, shorts, shoes or whatever aren't light, exotic or shiny enough. We become convinced they're holding us back: we're not going as far, or as fast, as we could be. The marketing narrative subtly insinuates that if we're not riding the 'right' bike, wearing the 'right' kit or doing the 'right' kinds of activities, we won't be seen as 'serious'. In short, we won't be Cyclists with a capital 'C', but mere people on bikes. And that, too, suddenly seems inadequate.

EVERYTHING IS ENOUGH

But why do we feel the need to justify ourselves and our riding in this way? Has life reached a point where something as simple and innocent as a bike ride needs a name – a brand, if you like – to lend it legitimacy? Is this why 'only' riding to the shops and back, or taking a gentle 10-minute spin round the block in ordinary clothes, suddenly feels like something we should apologize for? And does it help explain why so many of us insist on referring to our routine rides as 'training'?

When I'm really busy, and especially on short winter days, I may have just 20 minutes to spare; enough to do a short but hilly local loop of about four miles. Once upon a time, I'd have hammered round, angry with myself and the world, feeling it almost wasn't worth the effort, that somehow it didn't count. In other words, it wasn't enough.

But of course, it is. If 20 minutes is all I have, I'll take it. Any ride is better than no ride. I know I'm blessed to work at home: plenty of people don't have even that much time for the bike during the week. For them, the pressure to make the most of their weekend opportunities is overwhelming – hence the sportives, which are becoming correspondingly longer and more extreme every year.

Mindfulness is about accepting the present moment, and everyone and everything in it (including ourselves) as sufficient. So whatever it consists of, your ride today will be enough. You don't need to call it anything, get dressed up, pin on a number, record every detail, set a personal best or receive a free goody bag at the end. Nor do you need to film it in order to make it real. All that matters is that you were there.

A Meditation
on Suffering

Cyclists love suffering. There's something semi-religious, almost cultish, about their pursuit of physical extremity, privation and torment. On any given Sunday morning, you'll see them toiling up the longest, steepest climbs they can find – modern-day penitents seeking mortification of the flesh on two wheels. Three-time Tour de France winner Greg LeMond was once asked if training gets easier when you're competing at the highest level. He replied, rather testily: 'It never gets easier; you just go faster.'

In our cosseted, sanitized, ever more virtual world, there is much to be said for willingly subjecting ourselves to real, violent – and, yes, painful – physical effort. One of the most popular and charismatic riders ever to grace the professional peloton, Germany's Jens Voigt, famously declared: 'When my legs hurt, I say: "Shut up legs! Do what I tell you to do!"' His mantra encapsulates a natural, human desire to face down our own limitations, dig deep and find the gold that (we hope) lies concealed within ourselves.

THE AGONY AND THE ECSTASY

Hard riding is both enriching and purifying. It reduces life to its essentials: eat, drink, breathe, sweat, survive. And though my all-out time-trial efforts and day-long epics are behind me now, I still love coming home some days, knowing I've left it all out there on the road.

Some might argue that hard riding and mindfulness are mutually exclusive. I actually find the opposite is true. When I'm just tootling along on my vintage bicycle, my mind tends to wander. I find myself replaying conversations, composing bad poems or trying to recall some random song lyric. On my road bike, however,

I have to be wholly present in the moment, which is the very definition of mindfulness. When you're tearing downhill at 40 miles an hour on tyres less than an inch wide, you really can't be thinking about anything else. Riding hard means being fully aware of your breathing, the road surface, the lactic acid building up in your legs, the evenness and cadence of your pedal strokes, and making constant tiny adjustments to your position, effort and line. It may not sound much like meditation, but 20 minutes of riding 'on the rivet' is the best way I know to focus, clear my head and reconnect with myself and the world.

SIGNS WE ARE TRULY ALIVE

It is, of course, perfectly possible, and acceptable, to ride without breaking a sweat or raising your pulse by more than a few beats per minute. But that's not really what we were designed for. The legs may burn, the lungs labour, and every nerve and fibre scream at us that this is ridiculous, unnecessary and entirely within our power to stop. Yet these are affirmative signals, telling us we're functional and truly alive. As humans, we are hardwired for exertion, genetically programmed to endure.

And the bicycle simply, gloriously, magnifies our inbuilt biological capabilities, however modest they may seem. Derailleur gears convert energy into motion with 98 per cent efficiency, compared to just 18 per cent for a typical internal combustion engine. It's been calculated that, at a steady 15 miles per hour, the bicycle returns the equivalent of over 900 miles per gallon. Given sufficient food and water, any reasonably healthy person can ride at a pace faster than they could ever run, and sustain it almost indefinitely. Even a gentle jaunt puts you several leagues ahead of those who congratulate themselves on occasionally taking the stairs instead of the lift.

IN TUNE WITH THE BODY

Yet paradoxically, it's precisely the mechanical advantage the bike confers that makes it such a potent source of physical suffering. Unlike us, the bike does not experience pain, fatigue or boredom, but will keep going literally until we drop. The bike doesn't care, the mind whispers, so why should we? Hence there is always the temptation to push that little bit harder, go that little bit further. To do so mindfully is to find that precise point of balance between what we can do, and what we just can't.

It is important to note, however, that this kind of positive suffering is not the same as actual bodily injury. The mindful cyclist is always minutely in tune with his or her body. Warning signals from back, neck, shoulders or joints should never be ignored. Cycling is hard enough, without subjecting yourself to clothes that chafe or a bike that's the wrong size. That is simply misery. And who can truly profess to love that?

It's Not About
the Bike

Although this isn't a novel, you could say the bicycle is the hero of this book. That means, of course, we now require a villain, and since our setting is the world of cycling, there's really only one man who can play the part.

I didn't want to mention Lance Armstrong, and you've probably read all you ever want to about him, and more, elsewhere. Suffice to say I spent (wasted?) several years as a true believer, and witnessed his fall from grace with a mixture of horror, sadness, *schadenfreude* and embarrassment at my own credulousness.

Yet the shadow he casts remains long, transcending the sport – and for good or ill, he had an enormous influence on my formative years as a 'serious' cyclist.

I still own the team-issue US Postal Service carbon-fibre bike I waited five years for, then rode for more than 25,000 miles. Like millions of others, I was inspired by his exploits at the Tour de France, starting with his comeback victory in 1999. That his story of triumph and redemption turned out to be less fairy tale than fabrication is a betrayal many of us may never forgive.

A HUMAN DRAMA

Still, one truth remains inviolate. It's the title of his autobiography, lauded (ironically in the light of later events) for its candour and humanity, which became both a global blockbuster and a central pillar of the Armstrong mythology. Like the man said: *It's Not About the Bike.*

In choosing that title, Armstrong laid down a marker. This is a human drama, he was saying: if you want to read a book about bike-racing, this ain't it. He wanted us to focus on his miraculous recovery from cancer, and the tough Texas upbringing that fuelled his competitive urge – to look at the man, not the machine. It was a master stroke. As well as helping to raise hundreds of millions of dollars for his eponymous foundation, it placed him on a pedestal so lofty and impregnable it would be years before we discovered It Wasn't Really About That Either.

But if it's not about the bike, then what is it about? One could ask the same question of any sport or activity. Is angling purely about catching fish? Is mountaineering just about reaching the summit? Is writing a book merely about getting the required number of words down on paper? To which the answer is: of course not.

WHAT CYCLING IS REALLY ABOUT

So in this final meditation, and in no particular order, let's consider what cycling is really about.

It is about freedom. The bike provides a means of escape from the confines of home, work, the phone and the inbox – a chance to, temporarily, drop off the radar and disappear. It is also about reconnecting with and being aware of feelings, physical sensations, and the world around us. It is about confronting and overcoming challenges, fears and limits. It is about self-reliance and independence, and also the company of others, and encounters with strangers. It is about recapturing a sense of childlike wonder, and turning back the clock to simpler, more innocent days. It is about being in nature, on her level and terms, and directly sensing the long, slow roll of the seasons. It is about a new appreciation of the laws of physics, and finding ways to bend them, even while they remain unbreakable. And that's just my list.

It is, above all, about awareness. The modern world sometimes makes this difficult, with its constant distractions, pressures, demands and expectations. The bike gives us so many other, different things to focus on. How the legs are feeling, the texture of the road, changes in temperature, an approaching vehicle, a wild creature briefly glimpsed, a new sound from the transmission, a tight bend on a steep descent – all bring us back to the immediate moment. And when we're in that present, mindful state, all else fades into the background. If, at this moment, the bike is still moving forwards, I am climbing the hill I thought was impossible. If, at this moment, I am riding along safely and in one piece, the traffic I'm afraid of has not harmed me. From this realization comes resilience.

SUFFICIENT UNTO ITSELF

For Lance, it was All About Winning – on the road, in courtrooms, financially and within personal relationships. We are constantly exhorted, by business, the media and society, to want and expect more, both from the world and from ourselves. The awareness we can cultivate on the bike can help us to detach ourselves from desire and entrenched thought patterns and view things more objectively. It's raining. It's cold. This hill is steep. I am travelling at 15 miles per hour. That's it. No value judgement, no good/bad, right/wrong. The moment is sufficient unto itself. Does it need to be about anything else?

ACKNOWLEDGEMENTS

This book exists only because of the following:

The wonderful team at Ivy Press: my editors Tom, Jenni and Jenny for their wise words, impeccable guidance, astonishing faith and gentle persuasion; and Monica for reviving a dream I thought had long expired;

Paul Fournel, who opened my eyes to the poetry in cycling, and whose wheel I have always aspired to follow;

Mike Plumstead, with whom I had the honour of sharing the longest, hardest and greatest days I've ever had on the road;

Kevin Smith, for his unfailing good humour, common sense and companionship. 'The Rain it Raineth' is for him.

Isobel and Ingrid, who are the true reasons for everything;

And of course, the bikes.